lesh
into
Fire

JA *Huss*
Johnathan McClain

Julie & Johnathan

HUSSMCCLAIN.COM

Copyright © 2018 by JA Huss & Johnathan McClain
ISBN: 978-1-944475-45-1

Edited by RJ Locksley
Cover Design by JA Huss

FLESH INTO FIRE

JA HUSS & JOHNATHAN McCLAIN

CHAPTER ONE

TYLER

My neck itches.

I hate wearing a fucking collar. I really do. I think it comes from my time in the service and all the gear. I had so much shit all up around my neck and face all the time. Always made me feel like I was being choked. Or suffocated. Sometimes I was, of course, being choked. Or suffocated. So it's possible that it's really just a Pavlovian association of some kind, but regardless, I hate wearing a fucking collar.

Good thing I never considered becoming a priest. For, like, a hundred reasons, but the collar thing is one of them.

But I'm wearing a collar today, for the second time in the last week, because I want to show the proper respect to the deceased. So I borrowed one of Evan's fourteen-thousand-three-hundred-and-forty-six-dollar suits (I asked), and God-knows-how-much-they-cost shirts and ties, and stuffed myself into them. (There wasn't actually a lot of stuffing to be done. They fit great. Evan and I are almost exactly the same size, as it turns out. He and Robert went to Italy—Naples, I think—so they could both have several custom suits made by some famous bespoke tailor. So the suit is designed for *his* frame, but it might actually fit me just a little better. At least that's what Robert said. But he may have just been fucking with Evan. Anyway.)

My neck itches.

I gotta shave again someday.

Jeff's funeral was rough. Even though we didn't really know him at all, we went. Maddie and I, that is. Seemed like the right thing to do. For a lot of reasons. Not least of all the fact that, even though we didn't talk about it, I think he reminded Maddie of Scotty just as much as he did me. On some very evident level, it was a makeup funeral for the one I missed seven years ago.

A first responder funeral is a lot like a military one. There was a procession of fire trucks and police escorts all the way to the grave site. All of Jeff's brothers-in-arms from all the station houses in town wearing their dress uniforms. There were bagpipes. Which is kind of weird. I know it's a thing they do, but I don't think Jeff was Scottish. Turns out his last name was Rossi, so I guess he was Italian, but... Whatever. Doesn't matter. The bagpipes were a nice touch.

Evan gave a eulogy. He talked about dedication and commitment and honor and all the things I'd expect, but then he did something I wasn't expecting at all. He talked about Jeff's twenty-first birthday. The night we went to the strip club. The night I saw Maddie dancing and fell in love with someone I knew but didn't know I knew. The strip club that burned down and killed Jeff in the process. The strip club that was burned down by people who did it to punish Maddie.

Fucking hell.

So understandably, I was a little nervous when Evan began telling the story. And not just for all the personal reasons, but also because telling a story about a guy at a strip club feels like it's better suited for a bachelor party than a funeral.

But goddamn if Evan didn't somehow manage to make it sweet, and kind, and insightful, and full of heart, and when he got to the part about Jeff throwing up on his expensive shoes, everyone was laughing and crying at the same time. It was perfect and made us all feel like we really knew Jeff, whether we did or not.

I don't believe in heroes, but if you held a gun to my head and told me that I had to pick someone to claim as my personal hero, it'd have to be Evan Silver. (Actually, if you held a gun to my head and told me to do anything, I'd tell you to go fuck yourself, but privately, inside, I'd be saying Evan Silver was my hero.)

Maddie was pretty beat up by the whole thing. The funeral, that is. When Evan started in on the strip club stuff, she gasped a little and squeezed my hand tightly. But she was hanging on, not crying too much, being a total champ, especially given how complicated I know her feelings must have been. She managed to stifle her tears pretty well. Right up until...

Jeff's dad got up to speak.

"Um," he said, "I, uh, I'm not typically inclined to talk a lot, so I'll keep this short."

And he did. Because that was it. That was all he was able to manage.

He stepped in front of Jeff's casket, all draped in the American flag, Jeff's picture on an easel beside it, very classic and traditional, and he readied himself to speak. But he couldn't. He just flat-out broke down. It started with little spasms in his shoulders, but within seconds he had collapsed onto the coffin and was sobbing uncontrollably.

Turns out Jeff's mom passed away a couple of years ago after being hit by a drunk driver, so for the second time in two years, Jeff's dad had someone he loved taken from him with absolutely no warning at all.

The whole scene had me flashing for half a second to what my dad would've done if I had somehow died after my mom did. It wouldn't have been the same, of course. Not least of all because Barbara Morgan (née Hudson) died of cancer, so my dad had time to accept that it was coming, but still… I wonder, if I had died in Iraq or Afghanistan and my body had been flown over for the funeral, would he have gotten all busted up over it? Would he have even shown up to the service? Would he have even known it had happened? But then I quickly remembered:

Fuck it. Doesn't matter. Not about me.

The person to go and comfort Jeff's dad was Brandon. New-guy Brandon. Creepy never-says-nothing-to-nobody Brandon. Brandon who ran into a burning building to try to save Jeff and carried his limp lifeless body out of the jaws of hell. Which is the only reason that Jeff is even inside that pine box and not pulverized and burned to a crisp inside the wreckage of a torched strip club.

We couldn't hear what Brandon was saying. He just draped his arms around Jeff's pop and whispered in his ear until eventually the poor guy calmed down and Brandon led him away.

(I swear to God, I'm gonna figure out what Brandon's story is. Because it's gotta be fucking fascinating.)

Anyway, seeing Jeff's dad lose it the way he did put Maddie over the edge. She moved around behind me, sobbing into my back, all over Evan's custom-made suit, and I did my best not to let her feel how much I was crying too.

So that was a fun day.

Today we're in my car headed to Raven's house for Pete's wake. Maddie's fidgeting in the passenger seat, chewing her nails. Is it fucked up to say that she looks beautiful and sexy in her black dress that cinches tight at the waist and showcases her fabulous tits? Or that the tulle or whatever it's called at the bottom causes me to imagine what it would be like to pull the car over to the side of the road, open the passenger door, lift all the poofy fabric over my head, and eat out her glorious pussy?

Rhetorical question. Of course it's fucked up. We're going to a goddamn wake. But I feel like if Pete knew that this was what I was thinking, he'd give me the thumbs up and tell me to go for it.

"No," says Maddie, out of nowhere.

"No, what?" I reply, still thinking about pussy eating.

"You're thinking about eating my pussy. Not now. OK? We're going to a wake."

How the fuck did she know—? "How the fuck did you know—?" I start, before she cuts me off.

"Because you're staring at my lap, kind of swirling your tongue around."

Jesus. Really? "I was?"

"Hey," she says, "I'm flattered and honestly, I'd love you to go down on me—"

I start to veer the car off to the side of the road.

"But—!" She puts her hand on the steering wheel and directs us back into the flow of traffic. "We're going to a *wake*." She really emphasizes the word. "And…" she starts, but then stops herself.

"And what?" I ask her, noticing a little furrow in her brow.

"I have... a lot of shit on my mind."

I nod. I don't have to ask. I know what she's talking about. Carlos Castillo. The money she owes him. The fact that he and his dipshit nephew, Logan... Huh. I should find out Logan's last name. The more you know about a douchebag, the better your shot at wielding some power over him. Anyway...

She's thinking about the fact that both Jeff and Pete are dead because of the debt she owes Carlos. It's not her fault, of course. On some deep level, she's aware of that, but she still feels guilty. Shit. How could she not?

I tell her, "I've told you, I will"—I stop myself and autocorrect—"*we* will pay that dick-sucker back, OK? And then you'll be clear and then—"

"Fuck that," she says decisively. "I'm not giving that asshole one penny of my money."

Technically it's my money, I think, but wisely avoid saying out loud.

"But I do owe him. Do I fucking ever," she says, staring out the window, still biting at her nails.

Which concerns me just a tad. She's been saying stuff like that since the fire. I've made the choice not to question her too much about it, but I'm getting a little worried that her hinges might have gotten knocked a bit loose with everything that happened and that she might actually be considering doing something like... oh, I dunno... murdering a Mexican drug lord. Which, hey, I get the impulse. I wanna kill the fucker too. But to me, actually *doing* it seems ill-advised.

"Hey," I say, reaching over and patting her knee. Which gets me hard. And which I've just accepted is what's going to happen every time I'm near her for the rest of my life and I've made my peace with it. "It's all going to be OK. OK? I promise. One way or another, we're going to handle this Carlos thing."

She keeps staring out the window.

"OK? Maddie? Madison? Mads? Angel?"

"Mm-hm," she mumbles, still biting her nails.

Shit. I really thought I was done helping kill people.

Raven's house is nice. I don't know what I expected, but it's just totally suburban and basic and kind of sweet, tucked away in a cul-de-sac that's all decorated with holiday lights, looking kind of like a Currier and Ives Christmas postcard. If Currier and Ives had made postcards set in the desert, with cacti and iguanas instead of pine trees and horses and shit.

We stride up the walkway, Maddie in front of me, her ass swaying along with her skirt, causing me to hold the flowers I'm carrying in front of my junk so that when she opens the door, the first thing Raven's greeted by won't be me and my big old pal, Chuckie Stiff. (I used to call it Johnny Butch, but Chuckie Stiff sounds funnier.)

We reach the door and Maddie rings the bell. It gives one of those cathedral-like chimes, which is a very Vegas thing for a doorbell to do. I love it.

The door swings open and Raven is there. Not unrecognizable, per se, but certainly more like someone masquerading as Raven and less like Raven herself. She's wearing a dark blouse and black, silk trousers, with what look like closed-toe black shoes. The blouse has a high, ruffled collar and one of those silky cravat/bow things that society chicks will occasionally wear. I got invited— by terrible accident—to a party in the Hamptons once, and there were a couple of older broads wearing that kind of shit. What's surprising about seeing it on Raven is that it doesn't look out of place at all. It looks right at home on her. And suddenly, the idea that she works… worked… in a strip club is actually what feels weird.

"Maddie," she says, and gives Maddie a hug, which seems to take Maddie by surprise. She lets her arms dangle for a second before she realizes herself and hugs Raven back.

After a long moment, they release their embrace and she waves us inside. When she takes the flowers from me, she gives me a hug too. Which I was definitely not expecting, and I kind of shift to the side so that I don't poke her with my man, Chuckie.

The house is pretty full of people milling around. Mostly girls I recognize from the club. I got kind of familiar with the regular dancers while I was sitting around on stakeout, so I see faces I recognize even if the non-wigged hair and the pasties-free tits force me to take a second to remember the names.

I nod at Monet, and Roxy, and the delightfully-monikered Cessna, as Raven brings us into the living room. She takes a seat on the sofa, Maddie sits beside her, and I plop myself in a chair, facing them, on the other side of the glass-top coffee table.

"You guys want any food or anything?" she asks us.

We both decline politely and then Maddie asks, "How you doing?"

It takes her a second to answer, like she's debating the response. Then, "Um, pretty fucking shitty. How about you?"

"The same," Maddie says with a smile.

Then Raven smiles too, and then I smile even though I don't really want to, but I'm trying to be a good boyfriend. Which, over the last couple of days, I've decided is what I am. I've never actually been anyone's boyfriend before, but I mean… once you put on suits and go to funerals and shit with a person, and hold them while they cry, and listen to them as they pace around their living room muttering about maybe killing people, I dunno. That sounds like some boyfriend shit to me.

"Do they know what happened yet exactly?" Raven's asking me. And Maddie's looking at me too.

"Oh, uh, yeah, I'm not really sure to be honest. They're still waiting on the inspection report and, y'know, this shit takes time. So…" It's not a total lie.

"Yeah," she says. And then, looking back to Maddie, "Can I ask you a question?"

"Sure. Of course," Maddie says.

"What exactly is your story with Carlos Castillo?"

I don't know why it feels like we just crested the first major drop on a roller coaster, but it does.

"Um, what do you mean?" asks Maddie.

"How did you come to fall in with him on whatever it is that you're in with him on?"

"Uh…" Maddie looks at me. I look back at her with a very helpful 'fuck are you looking at me for' expression. (Nice job, Ty.) Maddie goes on, "He, I mean, I was trying my hand at running a wedding planning business and he just, like, found me."

13

JA HUSS & JOHNATHAN McCLAIN

Maddie gives her the whole story. How she planned the wedding for his skank daughter (I've actually never met the daughter, she might be a lovely person, but her dad has totally fucked Maddie's life, so I'm being petty), and how she went off and got pregnant with some other dude's baby, and how Maddie had already spent most of the preposterous two hundred grand he gave her for wedding shit, and how he's being irresponsible and irrational about getting it back.

Maddie tells the whole story unemotionally, being careful to omit anything that might let Raven know that it's Carlos who killed Pete and burned down the club. Raven sits and listens, barely blinking the whole time.

Once Maddie finishes, Raven asks, "The money. When did he start demanding it?"

"What do you mean?" Maddie asks.

"I mean, did he lean into you the way he has been before you started working for Pete? Or after?"

Maddie thinks for a second. "I dunno. Um…"

"Like, sending that dickhead Logan to find you and all that noise. When did that start? Was it after you started dancing? Or had you seen him before?"

Again, Maddie considers this. "I—I mean, I don't necessarily remember the timeline, but I guess I don't remember meeting Logan until after I started dancing at Pete's."

"The night you flashed him your pussy. Was that the first time you saw him?"

"The night you did what to who?" I ask. Which seems reasonable.

"Doesn't matter," Maddie says. (I disagree, but there's clearly other shit at work here, so I will choose to table it for later.) "What's the deal?" Maddie goes on. "Pete said a bunch of stuff to me about Carlos too. Like he knows him. Knew him, I mean. What's going on?"

Raven sighs. It makes the bow and ruffles rise and fall with her breathing chest. And just like the night she approached me in the parking lot of the club, she looks younger and softer somehow. It makes me sad for a reason I can't quantify.

"So…" she begins. "Pete had a wife. Carolina."

"Is she the one he kept in his office?" I ask.

"What?" responds Maddie. I shake my head at her. I don't wanna get off track right now. (Besides, my dear, two can play the "Pete's Secrets" game…)

"Yes," says Raven. "That's her. She passed away a few years ago. Pete loved her more than… well, hell… more than anything. The club? That was her idea."

"Really?" asks Maddie. "Running a strip club was his wife's idea?"

"Yep. She was a dancer herself, back in the 70s. And she experienced some pretty rough treatment, I guess. Which is par for the course. But it doesn't have to be, and she wanted to have a place where girls could work and not be exploited and not be judged and not deal with all the garbage that girls have to deal with. I mean, let's not over-inflate it. We gotta be real, she was opening a strip joint, not a convent, but still…"

If you asked me to pick a moment when I decided that I thought Raven was awesome, I might have to put this one high on the list as a contender.

"OK," says Maddie. "So what—?"

"Carolina was Mexican. She lived in Mexico. And that club she was dancing in was owned by a young, Mexican guy who was just starting to make a name for himself in the entertainment, tequila… and drug-running business."

"You. Are. Fucking. Kidding me," says Maddie. Or it might be me who says it. Either way, it's the right reaction for both of us to have.

"I am not fucking kidding you," says Raven. "And more importantly, he kind of fell in love with Carolina, and he tried everything he could to make her love him back and blah, blah, blah. Just a plain old sappy story of unrequited love, honestly."

This shit is blowing my mind. "And Pete…?" I ask.

"Pete was a recently discharged war vet who was down in Mexico doing… whatever guys do when they come back from war." She tilts her head at me like it's a secret code or some shit. I just wave my hand at her to continue. "And, y'know, it's not real complicated after that. Pete and Carolina fell in love, he and Carlos had a lot of bad blood between them, Pete got her the fuck out of Mexico, they settled in Vegas, built a strip club and lived happily ever after."

I start to point out what Raven already knows.

"Yeah," she says, "That is until Carolina died and then Carlos found *you*"—she points at Maddie—"totally coincidentally, I suppose, working at the goddamn symbol of his onetime heartbreak and failure, for probably the one guy he ever met in his life who he couldn't intimidate or bend to his will, and somehow in Carlos' warped fucking mind, he saw this as a chance to get even somehow, I suppose, and so he tried to fucking win *you* instead, and when he couldn't do that, he burned down Pete's with Pete inside."

I hate it when I know I have a dopey, slack-jawed look on my face but can't stop it.

"OK, thanks," Raven says to me. "I was just taking a shot, but you confirmed it for me with the dumbfounded mug you're wearing there."

I snap my mouth shut. Then open it again to ask, "But how——?"

"Dude, I've been around a long time. I've seen shit. And all the shit with that fucker, Logan... I knew it was only a matter of time before it all went pear-shaped. Especially after I saw *you*"—she points at Maddie again—"show back up after he made off in his car with you on Halloween."

"What... What do you mean?" asks Maddie.

"Sweetie, no offense, but if Carlos wanted your money, you dead, or *you*, he'd have it. He was just fucking with you to torture Pete, is my guess."

"But that doesn't—"

"What?" Raven asks. "Make sense? Babe, Carlos is a lot of things and one of them is crazy. With a capital kray. You know he won't get on an airplane, don't you?" And then she gets solemn suddenly. "But I never thought..." And goes silent. As do we all.

This is a lot to take in. Even with all the surreal shit that calls itself life swirling around me lately, this is a bridge farther than I could imagine having to walk. Carlos was using Maddie to torture Pete? Because of a girl? From, like, over forty years ago?

Know what? When I stop to think about losing Maddie to some other asshole, it doesn't seem so nuts. The way I feel about her, I'd spend the rest of my life trying to make that other guy suffer. He's not even real, he's just a figment of my very immediate imagination, and I'm already thinking of ways to make his life miserable. So, in that regard, I get it.

"What are you gonna do?" Maddie asks Raven, thoughtfully.

"Me? Oh, I mean... I'll, y'know, rebuild."

"Rebuild what? Pete's?" Maddie asks.

"Of course. What else am I gonna do?" She smiles. "But there's not gonna be a place for you, I'm afraid."

Maddie smiles back. "Good."

"You know why I busted your balls so hard, don't you?" Raven asks her.

"Yeah," says Maddie. "I do now."

"Good," Raven says and they take each other's hands.

I don't know. I honestly have no idea what the fuck is going on. This is some straight-up girl shit happening, but fine. Not my place to ask. Is it fucked up that seeing them both dressed in black and holding hands gets me hot? Again. Rhetorical. Of course it is.

Then Maddie asks, "Raven? How did you come to—?"

Raven shushes her. "That's a whole other story for a whole other time," she says.

Maddie sniffs and laughs. "OK," she says. "But," she goes on, "can I ask you one thing though? For real?"

"Sure," says Raven.

"What's your real name?"

The question hits me in the gut. I don't even know if she's aware of it, but that's the exact question she asked me in my kitchen on Halloween. The night we found out who we are. Both to each other and to ourselves. The night she went off and got into a car with Carlos Castillo. The night that everything irrevocably changed forever. In both wonderful and terrible ways.

An unsettling smile unfurls slowly along Raven's lips. She regards Maddie, looks over at me, and then looks back

18

at Maddie again. And it reminds me of the last time we saw Pete in his office, and how he did the same thing. The weird déjà vu I feel at this concurrence of events is both bittersweet and ominous. I've got a sinking feeling that she's going to say, "Carolina Flanagan," or something equally unnerving and disquieting that pastes yet another layer of complexity onto this already far too complicated story that keeps unfolding for us. Shit, she might just say, "My name's Tyler Morgan," and send me spiraling off into *The Twilight Zone* for good. Never to return.

I brace for who the hell knows what, and after a few, profound, filled beats, her grin grows even wider and she says…

"It's just Raven."

CHAPTER TWO

MADDIE

After story time is over, we mingle a little. Raven moves quietly into, and between, the small groups of people talking in hushed voices. She touches them all—a gentle hand on the arm or shoulder, a small smile.

She brushes a piece of hair away from Raquel's face and it drags a tear along her cheek, which smudges her makeup and leaves a trail of evidence. Raquel cries softly, her uncertain eyes darting anywhere, everywhere, but directly at Raven. Like she's embarrassed.

Raven comforts her. Refuses to walk away until they are face to face, and Raquel is nodding her head, and looking her in the eyes, and using the tissue handed to her to dab at her cheeks.

They hold hands the ways girls hold hands. All ten fingertips fitting into other fingertips like a puzzle. And for some reason it reminds me of Girl Scouts. When you made a pledge to your troop buddy. You held her hands that way, and you swung your arms a little, like it was a game, and chanted something simple and pretty about promises and friendship to her.

I watch from across the room. Mesmerized.

I know every woman here. Which is… surprising, I guess. But not.

Kinda like everything else about this day.

I mean, I was the morning manager at Pete's. Only for a few weeks, but basically, Pete's was my life. Was really the only thing I had. Yeah, Tyler was there, but he was something to be avoided and Pete's was where I went to avoid him. Where I went to avoid the past. And the present. And probably the future, too, if I'm being honest.

Pete's gave me direction. Pete's gave me purpose. Pete's was a place I could count on.

And now there's no place for me there. Words straight out of Raven's mouth.

I'm not sad about retiring as a stripper. That would be dumb.

But I lost something more than I can quantify in that fire. More than a sense of purpose.

I lost... I dunno. Something akin to family, but not. Because family is just something you have, or don't. And the people at Pete's are... friends.

I had Annie. But I never put a lot of effort into Annie. Same for Caroline and Diane. They were just there. I never felt needed by them. I paid my rent, we sometimes ate and drank together. We tanned out by the pool and pretended we were living the dream.

But that wasn't real. This, these people, these women who take off their clothes every night and pretend to love their jobs for the sake of their sanity—this is reality.

Cold. Hard. Truth.

I love them all in some weird way I've never felt before.

Which is curious. That this room, filled with dozens of women just as messed up as I am, is what really matters to me these days. Their daycare bills, their boyfriend problems, the past they're all running from. It matters to me.

And I wonder if I'll be letting them down when I'm not in their life anymore. Will they miss me the way I'll miss them? Who will settle shoe disputes? Who will put them on the schedule? Who will listen with a sympathetic ear when they have to beg for more stage time so they can make the rent?

Clearly, there will be someone.

Right?

Raven will be there.

Maybe I'm just worried that they won't miss me. They don't need me. Never did need me. I'm just another person in their life with a little bit of power to make it easier and none of it was about family, or friendship, or…

"Mads," Tyler says, placing his hand on my elbow to direct me over to the kitchen island where there's drinks and food laid out. "You should eat something. Want some crackers?"

I look up at him through a blurry haze and realize I'm crying. And even though there's a lot of reasons to cry right now, I don't even know why I'm crying. Is it Pete? Sure. It's Pete. Is it Carolina? Yeah, I think so. Is it Raven, who isn't the person I thought she was? That too.

It's all of it.

It's Carlos, and Logan, and Ricky, and the Mexican compound, and the debt, and the drone, and my parents, and Scotty, and Jeff, and the funeral, and the wake, and how the past is so fucked up and the present looks pretty bad too. And the future? Jesus fucking Christ, what future?

"Here," Tyler says, handing me a cracker. There's some fancy topping on it. Chopped-up cucumbers and mayonnaise with sprinkles of paprika. I eat it, because that's just what you do with a cracker. And it's delicious. Did I ever doubt Raven would serve anything but delicious finger food at Pete's wake?

"Mads," Tyler says, bending down a little to look me in the eyes. "Are you OK?"

I nod my head, sniffling as I wipe away the tears. No fucks to give about the makeup I just smeared across my cheeks. But in my head I say, *No. I'm not OK. Not yet. But I will be.*

I'm not entirely sure what I mean by that. I have an idea. But it's vague. It involves a lot of anger, and hate, and violence.

"Maddie," Tyler says, trying again. Because clearly I am not OK. And that stupid nod wasn't enough to convince him. Can't get anything past Tyler Morgan. "Should we leave?"

"Leave?" I almost laugh. "I don't ever want to leave. I want to stay here forever."

He nods back at me. Slowly, like a hostage negotiator dealing with unreasonable demands. He opens his mouth to say something back, but he's interrupted by silverware clanging on crystal.

We redirect our attention from each other to Raven, who is standing in front of her fireplace, glass and spoon in hand, like she's gonna give a speech.

Which she does. And soon, every woman in the room is crying. Because Pete was one of the good ones and we all knew it. Felt it, at least. And now he's gone, and our lives have been upturned, sure, but we're not lamenting the loss of our jobs, not really. Because Pete's was more than a job. And we all knew that too.

Raven doesn't elaborate on her plans for rebuilding. Or talk about Carlos or Logan or anything like that. It's just the good stuff.

Everyone takes a turn telling a story about Pete. We collectively stop crying and start smiling. Some of the stories even make us laugh. Leave it to Raven to fix an entire room of lost women in under ten minutes.

I think that might be her superpower.

Soon, everyone has told a story but me. And even though they all know I didn't tell one, they don't look at me expectantly. There's no uncomfortable silence. It's like… it's like they understand I can't do it right now. Even though every single one of them managed, I'm not able to manage.

The crowd breaks up after that. A few people leave. Tyler and I stand there, silent. So many things to say, unable to say them. And finally he takes my arm at the elbow again and says, "Let's say goodbye," as he leads me over to Raven.

I hug her tighter than I probably should, unable to say what I want to say, but the squeezing makes her understand. She pulls away and smiles. It's the smile of a champion, I realize. A winner. Someone who knows things, has been through things, understands things. "Call me, OK? You've got my number?"

I nod, dumbly. I didn't, before the fire, I mean. But I do now. Because she's been texting me the past few days. Checking up on me, maybe?

Which makes me start to cry again.

"It's OK," she says, wiping that tear from my face. "It's gonna be OK."

Tyler says a few words to her. Thank yous and stuff like that. And then he leads me out of her house and down the street to where we parked. He opens my door, waits for me to get in, then closes it softly and walks around to the driver's side.

In those few moments, something changes. The Devil pops up on my shoulder and I think it's just... his presence. Knowing he's still with me. I think that's what changes.

We good? he asks.

Yup. We good.

The driver's side door closing makes Devil disappear and I take a deep, deep breath as Tyler starts the engine.

"So," Tyler says, pulling away from the curb.

"So this is how it's gonna go," I say.

"What?" Tyler glances at me as he turns right onto a main street.

"We're gonna kill that motherfucker."

"*What?*"

"I mean, he deserves so much worse than death, but I'm just not sure I have it in me to torture a man. But if that moment comes, you know, when we've got him? And he's begging for his life? I might. Yeah," I say, almost talking to myself. "I might be able to like... pull his fingernails off with a pair of needle-nose pliers, ya know? So we won't rule it out."

"Maddie, we're not killing Carlos." Tyler says this like it's normal to consider it. Which I take as a good sign.

"Not Carlos, Ty. *Logan.* Carlos... I haven't decided what I want to do with him yet. I mean, there's so many options. And the devil has my back, so I'm pretty sure he's gonna come up with something pretty cool."

Tyler huffs out something that might be a laugh, but might not. Might be one of those noises one makes when the person riding in the car next to them has gone off the edge and they have no good comeback for the insanity she's spewing.

But I don't mind. Or take it personally. Because Tyler hasn't really seen me yet. I'm sure on some level he still thinks I'm that innocent teenager he left behind when he went off to war. He still thinks I'm good, and pure, and sweet. Even though he should know better.

Because I'm not. I haven't been that girl for a very long time. Even though I've been holding onto that image of myself for years, it's gone. In fact, I'm not sure I was ever the girl next door. I was never the angel.

But it's not his fault he doesn't know. I've come to understand that I hide it well, ya know? I'm just really good at that.

His moment of reflective silence gives me an opportunity to elaborate. "Look," I say, turning in the seat to see him better. My tears are gone. I'm sure I look a mess, but the sadness stayed behind at Raven's house. I'm a different person right now. "I'm not gonna say something stupid like this is all my fault. It's not. And I'm not gonna try to sell you on the idea that this is just about Pete, either. Or Jeff. Or Scotty."

Tyler raises one eyebrow at me.

"It's not. This is called *payback*, Tyler." I kinda seethe the word. It comes off angry because it is.

Tyler sighs. "No. This was about Pete and Carlos, Maddie. Not you."

"Bullshit," I say. "Carlos found me online. How?"

"Whattayou mean? He has a computer? He knows how to use Google?"

"*No*," I say, louder than I should. "No. Look, Raven's story about the bad blood between Pete and Carlos… That's the whole point. Carlos found *me*, Tyler. First. I didn't take the job at Pete's until after the wedding stuff went sideways."

"OK. So? That doesn't... You're not making any sense."

"You don't get it. Listen. I was at the drone store—"

Tyler's laugh is so loud, it startles me. "Drone store? The good old drone-porium?"

"Fine. It was a warehouse. But whatever. Warehouse. Store. Same thing."

"Uh-huh. And who runs this 'drone store'?"

I think back, trying to remember the guy's name. "Slade?" I say. "Slate? Slayer? I'm not really sure. Something like that. He was one of those mumblers, ya know? Kinda slow, with a drawl. Not Southern, but... redneck, maybe?"

"OK." He sighs. "So you're buying a drone for the real estate stuff—"

"No. For the wedding planner class I took. That's the point." I say it like, *Duh.*

He shakes his head, like he's trying to wrap his mind around my totally logical explanation. "Wait. No. What? No. I thought you bought it for real estate."

"No. I started thinking about it for the wedding stuff, but then that went south with Carlos and shit, and then later I thought I'd do something cool for tourists on the Strip, right? Like chronicle their crazy drunken adventures. But the drone laws are pretty strict, OK? So that wasn't a good idea. And I was just randomly wasting time one day looking for my dream house on Zillow and... *voilà*. Real estate was the answer."

He pulls the car over by the curb, stops, pulls up on the e-brake. He blinks at me. Three times. Slowly, like this makes no sense, even though it does. "Ok, I'm sorry, I think maybe I need to focus. So let me get this straight. You took a wedding planner class, which gave you the idea for a drone to make videos of weddings."

"Yes."

"And then you went to find a drone at a drone warehouse where some hillbilly called Slayer was running the joint."

"Well, it might've been Slate. Or Slade. But yes."

"Super. Then you bought a drone, and—"

"No! That's the thing. I didn't have the money for a twelve-thousand-dollar drone back then. I was broke. I didn't get the money until after I was working for Pete."

Tyler sighs. Pinches the bridge of his nose. "So *when* did you buy the drone?"

"After I started at Pete's. I just told you that. Jesus. I went in—"

"Was Slate there?"

"Coulda been Slayer, or Slade, but no. Some other guy. And I told him I'd been there before looking at the 900XZ, and I wanted it. Oh, and I had cash, because these guys only dealt in cash."

Tyler blinks again. Twice this time. "So you bought a *stolen* military drone?"

"It was not stolen!"

Tyler sighs. Longer and louder than before.

"It wasn't stolen. I have a warranty, OK? I registered it and everything. These guys were legit."

"Terrific. So—"

"Hey! I'm serious. I got a warranty. They had to register it to me before they sold it. It was like a big fucking deal, too. Took them forever and they had to call a bunch of people and... I'm telling you, it was legit! I am not stupid, OK?"

JA HUSS & JOHNATHAN McCLAIN

"OK, OK. Jesus. So, fuck, I'm—I'm just trying to understand what this has to do with Carlos and Pete."

It feels like I'm talking to myself. "The first time when I went in and talked to Slater—"

"Slater?"

"Whoever. And I didn't have the money, and I didn't know how I was gonna get it, there was a flyer for Pete's on the table."

"A flyer?" he says.

"Yes!"

"For strippers?"

"Yeah, it was like… a help wanted ad. Maybe not really a flyer. It was like a call for strippers."

"So… You're saying that… *Pete's Strip Club* was looking for potential *strippers* at the *drone store*?"

"Yes! That's what I'm saying!" I push him on the shoulder. He's finally getting it.

He puts his hands together like he's praying, interlocking his knuckles until they turn white. "OK. Like, seriously, I don't—"

"My point is… I took the job at Pete's *after* the wedding thing went weird. That's all I'm saying. So Raven's story, good as it is, doesn't really add up, does it? I mean, I *already* knew Carlos when I took the job at Pete's. See what I'm saying?"

He takes a slow breath like he's trying not to yell or something. "So, OK, lemme work out what I think you're saying. You're saying… that, like, somehow Carlos steered you to the 'drone store,' knowing that he was going to demand his money back for having to cancel the wedding, but that you wouldn't be able to pay him, and so he… planted a flyer there for Pete's, knowing that you would then have to go become a stripper at the club of his old archnemesis and that that would eventually lead him to burn the place down? Is that basically what you're saying? Because that *is* basically what you're saying."

"Well, when you put it that way…"

"So did you know Logan at the time?"

Where did that come from? "Logan? No," I say. "No, I don't think I saw him until the night—"

"The night you flashed him your pussy?" Tyler adds.

I narrow my eyes. "Really? You want to do this now?"

He gives me this look that says quite clearly that yes, he does indeed want to do this now. But he's gonna be patient and leave that fight for later. And I'm sure he's feeling magnanimous about that very adult decision he just made, but I'm thinking he'd be very stupid to call me out on flashing Logan right now. Because I'd go all redheaded devil on him.

But I, like him, know when it's time to adult, so I do that. "I'm just saying that it's all *too* coincidental to be a coincidence. Y'know?"

He looks at me like he's not so sure. "I thought we all agreed that sometimes things just happen. You, me, your shitty shrink, all of us. We all agree that everything doesn't always have a deeper meaning."

"Yeah, well, I'm not sure that does it for me anymore. OK? I don't wanna believe that I'm just floating along and shit happens or it doesn't and it's got nothing to do with me. I can't fucking believe that anymore. I just can't."

He reaches across and strokes my cheek.

"I can't," I say again.

"OK," he says, "I get it. Look, let's just go back to your place and forget about drones, and Slayers, and everything for now, OK?"

31

I sigh. Leaning back into my seat. Because this has been a pretty fucked-up day. And say, "Yeah, sounds good to me."

By the time we get back to my house it's almost dark. Caroline and Diane aren't home, both cars are gone, so they must be at work early tonight. But that's OK. Just means Tyler and I can have the place to ourselves.

When we get inside I reach for the lights, but Tyler's hand on mine stops me.

"Leave 'em off," he says, pulling me into his chest. "Let's just go straight to bed."

I lean up on my tiptoes, kiss his mouth, and whisper back, "Sounds perfect," as I reach down and grab his cock. He's hard. When isn't he hard?

But when I try to pull away, he doesn't let go. His hands come up to my face, palms on my cheeks, and he kisses me back. It's a long kiss. A nice kiss. But there are a lot of promises in that kiss too.

He reaches up under the tulle of my dress and rubs his hand along the inside of my thigh, his cool fingertips tracing the edge of my panties, making me shudder.

I kiss him harder. Needing him tonight. So glad he's here. He backs me up, pushing me in the direction of my bedroom, ready to make good on his bed idea…

When the doorbell rings.

We break apart, both of us staring at the door. There's a small window, through which we can see the top of a head. Dark hair. Probably male.

"Who the fuck is that?" Tyler asks.

"I dunno," I say, breaking away to go see.

But Tyler pulls me back, says, "Stay here," pointing a finger down at the floor, and walks over to the door and peeks out the window.

"Oh, motherfucker," he says, more to himself than me. "You've miscalculated badly if you think you're gonna start shit today."

He pulls the door open, and I have a second to recognize Other-Guy Ricky Ramirez on the other side of the stoop just before Tyler's fist crashes into his face.

CHAPTER THREE

TYLER

As I drag him inside and slam the door, I think that I've just about had it with this whole Carlos Castillo gang of idiots. I immediately recognize this dummy as the same t-shirt-wearing jackass I knocked out in the alley behind Pete's. The one I so cleverly dubbed "T-Shirt." And even though he's wearing a light sweater today, I'm still gonna call him T-Shirt. Y'know, for simplicity. You start handing out too many nicknames and shit gets confusing.

Anyway.

On the one hand, it's nice of him to ring the doorbell and stand there like a dumbass, allowing me to see who's there *by looking through the fucking window* and then punch him in his stupid, drug-dealing face for a second time.

But on the other hand, it really, really bugs me that these are the dipshits we're dealing with. That these cock-knockers are the ones who killed Pete. And Jeff. And are threatening Maddie. I dunno. Maybe it's just ego, but I think everything would go down for me a lot smoother if it didn't seem like *Amateur Night at the Apollo* every time I had to confront one of these clowns.

And right as I'm thinking this, I get a powerful reminder about the dangers of hubris.

Because just as I'm about to tap him up again and give him a middle-of-the-day nap with a rock-a-bye-baby, he spins out of the way with some, like, crazy Krav Maga-looking shit, grabs my arm, pins it behind my back, and then slams me against the wall.

Honestly, apart from the fact that my hard-on slamming into sheet rock instead of into Maddie is a huge bummer, I'm pretty stoked. I may have misjudged the guy, and the fact that I now might have a chance to win something resembling a fair fight makes me feel a little less bad about the ass-kicking I'm about to hand out.

And then, for the second time in five seconds, I am again taught a lesson about over-confidence.

Because just as I'm about to push backwards, driving this knobgoblin across the room so that I can break free and see just how much pressure his windpipe can take before it snaps… He throws *me* into a choke-hold and presses a SIG P320 against my temple.

Well, shit.

It may be strange, but the only thought I have in this moment is, *Eh, this'll be quick. That's a really good gun. I hope the blood doesn't ruin Evan's suit.*

But before he can pull the trigger, Maddie screams, "No!"

And in return, T-Shirt says, "Dile a tu amigo que se calme, Madison."

Now here's the thing: I like to think of myself as pretty multi-lingual. I can say "hello," "thank you," "give me a beer, please," and "I didn't know she was your daughter," in like six different languages. But it turns out that while those phrases are more or less all you need to get by in most situations, they don't really help me much in the one I'm in now.

"What?" I ask. Then I tell him, "Fuck you, dude. What'd he say?" I ask Maddie.

She ignores me. "What are you doing here? I still have two weeks for the money and you've already taken a more than sufficient deposit, don't you think?" She spits out the words, and then she actually spits at the guy. She's fucking awesome.

"Maddie, calm down. I'm just here to talk," he says.

Huh. Either I speak more Spanish than I thought, or this dude's speaking English now.

"What the fuck do you want to talk about?" She steps toward him. He spins me around, putting my body in between him and Maddie. She stops, but doesn't take her eyes off T-Shirt. And I can't help but smile. I twist my neck to talk in his direction.

"Bro," I say, "you need to think real hard about what your next move is, because if I'm still standing in ten seconds, you won't be. And if I'm not, then you *really* won't be." And I wink at Maddie.

(Shit, that was awesome. That's better than most movie dialogue. Maybe I should write screenplays. If I don't die in the next couple of minutes, I'm gonna put some thought toward learning how to be a screenwriter.)

There's a tense beat where I think he's gonna call what he believes is my bluff (it's not, she'll totally kill him if I don't) and blow my brains out, but then he wisely thinks better of it and pushes me forward, toward Maddie, while keeping the gun on both of us.

"Jesus," he says, "Do you think if I came here to hurt anybody that I would've rung the goddamn doorbell?"

"Yeah, I do," I say. "From what I've seen, you guys are really bad at your job."

"I just want to talk, OK? I'm gonna put the gun away."
And he commences slowly lowering the gun. I'm just
about to Conor McGregor the dude one more time when
he asks me, "Were you Special Forces?"

The question grabs my attention and I stop calculating
his demise for a second.

It's not that I trust his actions, or really even the
question itself that stops me from turning his day into
night. It's the way he asks it. Without an accent. At least
without a Spanish one. Or Mexican. Or whatever. My ear
is not well attuned enough to regional dialects to be able
to discern precisely where this dude might be from, but I
likely would *not* have said Wisconsin. Which is where he
sounds like he's from now. Or Ohio. Illinois. Idaho.
Wherever. I dunno. Someplace that my high school
speech and debate coach would've called Standard
American. Which is dumb. There's no such thing as
Standard Americans. I hate generalizing.

But then again, I was just kind of generalizing where
T-Shirt might be from just because he was speaking
Spanish. He could be Russian and just speaking Spanish
to throw me off for all I know. I have no idea.

Ugh.

Rambling.

"Ty...?" Maddie looks up and nudges me to bring me
back to the present.

"Uh... No. Special Forces? No. EOD. Navy. Why?
Fuck do you care?"

"Because you punch like a Ranger," he says. And,
rubbing his jaw, he gets a little smile and adds, "It's a
compliment. Only been knocked out twice in my life.
Once by a Ranger in Mosul and once in an alley behind a
strip club in Vegas. By you."

This whole exchange just took some unexpected turns.

"Fuck were you doing in Mosul?" I ask him.

"Fighting ISIL," he says, tucking the gun away in the back of his pants and raising his hands in a gesture of surrender.

"Ricky?" says Maddie, shaking her head. "What the fuck?"

"You know his name?" I ask, confused and mildly agitated.

"He drove me back after I convinced Carlos to give me time to get his money instead of being his sex slave or whatever."

"What?" What is she talking about? "Um, I feel like there's a lot I still don't know about what's going on," I say.

"Not now," she says, waving me off. OK. That's fair. I still haven't told her I burned my apartment down. I'm in no position to judge. "His name is Ricky Ramirez," she says. "His card says he's a distributor for Castillo Tequila, which means that he actually distributes Carlos's meth, or cocaine, or whatever the fuck it is."

Ricky nods carefully and volunteers, "Yeah, well, I also have another card. Which is what I'm reaching for now, OK?"

He leans over slowly, unbuttoning the side pocket of the cargo pants he's wearing. I take a step toward him, just in case. So does Maddie, which makes me hard again.

Fuck! Jesus Christ. Not now, Chuckie.

Sure enough, he pulls out a business card, cautiously, and hands it to me. I hold it so that Maddie and I can look at it together. It reads…

JA HUSS & JOHNATHAN McCLAIN

"United States Department of Justice. Drug Enforcement Administration."

I glance up at him without lifting my head. He nods just enough for it to register as a nod. I shift my eyes back to the card. Underneath the header is...

"Richard Martinez. Special Agent."

CHAPTER FOUR

MADDIE

I take the card from Tyler and read it again just to make sure I'm seeing this right. Yup. DE fuckin' A.

And then I swing, and my little fist crashes into Ricky's tightly-clenched jaw. And there's this weird moment when Tyler looks at me in surprise, and Ricky looks at me in surprise, and I have to collect my thoughts so I can put into words what that punch really meant.

But I do it. I smooth an imaginary wrinkle out of my dress, raise my chin, and say, "Eso es por mentir."

Ricky rubs his twice-punched jaw.

"What?" Tyler says. "What'd you just tell him?"

But I ignore Tyler and take another step towards Ricky. I point my finger in his face and say, "I hate liars."

"I get that," he says. "I'm sorry."

"We spent like eleventy-billion hours together driving back to Vegas. You couldn't tell me this *then?*"

"I can't risk talking in one of Carlos's cars. I'm risking enough by even being here now and having the damn card on me."

"And then—" I'm so angry, I'm seeing red. "And then you threatened to kill me if I didn't have the money in time when you dropped me off." I swing again, but Tyler catches me by the wrist before I can make contact.

"What?" I snap, turning my head to glare at him.

"Why are you mad at me?" he asks.

"I'm not mad at you," I snap again. I walk right over to the couch, plop down, causing my dress to flounce out over the sofa cushions, and I hug a pillow to my lap. I'm so mad.

"OK..." Tyler says. "Can we try again? Without the Spanish this time?" He points to both of us with two fingers forming a V-shape. Ricky nods. "So, OK. So, you're a fucking DEA agent?"

"I am. And, just so you know, nobody knows I'm here today," says Ricky.

"How'd you know we were here? Were you fucking trailing me?" I ask him.

"I was. I read that Pete's wake was happening and assumed you'd be there."

I am so, so mad.

"OK. Good for you," says Tyler. "So whattayou want? If you're so goddamned worried about blowing your cover, then why *are* you here now?"

"Because it's important." Ricky takes a breath, then says, "So I work out of the San Diego field office. I've been inside the Castillo organization, working my way up, for the last eighteen months."

He looks at me like I should care. Fuck him. He threatened to kill me. A threat I took seriously. I made decisions based on that fucking threat. Like stripping in the morning at Pete's.

Ricky continues, "And it's been tough. Like real tough. We're getting shit."

"Why?" asks Tyler.

"Because Castillo's crazy but he's careful. You know why he won't fly? It's not because he has some innate fear of flying, it's because he thinks the US government will shoot him down."

"What? Why?" I ask. "Would you guys really do something like that?"

There's a pause before Ricky says, "Probably not. But it's what he thinks."

Jesus. This whole thing is insane.

"Point is, he doesn't trust anyone."

"What about his nephew? Unlucky Logan?" Tyler asks. I look at him to explain himself. He shrugs and adds, "My nickname for him. How I keep people straight. This guy was just T-Shirt until a second ago. Now he's Ricky DEA."

"Logan's his own thing," says Ricky.

"Fuck do you mean, 'his own thing'?" I snap at him. "You know he burned down the club and killed Pete, don't you? On his uncle's orders."

Ricky hangs his head and says, "Yeah. Yeah, I know what he did."

"So then fucking arrest him!" I shout, standing up. Tyler puts a hand on my arm to hold me back. But I'm about two seconds from being able to be held back by anyone.

"We can't. I can't. If Castillo goes down on a murder charge, which is a state charge, then we blow up our whole investigation. Not to mention the fact that he's not a US citizen. Trying to extradite him would take months, or longer, and in the meantime, he'd move pieces around so that we'd have to start our work with him all over again. It's... We can't. I'm sorry."

I pull myself free of Tyler's grip and get right in Ricky's face. "Fuck. You."

"OK, OK," Tyler says pulling me back. I jerk free again and throw myself back onto the couch. Tyler goes on, "Look, what are you doing here today? What do you want?"

Ricky looks around then spies a chair across from the couch. "May I sit?"

"Whatever," I say, panning my hand to the chair.

Ricky places himself in the chair and looks at me. "Maddie, I've been working this thing for a year and a half. And in that time, I've known Carlos to be singularly focused on running his business and keeping his competition in place. He eats, drinks, and sleeps work. Talks about nothing else."

"So. What does that have to do with—?" I start.

"Until you," he interrupts.

If Ricky Ramirez-Martinez-Whatever-His-Last-Name-Is wanted my attention, he has it now. "What are you talking about?"

"Yeah," says Tyler. "Fuck are you talking about?"

"He's... obsessed. With Maddie. He talks about her all the time. Maddie, he doesn't care about the money you owe him. He wants you."

"Well, yeah," I say. "I kinda figured that out when he tried to abduct me."

"No, that's my point. He doesn't *try*. He doesn't negotiate with anyone. Nobody leaves unless he wants them to. That he let you walk away...? Like, I'm saying he's in love with you, Maddie."

Holy. Fucking. Hell. This cannot be happening. And suddenly, I have a very bad feeling that I know where this is all headed.

"So… What do you want from me?" I ask, suspiciously.

"I'd like to ask you to help the United States government build its case against the Carlos Castillo drug cartel. By telling Carlos that you couldn't get together the money you owe him, and that you're willing to make good on your promise to… be with him."

There's a faint ringing in my ears, like something loud just happened next to me and it's going to take a while to get my hearing back. The next thing I can make out clearly is Tyler's voice saying…

"Um, I'm sorry. You think you're gonna get my girlfriend involved in your little government scheme to bring down a *Mexican drug lord?*"

That's *exactly* what Ricky thinks. Clearly. And—wait. Did Tyler just call me his girlfriend?

"It's neither little, nor is it a scheme," says Ricky. "It's a massive government *operation* that has already cost us millions of dollars and thousands of man hours. And what's missing for us to make our case is how Carlos is transporting his drugs."

"Whattayou mean, how?" Tyler asks.

"He's not flying anything, he doesn't use tunnels like his competitors, or at least none that we've been able to ID, and—"

"And what? Maddie is a fucking expert in drug trafficking methods all of the sudden?"

"No. But Maddie might be the one person we've found who's in a position to get the critical intel we need." Then Ricky takes a breath and says, "Look, I know it sounds ridiculous, but sometimes to catch the bad guys, we have to paint outside the lines. It's not ideal, I get it, but she'll be providing a service to her country and I'll be there the whole time in case things go sideways."

"OK," Tyler says, walking over to Ricky and staring down at him like he's gonna... I dunno, choke him until he dies, maybe. "First of all, this card," he says, holding up the business card, "is bullshit. I need a badge and then I need a supervisor, and then I'm gonna need a meeting with the supervisor, and then... maybe, if all that shit checks out, we can talk about how I, not her, but I, *might* help you. But until that happens, fuck you."

"Well," Ricky says, "I appreciate that, but unfortunately that can't happen. The deal is that I've got a lot of latitude to run this operation, so this is my call. Buck stops with me."

"OK. Then get the *fuck* out." Tyler is serious. Like, I haven't seen him in soldier mode or anything, but I've gotten glimpses of that particular side of him. And this is that side. This, right here, is who he's become since he left home all those years ago. Dead-fuckin'-serious I-will-kill-you Tyler Morgan.

"Wait," I say, throwing the pillow aside and standing up. "You're trying to take down Carlos?"

"We very much are," Ricky says, still calm.

"And Logan?" I ask.

"I mean, certainly he'll also go down if we can get Carlos."

I chew on my lip, thinking about this.

"No," Tyler says, coming to stand in front of me. Blocking my view of Ricky with his body. "No, Maddie. Not happening. We already agreed to just pay these nut-suckers the money you owe them and have that be the end of it."

"It won't be the end of it," says Ricky. "I assure you. Sorry. But that's the truth."

I step to Tyler and put my hands on his chest. "They killed Pete, Tyler. And Jeff. And who knows how many other people."

Tyler looks into my eyes, then says, "Fuck this," and starts pacing. "Fuck this. Fuck this."

"We need you, Maddie," Ricky says. "And if you—"

"Fuck this!" Tyler yells.

"—can get him to trust you—"

"Get the fuck out!"

"—and get him to think you're on his side... We *can* get him, Maddie. We can get him, and Logan, and all of them. All you gotta do is—"

Tyler jumps at Ricky, grabs him by his sweater and pulls him up out of the chair. Ricky doesn't resist. Just looks like he's bracing himself for another punch. Tyler screams at him, "The fuck are you talking about? No! The fucking answer is no!"

And then, out of nowhere, the Devil pops up on my shoulder. Smiling. Dancing a little jig. *Yes*, he hisses in my ear. *Yes. This is perfect.*

And he's right. It is, isn't it?

"Payback," I say, redirecting my gaze from Ricky to Tyler.

Tyler, still holding Ricky's sweater, looks at me. "What?" he asks.

"This is how we get our payback for Pete. And for Jeff. And for all the other people Carlos Castillo has fucked with and killed over the years."

"No, no, no," says Tyler. "What are you saying?"

"I'm saying..." My eyes shift back to Ricky. "My answer is yes."

47

TYLER

My grip on Ricky DEA's sweater remains tight, but it's less a threat and more so that I don't fall immediately to my knees when I let go. What the fuck is going on?

"Maddie..." I say. But she just keeps talking to Ricky.

"What do we do? How do we start? When do I go? Do I go with you now?"

Ricky taps me on the fist that's still holding his sweater, and I finally let him loose, trading places with him in the seat I just yanked him up from.

He says, "The Christmas deadline you guys have in place is coming up, and he's going to expect something. This is probably our best shot if we don't want him to get too suspicious. If he thinks you're going to him because you can't get the money together, we can likely sell it. We'll need a few days to brief you and get you ready for what you'll be doing. I'd like longer, but we don't have it, so we'll just have to do the best we can."

Fuck this. I can't keep it in. "The best we fucking can?" I shout. "That does not sound like what you want for someone when you're sending them into battle! 'Petty Officer Morgan, we know you haven't completed your diver training or ordnance disposal courses, but we're gonna just toss you out there in the field anyway, with IEDs and chemical weapons and so forth, and just have you *do the best you can.*' You can hear how that sounds stupid, right?"

"Ty——" Maddie starts, but she can wait for a second. She had her shot to be worked up. It's my turn.

I stand up, rip off my tie—because it's fucking choking me to death—and throw it on the ground. (Fuck it. I'll buy Evan a new one.) I pop the collar on the shirt, and get right in Ricky's face. We're about the same height, so we're basically nose to nose. "I don't know what the fuck they teach you assholes at the DEA, but this is not how shit is done. Read me? You were in the military?"

"I was."

"Yeah? Which branch?"

"Army."

"Oh, well, of fucking course you were. And what was your job? Besides getting punched by Rangers? Were *you* a fuckin' Ranger?"

"For a while," he says.

"Fuck does that mean?"

"It means that I left the Rangers."

"Why? To do what?"

"I was recruited by First SFOD-D. That's what I did before I got out."

First SFOD-D? Special Forces Operational Detachment-Delta? Seriously?

"You were a fuckin' Delta Force operator?" I ask him.

"I was."

"You were a fucking Delta Force operator, and went through everything that becoming *that* entails, and yet somehow you think it's a fucking banner idea to send an untrained *woman* into what is basically a combat operation?"

"What does me being a woman have to do with it?" Maddie asks sharply.

Oh, fuck. "It… That's not… Nothing."

"No," she says. "You made a point of saying 'woman,' like that has particular meaning. You somehow think because I'm a woman, I won't be able to handle it?"

Jesus Christ! "No," I say, taking a breath. "It's not because you're a woman. You just happen to be a woman. You are, in fact, a woman," I continue pointing out. "But the more relevant fact to this conversation is that you're not *trained*."

She eyes me. I don't know if she buys it, but I don't give a shit. I mean it.

"Hey, look," I continue. "I trained with two female techs in EOD school and I'd take either of them any day over half the jagoffs I graduated with. They were the fucking tits at the job." Oh, fuck me. "Not the *tits*. I didn't mean… I mean they *were*, but not… It's just an expression! Fuck it! My point is, you'd be amazing at anything you do, but everybody who does anything needs training! All I'm saying!"

"It's intel," says Ricky DEA, casually, from out of nowhere.

"What?" I ask, annoyed.

"It's not a combat operation. It's intel-gathering. Look, I will make sure that if it starts to look even a little hot, we get her the fuck out of there."

"And how will you do that?" I ask him. "Nobody knows you're here, right? You're in deep cover. How the hell will you get her out?"

JA HUSS & JOHNATHAN McCLAIN

"Tyler… It's Tyler, right?" I nod. "Tyler, at the end of the day, I do still work for a major US government agency. We have tools at our disposal. And she's not going in completely cold. My Vegas counterpart and I will give her a crash course."

"Crash course. Fucking super." I can't believe this.

"Besides," he says, "I've seen her handle herself with Castillo. I don't think it's *her* you should be worried about." And then he smiles one of those charming, good-guy smiles that I normally just want to punch off someone's face. But somehow, on this dude, I don't mind it. I dunno why. Maybe because he was Delta. Whatever.

"Tyler…" Maddie steps to me. "I need to do this. OK? I need to."

She takes my hand in hers and intertwines our fingers. Looking into her eyes, I can see the need she's talking about. I can see it. Her expression projects the truth that what she needs is so much greater than just avenging Pete, or getting even with Carlos, or anything as small and petty as that. It's about the need she has to stand strong. To lift herself up and move forward again. Finally. After all this time.

Well, she's sure picked one hell of a coming-out party for herself.

"I get it," I whisper, "I just… Dude, can you fucking go so we can talk about this shit? Please?" I say to my new pal, Ricky.

He nods. "Do you have a piece of paper?" he asks.

Maddie gets him one, and he grabs a pen from his other cargo pocket. He writes something down and hands it to her.

52

"This is the number to ring if you do decide you want to help us out. The woman who will answer is called Emily."

"Is that her real name?" asks Maddie.

"It's the only one I've ever called her."

"That's not an answer," I point out.

He nods. "I know." And as he grabs the door handle, he says, "I'm sorry this is happening for you, Maddie. I really am." He pulls the door open and pauses in the doorway. "But I suppose we're also lucky it is you and not somebody else. Give a call when you're ready to get going."

And then… he's gone.

TYLER & MADDIE

TYLER

The second the door swings shut behind Ricky DEA, she grabs her cell phone and starts dialing the number he left. And now I'm chasing her around the house like a maniac, trying to get the phone out of her hand. I feel like we're in a fucking Laurel and Hardy movie.

"Maddie, Maddie, Maddie, stop. Just stop and let me... Fuckin' stop!"

I finally secure the phone away from her and she spins on her heels and stares at me. "Give me. My. Phone," she says.

I hold it so that she can't reach it.

"GIVE. ME. MY. PHONE."

I suddenly wish Caroline and Diane were here. I would never, in a million years, harm a hair on Maddie's head, so it would be nice if there were someone else around to pull her off when she goes HAM on me in a second.

"Maddie, Maddie, please, just give me a second. I just wanna talk about this with you. Please."

She grabs my dick, which was starting to flag, but is roused back into action by her touch, squeezes, and says, "Give me my phone, or I will rip your nuts off."

"OK, OK," I say.

And I throw the phone across the room.

She shouts, "What is wrong with you? It's supposed to be a bad thing!"

"Sorry," I say, shrugging. "But are you still gonna jerk on my dick until you rip it off? Because I totally think you should. I deserve it." I smile a toothy smile at her and she lets go of my cock and flops back onto the sofa. Which is a massive let-down for me.

"Fuck!" she calls out. "Am I crazy for wanting to do this?"

"I mean... yeah," I say, matter-of-factly, as I sit at the end of the sofa, pulling her feet onto my lap and unbuckling her shoes.

"But... I think I have to. You get that, right?" she asks, looking at me earnestly.

"Yeah. I get it. I wish I fuckin' didn't, but I do," I say as I drop one shoe to the floor, then the other, and begin massaging her feet.

"Mmmm," she lets out, dropping her head back on a throw pillow.

"See?" I say. "You think Carlos will do this shit for you?"

She lifts her head and props herself on her elbows. "Are you... jealous? Is that what this is about?"

"No, dummy!" I say, flicking her big toe with my finger.

"Ow, fucker! I'm not like you. I feel pain and shit."

"Sorry, sorry," I say, kissing her toe. "You can stab me with something if you want."

"You'd like it." She grins.

"What? Is that weird?" I ask, kissing the other four toes now.

"Tyler, Tyler, stop," she says. I do stop. I don't wanna. But I do. She gets a serious look and says, "You really do understand? I *have* to do this."

"Yeah," I acquiesce, "I understand. I just…"

"What? What is it? You just what? Say it."

I can feel my heart beating in my dick. And not just because it's throbbing with want for her. My whole body is pulsing.

"I just… love you, Maddie. And there's about a million ways something like this can go wrong. And if anything happens to you… I'll…"

I'll kill myself.

It's not any more complicated than that. But that's not something a person needs to hear. Because it's selfish, and manipulative, and unfair. So…

"I don't fucking know what I'll do."

Sure. That's close enough.

MADDIE

He loves me.

He just said he loves me. He said it before, but it was desperate, from a place of panic. This is different. He's not panicked. He's worried. Because he loves me.

I smile but turn my head into the couch to hide it.

It's not like I planned this. It's not like I set out to seduce him. It's not like I've been dreaming of a Tyler and Maddie wedding since I was eight. Really.

But I've always loved him. In different ways throughout the years, but love is love.

He was... the perfect brother's-best-friend crush when I was a kid. I have always thought him cute. He was skinny once. Lanky and lean, more like a runner or a cyclist. Not bulked up like a soldier. But that was a long time ago.

Tyler grew up first, it seemed. Before Scotty or Evan. He just... burst into manhood when all the other kids were still boys. He became tall before my eyes. He filled in. Started lifting weights in his garage. He was the first to grow a beard, and that makes me smile even wider. It was a stupid beard. And I made fun of him. But he never took it personally. It was a joke. Something sweet. Like the way he called me Mads and made fun of my temper. Something just between us.

And even though he looks nothing like the kid I once knew, this is better. He's even better than he was. Because he's seen stuff, and done stuff, and learned stuff. And he's still here. He came back. Not for me, I know that. But he came home. Alive. And that's better.

Tyler Morgan is a good man. And I don't base that off some childhood crush. Everything he's done since we reconnected tells me all I need to know. Tells me he's one of the good guys.

That's what I've been telling you too, Angel says.

And I wish I had the words to tell him that right now because I have a feeling he doesn't believe it. But I don't have the words. And it's not the time.

He just said he loves you, Angel says. *It's the perfect time.*

"What?" Tyler asks. "What's with the face?"

"Remember that time when I was like six and—"

"Yes." Tyler's face widens with a grin.

"Liar! You didn't even let me finish!"

"My answer is still yes."

"I was six," I say again. "And I was sitting out on the front stoop crying over something, I don't even remember. And you came out of your garage. You were on your bike. Going somewhere. Wherever boys go on bikes. And you saw me, and you stopped, and you put that bike down, and you sat next to me, and you said—"

"'I'm selling smiles. Do you wanna buy one?'"

I buy one right now. "Yeah, you said that."

"And you bought one."

"I did. It was a good one too. Lasted me all day."

"Your fish," he says.

"What?" I ask, pulling myself out of the past.

"You won that goldfish at the carnival and it died the next day. You were crying over that goldfish."

I look at Tyler Morgan. See him for who he was back then. Who he is now. Cherish all the memories and appreciate the fact that he's been a part of all the most important moments in my life. Even when he wasn't. Because some people just stay with you, ya know?

Some people just find a place in your heart and call it home.

So I ask, "You love me?"

TYLER

I'm still rubbing her feet, but sort of absently, looking at her sweet, sweet face, that suddenly looks like it's about to welcome tears to start falling.

I shrug one shoulder and say, "Yeah. Sorry. It's true."

She gulps, lets out a huff of air through her nose, and says, "I love you too."

And that's it.

I grab her wrists and pull her into my lap. The fluffy black material at the bottom of her dress spills out around us. She takes my face in her hands and begins kissing me with a reckless hunger. Which is fine, because I'm starving for her too, and we can both feed the other with what we desire.

She's rocking back and forth against my erection, and the feel of her tight pussy rubbing against the light cashmere of the fourteen-thousand-dollar suit pants I'm wearing is like being wrapped in a cloud.

But since I absolutely do not want to come in Evan's suit, I lift her to the side and place her on her back on the sofa again. "Hold on," I say.

She looks up at me, rubbing her feet together, nibbling at her bottom lip, and every stitch of clothing I remove feels like it takes forever.

First, I kick off the shoes, taking off the jacket as I do and tossing it on the chair that sits across from the couch. Then I rip the socks off and toss them aside, and unbutton the dress shirt, popping the cuff links loose last, and toss it on the chair as well.

Me standing in front of her, wearing only the trousers, causes her to say, "You're so fucking sexy. Do you know that?"

"Nah," I say, "You're just seeing reflected glow." I wink at her as I unbuckle the belt and let it hang there. I snap open the trouser button, unzip the pants, and then pull them off along with the boxer briefs I put on because I was wearing another dude's clothes (I am nothing if not courteous. Everybody says so), and toss them to the side with everything else.

Then I take my cock in my hand and stroke it back and forth, watching her imagine that my hand is her mouth.

"I don't know where Caroline and Diane are," she tells me. "They could be home any minute."

"I can't imagine they'll be shocked. They are hookers and all."

"I don't know if they've ever seen a cock like that one," she says, tilting her head.

"You mean that in a good way, right?"

She giggles and nods. I bend down to my knees.

"What are you doing?" She asks.

I don't answer, just take her feet up with my hands and begin kissing them again and then sucking on them. Placing one big toe in my mouth and swirling my tongue around. Then putting the next in along with the first. Allowing my tongue to slide in the slender, delicate crevices that separate them. She whines with pleasure, and giggles as I lap and tickle the skin that lives here at the base of her amazing body.

And suddenly, I am reminded of the first night she and I reconnected, without knowing it was a reconnection. That night in the VIP room at Pete's, which is no more. I remember that when I held her hands, I *considered* them. Studied them. Wanted to learn and know them. And that's what I'm doing now.

I want to start at the bottom of her and work my way up, learning every possible millimeter of her flesh. Every line, curve, angle, perceived imperfection, everything.

And so, in looking at her feet, as I nip at her toes and she wriggles and moans, I notice a scar running along the back of her heel.

"Where'd you get that?" I pause to ask.

61

"What?"

"The scar. Here." I bend her knee so she can see, and she reaches down to touch it, remembering.

"Oh. You did that."

"What?" I ask, like, really surprised at her response.

"Seriously? You don't remember?" she asks.

"Seriously. No."

She laughs and says, "You remember the selling-smiles-goldfish thing and you don't remember how I got the scar?"

"I really don't. No. When did it happen?"

She huffs out another tiny laugh and says, "You know when you and Scotty and Evan all decided that you were gonna be volunteer firefighters?"

"You mean when we were like ten?"

"Yeah. And you idiots would ride around on your bikes going, 'woo-woo-woo'!"

"In fairness, I think it was only Evan who went 'woo-woo-woo."

She laughs again. She should. That was a good one.

"And you'd... I feel like I remember that... Didn't you guys actually *set* fires so you could go put them out?"

I put on an overly admonished face, like a kid who's been busted for doing something he shouldn't be doing. "Maybe," I squeak out.

"Yeah... Well, this was from the time you three were racing around the driveway at our place. Just, like, going in circles for no reason. Knuckleheads. And I came out to tell Scotty it was time for dinner and you didn't see me, or whatever, and you skidded to a stop, but wound up kind of rolling up the back of my leg. You really don't remember this?"

"No, no, I... kinda do? I dunno. I remembered the nice one! Cut me some slack."

She rolls her eyes. "Well, whatever, you took a huge chunk of skin off the back of my heel and that's what that's from."

I examine it again, more closely. Really favoring it and kissing it. Trying to go back in time twenty years and make it not happen.

"I'm sorry," I say. "That's probably why I don't remember."

"Why?"

"Because it caused you pain." She gives me a look like you give someone when you care about them but can't believe what an idiot they are. "I'm so sorry. I was an asshole."

"You still are," she says, smirking. "But don't feel bad. I loved that injury. Seriously. I loved it so much. Probably why the scar is even there."

"What? What do you mean? Why?"

"Every time it would start to heal over and scab, I'd pull it off."

I study her face and ask, "How come?"

She closes her eyes, kind of like she's embarrassed, and then says, "Because. You gave it to me."

That's it. Good night, fucking Irene.

Starting at her ankle, I begin licking. My head is hidden from her view by the flowy canopy of black that is her dress, but I can see every part of her. And waiting, at the top of my journey, are the black, lace panties she has on. The smell of her skin and her moist pussy swirls all around me, filling up my nostrils and making me fight back the urge to press my cock inside of her right this second. But, if I can hold out, there'll be time for that after I've let my tongue taste what it wants.

I lick my way up to behind her knee and start kissing her there. I swear, the sound she makes when I do causes me to think that she's coming right now. Which can't be possible. Or I suppose it could, and that would be wonderful and a nice trick to have up my sleeve, to know that I can make her come by just touching her there, but I don't have long to think about it because suddenly I can feel her hand on the top of my head, through the skirt, pushing my face up towards her pussy.

OK. That's no problem. Happy to oblige.

I work my hands up the outside of her thighs, reach the lace with my fingertips, and draw her panties down around her ankles. She kicks at them with her feet, kneeing me in the face in the process.

"Sorry!" I hear from somewhere out there in the air above my joy.

"All good!" I call back, and keep doing my duty.

She drops one leg off the sofa and onto the floor, and now I have a full view of what has quickly become one of my favorite sights in the world. I have seen the Taj Mahal, the Roman Colosseum, Machu Picchu, all that Seven Wonders shit. None of it holds a candle to the wonder that is Maddie Clayton.

I place my palms on the inside of her thighs, so that I can spread her wider with my thumbs and allow my tongue to burrow itself inside her. And just as I'm about to place my mouth on her tender, bare pussy, I hear a *riiiiiip*.

And before I can ask, 'What was that?' her hand comes shooting down into view, her index and middle fingers landing on her clit.

"Did you just rip your dress open?" I ask.

She ignores the question and her hand pushes my head forward before landing back on her clitoris again. I decide the only decent thing to do is to help her out, so I let my tongue stroke against the swollen flesh in time with her rubbing, alternately sliding it inside the pink walls of her pussy, lapping up the wetness that's starting to spill from her in torrents now.

MADDIE

His beard tickles my inner thighs. "That feels so good," I moan. I pull my hand away, giving his mouth better access, and slide my fingertips through his hair as his tongue flicks against my clit. And just when I think this moment could not feel any better, he places his whole mouth against me and sucks.

"Jesus," I whisper. "Don't ever stop."

A breath of air tells me he's laughing and happy about pleasing me. Which makes me want to please him.

"I want your cock in my mouth," I say.

He *tsks* his tongue, probably not meaning to drive me wild, but it does. I arch my back and fist his hair just as he says, "Plenty of time for that later."

So I lie back and enjoy it. I have no choice. Because Tyler Morgan has taken a masterclass in eating pussy or something. Every lick, every sweep of his tongue, every movement of his chin... all of it has me on the edge.

And then his fingers join in. My eyes roll back into my head. I lose time, I'm sure of it. I float somewhere unreal. Somewhere between then and now. Somewhere dreamy, and beautiful, and—

JA HUSS & JOHNATHAN McCLAIN

"Don't come yet," he murmurs, making my clit vibrate with his words.

And I want to say, *Don't worry. You can just make me come again.* And be selfish. And take everything he's offering.

But I hold back. I hold it in because if I come now it will upset the perfect balance of ecstasy he's created.

It's just that I can't hold on much longer. So I wiggle my hips a little and his tongue finds its way inside my pussy again as my fingertips wander down between my legs like they're in charge of what happens next. Which is me, playing with myself, as Tyler pushes his tongue in deeper, as my fingers find their rhythm on my clit, and all I can think of is… I never want this to end.

TYLER

She rubs harder and I stretch my tongue as far as I can, almost separating it from the inside of my mouth, straining as I swirl it around inside her. And on cue, her thighs come crashing together against my head, pinning me there, forcing me to stop moving, but allowing me to stay bound to her with my mouth. Which is all I want.

The vibration of her quivering thighs against my cheeks has me rubbing my dick into the sofa, unconsciously emulating the gyrating muscles in her legs. Suddenly, she pulls herself back from my lips, drawing the skirt up as she does, exposing my head to the room.

She presses her foot into my shoulder, forcing me to a kneeling position on the floor, and before I know it, she's pushed me all the way onto my back, picked her skirt up, and is mounting my throbbing cock. I can now see the rip she made in the top of her dress, and it makes my cock throb harder. It's torn down to her stomach, exposing her

66

taut muscles and her magnificent tits, still wrapped in the black bra she's wearing.

I reach behind her and, with a trick I learned back in high school and have never gotten sick of pulling out of my bag, in a snap of my fingers, I've unfastened the latch and freed her breasts from their confinement. She gasps and her eyes get wide for a second before she smiles and plants her mouth on mine.

"Is that what I taste like?" she asks, sucking at my lips with hers.

"Does it taste better than anything you've ever had in your mouth before? Then yes."

She bends her legs back, locking her calves to the inside of mine, allowing her the anchor she needs to grind my cock back and forth, back and forth, pulling her ass down my thighs until I'm *almost* out of her, and then rolling her hips forward and consuming me again. Back and forth. Back and forth. Back and forth.

MADDIE

I reach up, grab both my breasts, and squeeze. Tyler watches me, stupid grin on his face, which just makes me happy in ways I can't describe. "You like that?" I ask. "Do you like when I play with myself?"

"I like it better when it's me." He winks.

I lock eyes with him. Stare into him as I raise one breast up towards my chin. He tilts his head to the side as if to say, *You gonna go there?*

And I do. I go there. I lower my mouth to my nipple and swirl my tongue around, mimicking the way his tongue was swirling between my legs just moments ago. And when my lips descend, and I pull the hard nub into my mouth, we start fucking again. Hard. Like I made him forget for just a second what he was doing, but now he's remembered.

His hands grip my hips, pushing me back and pulling me forward as I continue to make my tongue dance over the peaked tip of my nipple... and I love it.

I want him to leave marks on my skin. I want to look down later tonight, or tomorrow, or next week and see bruises that bring it all back fresh in my head. I want to cherish those marks the way I cherished that scar on my ankle.

I want to make *memories* with him.

This makes me stop what I'm doing.

Not because anything's wrong. Not because there's so much to be worried about right now and we're here at my house having sex.

But because I just want to... look at him.

I place my palms flat on his cheeks. Study the colors in his eyes.

"What?" he asks. "What's wrong?"

I shake my head and smile. "Nothing," I say. "Nothing at all."

And it's true. It's perfect.

I take a mental picture for myself. To go with the possibility of bruises on my hips. Then I tuck it away for another day and resume our rhythm.

TYLER

On the next surge forward, I grab her around the waist and stop her moving. I put my mouth on her breasts and nibble at her pert, puckered nipples, making her struggle to get free. But I won't let her go free. I will insist on

68

keeping her here. Because I know that I won't be able to keep her forever. I know that ultimately, she will do what it is she wants, and while I will be there for her always, she is not mine to keep. So I savor this moment when she is. For this brief parcel of time, she is all mine. No one else's.

I pull back to look at her and stroke her hair out of her face.

"I love you," I say.

"I love you too," she says back. And then she shrugs like, *What're you gonna do?*

And I smile, grab her ankles, and begin moving her back and forth on my dick like she was doing herself moments ago. She leans forward, puts her hands on my chest, and allows her hair to collapse in my face, shrouding me once again. Her forehead is against mine and she whispers, "I'm gonna come again. Will you come with me?"

I don't answer, just tighten my grip around her legs and force her forward and back along my cock with a frantic push and pull. She's so wet that I think she's going to slide right off me and across the floor. The best waterpark ride in history.

"I'm gonna come again, I'm gonna come again, please, please come with me? I want you to come with me."

And even though I know she just means here, now, I decide that what it means to me is more than that. I decide that it means I will always come with her. Wherever she goes. Anytime she may be in need or want, she will never have to ask me to come with her, because I'll already be there.

But in this moment, I will also grant what she asks.

"Yes. Yes," I whisper out on a gasping breath. "Always."

And as she gushes out around me, I explode into her, our heads still touching, our mouths open against each other, sharing each other's oxygen.

We are unified. We are bound. We are one.

And no one has to declare it.

We know.

CHAPTER SEVEN

MADDIE

So. There was a phone call.

There was a lot of yelling. On Tyler's part, not mine. Because even though he said, "Yeah, I'm cool," when I asked him if he was cool, he wasn't. Which I forgave him for. Because this is kind of a difficult, stressful, life-altering kinda thing happening to us and it wasn't a lie. He was just trying to wrap his head around my decision to take down a drug lord.

I sigh.

So there was a phone call in which Tyler threatened to rain hellfire down on Ricky if anything happened to me. And the threat was directed to poor Emily, the person on the other end of the phone, not even Ricky. And the only reason he was going along with this crazy-ass idea was because I was a strong, capable woman who, if it came down to it, was one of two people he'd trust with his life. The other being Evan. And then there was a lot of mumbling about all the other guys in the firehouse, because he felt he'd somehow slighted them and he didn't want to give the wrong impression.

You know. Typical Tyler.

And at the end of the phone call, after he said, "Yes, we're in," he hung up, and he looked at me for a long moment. And then he said, "No," and shook his head and was already pressing the redial icon on his phone.

So I took the phone from him. Slowly. Carefully. Like he was a frightened wild animal caught in a trap and any wrong move would send him thrashing again. And I said, "We have time to say 'no.' We don't have to do it now."

Because I wanted him to know, if it really came down to it, and he decided that the head-wrapping around the taking-down-a-drug-lord thing was over and *his* answer really was 'no,' not 'yes,' then OK. I'd live with it.

And somehow, I don't really know how, he got that out of my two short sentences that said nothing of the sort.

So currently we're parked outside a strip mall filled with empty store-fronts, save one—but there's no sign, just some windows blacked out with shoe polish or whatever they use to black out windows—trying to decide if now is the time to stick with 'yes' or change our minds. Because suddenly, I'm not so sure either.

"You need to do this?" he asks.

I consider my answer carefully. Because even though I will say, "OK, we'll stand down," if he says no, he'll say, "OK, we're going in," if I say yes.

It's weird to be on such equal ground with someone. Someone's... partner, I guess. But it's completely awesome at the same time. It's called... like... mutual respect or some shit like that. I think. It's a pretty new feeling for me. So.

"I think..." I start to say, but then stop. Because I need to say this right. There's no room for mistakes or misunderstandings. "I think of all the people Carlos

Castillo has hurt. And then I try to add in Logan too. But I can't stop there, ya know?" I look at Tyler, who has a serious, solemn expression on his face. Almost sad. "I have to then think about all the other people who work for Carlos. And all the people those people have hurt in his name. And that's before I even get to Pete and Jeff. So I gotta ask myself." I swallow down the sadness creeping into my voice. "I gotta ask myself… how many Tylers and Maddies came before us who had a chance and didn't take it? And how many other people got hurt because they couldn't or wouldn't take a stand? And how many more people will get hurt if we say no and just try to live with it?"

Tyler nods. Understanding. "Yeah," is all he says. "But…" He shakes his head. "I mean, you're right. Of course, you're right. It's just you…"

He trails off and doesn't finish it. Maybe because he's worried I might take it the wrong way. Like he thinks I'm weak and can't handle this. Which is stupid. I *am* weak. Physically, I suppose. I mean, compared to the men I'm up against. It's just physiology. And I probably *can't* handle this. I'm a wedding-planning, dog-treat-baking, drone-flying stripper, not a secret agent or whatever.

So I'm not offended. Because I know he thinks I'm super-strong in other ways. Because I am.

Or maybe he doesn't finish saying it because he can't bear to think of what *could* happen to me. And let's be real. Killing me isn't the worst thing Carlos and Logan could do. And no one will be there. Not really. Ricky won't be able to save me. I don't care how many agents or whoever are waiting nearby. I don't care if they have helicopters or drones of their own spying overhead. I'll be all alone in that compound. With an insane killer. Who has a thing for me.

This is the stupidest thing I've ever done in my life. For sure.

"So..." Tyler interrupts my thoughts. "What are we doing?"

And I nod my head.

We get out of the car, holding hands as we walk to the door surrounding the shoe-polish windows. There's a camera over the door, so it opens as we get to the threshold, and then we're across and inside. We're entering a new life. Holding hands. Scared. Probably for very different reasons. And the door closes behind us.

"Hey. Thanks for coming," says Ricky. He's wearing gym clothes. A tight t-shirt that shows off his muscles and some cut-off sweats.

Which makes sense in context, because there are blue mats on the floor and some kickboxing bags hanging from steel beams overhead, and weight machines and stuff.

Tyler doesn't answer Ricky. He's busy taking it all in.

"Fuck is this shit?" Tyler says, panning his hand around.

"This is Emily," says Ricky, gesturing to the young woman next to him.

She's about my age, which surprises me. I don't know why I thought she'd be older. She's not wearing any makeup but is still very pretty. Like Ricky, she's also wearing shorts and a t-shirt. She's got on a baseball cap and has a long, blonde ponytail pulled through the opening in the back. Honestly, she looks more like a sorority girl going to a charity softball game than a DEA agent. I also notice she's staring at Ricky but trying not to at the same time.

She extends her hand and says, "We talked on the—"

Tyler walks past her outstretched hand and keeps yelling. "No! No! What the fuck is all *this*"—he gestures at the equipment and punches one of the heavy bags—"shit? What happened to 'it's not a combat op, it's just intel gathering?'"

Ricky raises his hands. "It is intel gathering. And we're going to go over all that. How we want her to do it. What we want her to ask. How she gets out of situations she's not comfortable in. All that. But, just in case she *needs* it, we'd like her to have a few tricks she can use."

"Tricks? OK, fucking David Copperfield! Jesus!" Tyler stalks around the space for a moment, kind of walking in circles. The three of us watch him.

"Tyl—" Emily starts.

"And what the fuck are you even doing here?" Tyler shouts, stomping over to Ricky and shoving his finger in Ricky's face. "I thought you were in *deep cover*," he says, drawing out the words 'deep cover' mockingly.

"I am," says Ricky coolly. "In fact, I'm on a job for Carlos right now, picking up four point six million dollars that's owed to him by someone whose name you probably know. Or that's where he believes me to be."

Tyler gives a slow clap. "Oh, yeah? Well, hoo-fucking-rah for you, pal. But you know something? You sure as shit don't look like a fucking drug dealer to me. Know what you *do* look like?"

"What's that?"

"A fucking DEA agent who I don't fucking trust!"

Ricky nods. "Fair enough. No reason you should, brother."

Tyler stiffens at the last word in that sentence. "I ain't your fucking brother. Know what? Fuck it. Let's just do this shit. Who's this?" He points at Emily.

Emily looks at Ricky, who shakes his head a bit, like, *Don't make a thing out of it.*

"Uh, I'm Emily," she says. "We talked on—"

"Yeah, yeah," says Tyler, walking past her and sitting down on an old leather couch next to a couple of mismatched chairs, and a table with fruit on it for some reason.

Ricky turns to me now. "You OK?"

I nod at him, feigning a confidence that he can surely tell is bullshit.

"Emily," he says, putting his hand out, gesturing for her to take the floor.

Emily nods and steps forward. "So—" she says, before Tyler shouts.

"And who the fuck is this? Looks like she just showed up from fuckin' rush week!"

"Tyler!" I say to him, with a clenched jaw. He gives me a look. I respond with a wide-eyed stare, and he nods and twists his head around in resignation. I see the kid I knew before and the man I know today all at once, and I almost smile. Almost. But I'm pulled back into the now by Emily saying...

"Mostly what we want to do today is give you some basic hand-to-hand skills you can use in the event things happen that require you to engage in force."

"Like, what kind of things are you thinking about?" I ask her.

She glances at Ricky, who nods slightly.

"Like any number of things," she says.

"You mean, like rape," I say. It's not a question.

She takes a breath and nods.

"Can I ask you something?" I say to her.

"Of course."

"How long have you been doing this? This job?"

"I've been an agent for two and a half years."

"And have you ever done anything like what I'm about to do?"

She looks at Ricky again.

"Don't look at him," I say to her. "I'm the one asking you the question. Have you ever done anything at all like what I'm about to do? Put yourself in a situation where you're basically bait?"

"No, ma'am. I haven't."

I stiffen at that. "How old are you?" I ask her.

"Twenty-five."

"Yeah, me too. Please don't call me ma'am." I don't say it in a snarky way, but this whole thing is already weird enough without somebody I could have partied with in college calling me ma'am.

"But," Emily says, "I was captured and held captive for eleven days in São Paulo by the Comando Vermelho and managed to extract myself and reach safety without being raped or murdered, so there are some ideas I feel like I can contribute."

I glance at Tyler, who raises his eyebrows with a look that says, *Well, shit. OK.*

I look back at Emily. "All right, then," I say.

She smiles a tight, official, government smile. "Over the next couple of days, you and I will talk about everything. Any questions you have, ways in which you can insulate yourself once you're inside, etcetera, but since Ricky can only be with us for today—"

"Deep cover," Ricky interrupts, and glances over at Tyler, who gives Ricky the finger.

"Since Ricky is only here for today," Emily continues, "we want to work on some self-defense tactics, in the *highly unlikely* event you need to utilize them."

The fact that she stresses 'highly unlikely' so much makes me highly nervous. Which is probably the opposite effect she intended for it to have.

I swallow and say, "OK," again.

Ricky steps up and says, "There are some gym clothes in a changing area over there." He nods to the back. "You feel like putting those on and then giving a few things a try?"

"Sure. In for a gram, in for a kilo," I joke. I'm not sure Ricky and Emily find it funny, but I don't care. It's my ass on the line.

I head to the back and as I'm walking by the sofa where Tyler is sitting, he stands, takes my arm and whispers, "*Are* you OK?"

"Yeah," I tell him. "I'm good. Promise."

He nods and gives me a kiss, and as I go to change clothes, I try to convince myself I mean what I said.

The whole time I'm changing, I hear a sound I can't quite identify, and when I come back into the space, sporting completely unflattering shorts that are far too baggy on me and a t-shirt that's two sizes too big, I find Tyler wearing boxing gloves, pounding the shit out of a heavy bag that's suspended from one of the steel beams.

Stuffing is coming out with every strike he lands, and it looks like he's going to send it flying off its mooring at any second. Ricky and Emily stand back and watch with what looks to me like a bit of... admiration.

He's all sweaty, and I step up next to him, wiping moisture off his cheek.

"Are you OK?" I whisper.

He nods. "Yup. Too good," he says. Then, referring to what I have on, "This is hot."

"Fuck you," I say with a smile.

"OK," he says and starts taking off his boxing gloves and heading to the back room where I changed. I grin, hit him on the shoulder, and turn to face Ricky and Emily.

Ricky stands on a mat and asks, "Have you ever taken any kind of self-defense course? Anything like that? Have any training at all?"

"Got approached about being a ring-card girl for MMA once. That count?" I laugh. Nobody else does. I clear my throat. "Um, joking. Sorry. I mean... Yeah? Some."

"What was that?" asks Ricky.

"I took a little Ju-Jitsu for a while."

"OK—" Ricky says.

"Also, some Tae Kwan Do. A little Aikido. Oh, and a few months of Wing Chun."

Ricky and Emily stare at me.

"I've tried lots of different stuff over the years." I shrug.

"All right," Ricky says on a breath. "Anything else?"

I think about it for a minute. *Ju-Jitsu, Tae Kwon Do. Aikido. Wing Chun...* "Oh! Yeah. And some Jeet Kune Do."

More stares.

"It's Bruce's Lee's thing. Means 'Way of The Intercepting Fist.'"

I glance over at Tyler, who's smiling a huge, shit-eating grin. He winks. And I get kind of proud of myself.

"OK," says Ricky. "Anything *else?*"

I shake my head. "Don't think so."

"And how much of that have you retained?" asks Emily.

"Guess we'll find out," I say.

I step onto the mat and Ricky steps on with me. "Have you ever had to defend yourself in a real-world environment?"

"What's the 'real-world?'" I respond. I mean it. I don't know anymore.

He nods at me. And then Tyler says, "We know she can handle Unlucky Logan, so at least we have that going for us."

"Whattayou mean?" asks Ricky.

"She kicked his stupid ass when he came to see her at Pete's a few weeks ago."

Ricky gets a surprised look on his face and says to me, "*You* did that?"

I shrug. "I guess. Yeah. I was pretty pissed off. I don't necessarily remember all of it. Everything kind of just went white. And the next thing I remember, Pete was pulling me off of him."

Ricky shakes his head and chuckles.

"What's funny?" I ask.

"He told us that Pete and his boys did that," Ricky says. "Told Carlos he was checking in on you to see what kind of progress you were making with the money, and that Pete got in his face and things got out of control. Said two big bouncers jumped into the fight too, and he fought off all three of them."

"Dude," Tyler says, "Pete pulled Maddie off of him. That bitch would be telling no stories to anyone right now if Pete hadn't been there."

And at that, Ricky's face hollows.

"What?" I ask him. "What?"

"That's the whole story Logan used to get Carlos to give him the green light on burning down Pete's."

"What?" I ask again, this time with more urgency in my voice.

"It wasn't Carlos's idea to burn it down. It was Logan's. He talked Carlos into giving the order by convincing him that Pete had insulted his family. Which, of course, Carlos sees as an insult to him. And then when you factor in their history…"

That ringing sound in my ears is back.

"Fuck. That. Fucking. Cunt," says Tyler. Which is the same thing I'm thinking.

"OK, well—" Ricky starts to say.

"Let's go," I blurt out. My whole body feels like it itches.

"What?" asks Ricky.

"Let's go. Right now. We're gonna train? Let's train. Come on. Come at me. Let's fuckin' do this."

"Maddie, why don't you—?" That's Emily. But the look I shoot her stops her mouth.

Then Ricky says, "You sure?"

"Fuck yeah, I'm sure! Put me in a choke hold. Grab my pussy. Whatever. Let's see who's made of what."

"Maddie," Ricky says, "One of the first things we'll actually want to address is your temper. It's not your friend. I know it feels like it is, but it's not."

81

He comes toward me with his arm out, like he's gonna calm me down, and I flash back to the morning he drove me home to Vegas from Carlos's compound in... wherever-the-hell it is. Back before he was Richard the DEA agent, when he was just Ricky the drug-dealing scumbag.

Ese es tu problema. Tienes mal genio, he said to me then. *That's your problem. You have a bad temper.*

Yeah, Ricky. You're goddamned right I do.

He reaches me with his outstretched hand and I grab his palm, twist his wrist, kick the inside of his thigh, and the next thing I know, he's flat on his back and I have my knee dangerously close to his fucking balls.

Emily gasps, Tyler claps and shouts, "Fuck yeah, baby!" And Ricky stares up at me with a look that's half-surprised, half-impressed, and says, "OK, then. And which was that? Aikido? Ju-Jitsu? Wing Chun...?"

Breathing heavy, and with no real clear image in my head of what exactly just happened, I let go of his arm, stand up, step back, and say...

"Pretty sure that was just Maddie Clayton."

CHAPTER EIGHT

TYLER

The mood in the firehouse is heavy.

I came by for lunch. I've been spending all my time with Maddie and I haven't even really seen Evan since the funeral. But the air in here is thick. Jeff's death is still fresh in everyone's mind. It probably will be for a while. Losing someone is always tough, but when it's a guy like Jeff, who was young, and eager, and had his whole life ahead of him, it's downright Shakespearean. So even though I'm losing my shit over Maddie offering herself up as a lure to reel in Castillo, I'm trying my best not to freak out about it in front of Evan and the guys.

"Dude, I am freaking out about this shit with Maddie," I say.

Fuck.

Evan nods. "Yeah, well, that's understandable. Be weird if you weren't. Who exactly is this guy?"

"Which guy?" I say.

"The fuckin' guy," Rod chimes in. "This fuckin' drug guy. Fuckin' Richie what's-his-name."

"Ricky," I say.

"Yeah, fuckin' Ricky. Ricky fuckin'-drug-fuck. What's his story?"

"His *story*? I dunno. He was in the military, got out, now he's a DEA agent. All I really know about him."

"Yeah? He trying to fuck your old lady?"

"Rod," Bear says, with some exhaustion in his voice, "go play in traffic."

"Fuck did I say? I'm just asking questions."

"No, Rod," I say. "I don't think he's trying to fuck Maddie. Of all the things I'm worried about with this whole setup, Ricky's prick is not one."

"Yeah?" says Rod, grinning. "Why? You seen it? He got a teeny peeny?"

Bear pushes Rod's chair with his foot and Rod falls over backwards. Nobody else moves. I get the feeling it happens a lot.

"Why you gotta be a dick?" shouts Rod.

"So you trust the guy?" asks Bear, ignoring his half-sized cohort.

"No. I didn't say that." I stand up from the table and start pacing a little. "Fuck should I trust him? He's recruiting an untrained asset off the street? That seems… I dunno. The whole thing just makes me uneasy."

"Yo, brother, lemme ask you something." That's Dean. "Are you supposed to be talking about all this shit to us? I mean, it's cool, pretty sure none of us are gonna say nothing to nobody, but still…"

"Oh, Yeah," I say. "I mean, yeah, I got a whole big lecture about secrecy and all that shit, but I'm assuming it really only applies to Maddie's roommates."

"Why?" asks Dean.

"Because they're hookers. You know how chatty pros can be."

"Nah, man," he says. "I really don't. Never paid for that shit."

84

Of course he hasn't. Fuckin' Dean. So fuckin' cool. Asshole.

"I gotta tell you," says Alex, lumbering to his feet, collecting everyone's empty lunch plates, "when people ask me why I don't believe in relationships, I'm gonna tell 'em this story."

"What?" says Bear. "You don't believe in relationships because a Mexican drug lord might fall in love with your woman and she could possibly get approached by an undercover DEA agent to become involved in an off-the-books op to try to bring him down?"

Alex grabs up the last plate, stares at the floor, considering the question, and after a beat says, "Yeah. Exactly," and then ambles off into the kitchen.

Bear turns to me and asks, "Is there anything we can do, man?"

"No," I say. "I mean, fuck, I dunno. But no. Of course not. I wish there was. Thanks."

"Well," says Bear, hauling his massive frame up to its full height, "we're always here for you if you need anything. You know that, right?" He sticks his hand out. I take it and we shake.

"Yeah, I know, man. Thanks."

He pulls me toward him with his monstrous grip and says again, "Right?"

Most people will say things like, 'I'm here for you if you need me.' Or, 'Let me know if I can do anything.' But Bear *means* it. And it means the world to me.

"Yeah, brother, I know. Thank you."

We shake, he pats me on the shoulder, and then he walks off toward his office, Rod trailing him, bitching at him the whole way.

"Yo," says Dean, putting a leash on Gladys the French Bulldog, to take her for her post-lunch constitutional. "Real talk? You know he's not bullshitting? We got you, man. You feel me?"

I shake my head and laugh a little. Because I know he means it too. They all do. But the thing is, it's not because of *me*. It's because of Evan. They love Evan so much that they're honor-bound to have my back too. And I couldn't be more grateful for that.

"Yeah, bro," I say. "I feel you."

Dean goes to dap me off, but I kind of fuck up the handshake because I am a lot of things, but as cool as Dean is not one of them. Finally, he just slaps me on the back and says, "All good, baby," as he takes off with Gladys.

I take the balled-up napkin that I've been fiddling with in my fingers and lob it across the station house. It lands dead in the middle of the trash can on the other side of the room. Three points.

"We should go shoot around sometime," Evan says.

"You hate basketball," I remind him.

"Yeah, but I love bumping up against sweaty guys." He smiles and nudges me. "You gonna make it?" he asks me.

"What do you mean?"

"I dunno. Just… Are you?"

I take a deep breath and let it out on a long sigh. "Shit. I have no idea. I'm fucking trying. It's been an… eventful… couple of months."

Evan chuckles, "Yeah. I guess it has."

"Hey, what are they saying about the fire?"

Evan looks down and shakes his head. "Electrical."

"Are you fucking kidding me? Fucking electrical?"

86

"I know," he says, "I know. But the official inspection report says that there was most probably a faulty outlet and that the breaker box wasn't up to code and blah, blah, blah. That's the official cause."

"Dude, there was a fucking explosion. I saw it."

"Caused by the chemicals contained in a stockpile of cleaning supplies."

"Jesus." I walk forward a few steps and then track back.

"I know, man," he says. "I know."

"And that doesn't fucking piss you off?"

"Of course it does," he tells me. "But I'm not the commissioner. What am I gonna say? 'I have no hard proof I can provide, but I'm pretty sure that this was arson and that your inspector is on the take, being paid off by a Mexican fucking crime boss?' Yeah, that wouldn't go over real well. I gotta work in this town, man."

"Dude—" I start, but Evan cuts me off.

"Bro, it's Vegas. We do the best we can. I'm a firefighter. Not a cop. I'm sorry."

Shit. Of course, he's right. It's not his fault, and it's not his problem, and there's nothing he could do about it anyway. The only thing that any of us can do about it is already being done. By Maddie.

"So when does all this go down?" he asks.

"Day after tomorrow."

There's a long moment where we both stand in the open door of the station, staring out at the sky. The winter sky in the desert *looks* like air. There's really no other way to describe it. Even with all the ways that we have polluted and fucked up the planet, tried as hard as we can to run it into fucking oblivion, there's something about a winter sky in the desert that looks pure, and untouched, and tranquil.

It's an illusion, I know. There is no tranquility, there is no purity, and there's no place we can go that hasn't already been altered by our merely having been here. But sometimes it's nice to pretend.

And then I look across the street and I see Brandon, New-Guy Brandon, sitting by himself on a bench in the park, eating a sandwich.

"What's that all about?" I ask.

Evan shrugs and presses his lips together. "Since Jeff, he's been quiet. Just kind of keeping to himself."

"Unlike usual?" I ask with the one eyebrow I can arch lifted to its maximum level of suggested sarcasm.

"*More* to himself," says Evan. Then he asks, "You wanna do anything special for Christmas?"

"Asks the Jew."

"Bro, I'm married to a dude who's so WASPy that albinos are like, 'That guy is *white*.' Christmas is like a whole thing. My hope is that with you there, we can make up some weird Christmas tradition where you make Robert, like, put live swans in the pool or something. That'd be hilarious. Swans are assholes."

"Honestly, man, until I know that Maddie's gonna be OK, I doubt I'm gonna have a lot of Christmas cheer to offer. Though if we really wanted to do something funny, we should try to force him to do a living manger, with me as Joseph, you as Mary, and make him be the baby."

"I like it. Feels like a long shot though," Evan says.

"I know. I'm just spitballing."

And suddenly I feel like I can't stand still. I'm thinking about Christmas without Maddie, and more importantly, what Maddie's Christmas is going to be like, stuck alone in a fucking compound somewhere with Carlos. And Logan. And then I think of all the Christmases I spent in the Middle East with no one to talk to. And all those Christmases I spent drifting the planet with no one to talk to. Christmas after Christmas alone. No family who gave a shit, nobody to call back home…

Except now I realize that I did have someone there all along. Someone waiting for *me* to reach out. And I blew it. I just fucking blew it. And now that we've found each other, and we're together, we're being pulled apart again.

But if recent history holds its course, I guess there's some hope. Because Halloween was an *actual* horror show. But then Thanksgiving was a true moment of thanks and reparation. So, possibly, if we're lucky, we can believe that we might get handed some kind of Christmas miracle. Jesus, I hope we can all just make it to the new year. Because then, just maybe, everything can start fresh for all of us, and—as Nadir would have said—joy shall cometh with the morning.

Or else the whole goddamn world will just up and explode. Could go either way.

"Dude, I need to get back to Maddie," I say.

"Right on," Evan says, giving me one of the loving hugs only my brother can give. "Come over the second she leaves, OK? I don't wanna have to go chasing you down to make sure you're all right."

"Respect," I say, and slap his hand.

He heads back inside the station, and I start off for my car, but then I glimpse Brandon again, just sitting there, eating his sandwich.

Fuck it.

I trot across the street and come up to the side of him cautiously. I still don't know this dude at all and I don't wanna go sneaking up on some physically jacked, psychotically quiet firefighter I don't know.

89

"Dude?" I say, kind of waving my hand and leaning in to let him see it's me. "You mind if I sit for a second?"

The plastic grocery bag that holds the rest of his lunch—a banana, a bottle of apple juice, some animal crackers—is sitting on the bench beside him. He twists his head to look at me, chewing a bite of sandwich, then he looks back in front of him and picks up the bag and moves it to the other side of him without a word. I take that as my invitation and sit down. Brandon takes another bite of his sandwich and continues staring ahead.

I look to see what's in front of us. It's a dog park. There's five or so dogs and their owners inside the fence. The dogs are playing, running, y'know, shit dogs do.

And then, out of nowhere, just as I'm about to try to make some kind of overture to get the guy into a conversation, Brandon says, "They just are what they are."

"They... Sorry, what's that?"

He takes the final bite of his sandwich and he says, "Dogs. They're just... dogs."

I'll be honest. I'm not sure what my next move is here. Fortunately, and to my surprise, Brandon keeps talking.

"They don't try to be something they're not. And nobody expects them to. They don't judge themselves and they aren't judged. They run. They play. They eat. They sleep. And they love you if you don't hurt them. That's it."

There's a long moment where we both watch the dogs all chasing each other. And then he says, "I hope, if there's another life after this one, I get to be a dog."

Shit.

Brandon.

"So, hey," I start, "Um, what you did with Jeff—"

"Was my job," he says, still looking straight ahead of him.

I don't say anything. I just nod. Because he's right.

"What do you want to know?" he asks me after a moment.

"Sorry?"

"You wanna know something. What is it?"

He's right. I do wanna know something about him. Anything, really. Everything. I've been watching this dude for weeks now and every time I see him I wonder what his story is. And now that I'm sitting here with him, and he's inviting me to ask him, I find myself unable to make the words.

"Um," I mumble, "I… I dunno. Why did you come over here from Heavy 44?"

"Shortage of manpower. They needed some volunteers to go to some other stations, so I went."

"Yeah?"

"Yeah," he says. "Sorry if you wanted some big, dramatic story. There isn't one. Help was needed, so I helped. What else?"

"Uh…" I seriously don't know what to say. "Are you doing… OK?"

He turns his head to look at me again. "Whattayou mean?"

"Well, Jeff, and… Are you doing OK?"

He stares straight at me for a long time, just like he did on Halloween night when I asked him how he was doing. I don't look away. I just look into his eyes to see if I can find anything hidden there that I can understand.

Finally, he says, "It's because people are easily disappointed."

"What?" That was an answer to a question no one asked. "Sorry. What?"

"That's why I don't talk to people. Which is what you want to know. Why I don't talk to people. It's because then people expect stuff from you. Because they feel like they know you. Or they understand you. But they don't. Nobody knows anybody. Not really. Because what can they know? The things you think? The things you say? None of that is *you*. You're not your thoughts. You're not the stuff you say. You're more than that. But people get attached to the stuff they think they can assign to you and then that becomes who you are in their minds. And once they develop that attachment, they come to have expectations. And once someone has expectations, they can be disappointed. If you don't take that first step, then there won't be a second, and people go away and attach to somebody else who can disappoint them instead."

I don't speak. Not because I don't have anything to say, but because I have too much to say to put it into coherent language.

"So that's all. That's why I don't talk to people."

"I…" I begin. But he cuts me off before I can continue.

"But you already know all that," he says.

He turns and looks at me. I look back. Then he reaches into his plastic bag and opens the box of animal crackers. He pulls one out, then another, then another, and places them to the side. Finally, sifting through, he finds a lion. He hands it to me. Then he digs out another lion, and then places the rest of the box down as well.

He gives me a short, curt nod, then he bites the head off the lion and turns back to look at the dogs playing in the park again.

I slowly, carefully take a bite of my lion as well, and even though I'm anxious to get back to Maddie and be with her as much as I can before she goes...

I sit for a moment, watching the dogs play without a care in the world, and devour the king of the jungle.

CHAPTER NINE

December twenty-second. Three days before the artificial deadline that Carlos created in order to wield power over me. Three days before I have to give him money I don't owe him or give him my body. So I'm packing to get ready to go.

Ricky, Emily, and I have decided that I should go ahead and deliver myself to him tomorrow. Waiting doesn't make any sense and this way we can create something resembling a strategy. Waiting just delays the inevitable.

So the plan is to tell Carlos that I called the number Ricky gave me, told him that I'm not going to be able to come up with the money, and that he convinced me to just bring myself to Carlos now. It will have the added benefit of gaining Ricky additional favor within the organization. Because what I've also found out is that Carlos is none too happy with Logan about what happened to Pete.

Apparently, killing Pete was never supposed to be part of the deal. Logan was supposed to make sure that Pete was out of the club before he and his goons burned it down. But we all know what happened there.

So I guess Carlos is keeping a tight chain on his nephew now and Ricky has been given most of Logan's old duties. Notably, keeping an eye on me. Which is how he's been able to get close enough to recruit me into this whole thing without arousing suspicion.

Christ. I feel like I'm in a fucking Jack Reacher book or some bullshit.

"How long are they saying you're going to be there, though?" Tyler's standing in front of my bedroom door watching me pack. His arms are crossed. He looks like a sentry guarding the exit. Which, I suppose, he is. I know when it comes time for me to leave in the morning, he's going to raise holy hell.

"Emily and Ricky argued about that. Ricky's saying as long as it takes, Emily says that if I don't have anything useful in two weeks, they should pull me and then I disappear."

"Disappear? Fuck does that mean?"

"I dunno. Witness protection, I guess? I get the sense that she's capping it at two weeks because that's about as long as she was able to keep herself safe with that drug gang that held her captive, and she only feels like she's got enough tricks to help me keep Carlos at bay for that long."

I also get that sense that she and Ricky have a little something between them. Nothing I can prove, but the way she argued with him over the phone sounded familiar.

"This is fucking stupid!" Tyler yells. Like I said, familiar. "And so you wind up in witness protection and then what? Do I ever see you again?"

He's pouting a little, I think. Hard to tell behind the beard, but the voice sounds pouty. I cross over to him and put my hands on his chest.

"What? You won't come with me?" I ask.

He looks at me, a little surprised. "I'm invited?"

"Of course you're invited. Don't be dumb. If I wind up having to spend the rest of my life on the run, I'll want someone there to go the grocery store for me and shit."

He laughs a little, and while I do too, I'm also struck by the gravity of this whole thing for the first time. Hard to believe it's the first time it's dawning on me that this might result in me never seeing anyone I love again. Which I guess really only consists of my mom and dad. There isn't anyone else. Except Tyler. Which is still a new concept. That he's here, I mean. Not that I love him. If I'm being honest with myself, I've known I love him for a long time. The fact that he's here is what's taking some getting used to. But he is here, and even though it makes me nervous to believe it, it doesn't look like he's going anywhere.

But that's it. That's the whole of my world. Hell, I don't even really see anyone else. I haven't seen Caroline and Diane for days now. I don't know if they even still live here. I should poke my head in their rooms to see if their stuff is still there.

God. Have I really been so successful at walling myself off all this time? I guess so. Wow. Well, good for me. I suppose.

"Hey," Tyler interrupts my thoughts. "Listen, if there's a possibility we're just gonna wind up on the lam for the rest of our lives anyway, why go through with this? Let's just go now. I've got enough money to take care of us, and I've seen places on the planet where no one would ever find us. We could go to one of those, build a cabin and shit, and I'll hunt food for us. It'll be rustic as balls."

He tugs at my arms, but I pull away. He's being sweet and charming, and if I let myself I'll just fall under his spell and take him up on the offer. And that would be the easy way out. And I've never been one for doing things the easy way. Which is fine. As long as you're smart about it. Which I think I am. But which I haven't been.

"Do you know the difference between hard work and struggle?" I ask him.

"What?"

"Hard work. And struggle. Do you know the difference?"

"Uh, yeah," he says. "Hard work is, uh, so you're working and, you know, it's... hard. And so you do that, but when you struggle you have to, uh... Sorry. No. What's the difference?"

Dork.

"Hard work," I tell him, "is when you dig in and roll up your sleeves and you face down a problem. You engage with it and you figure out a way to get around it and even if it's scary or difficult you do it anyway. I think it was Einstein who said, 'You can't solve a problem with the same level of thinking that created it.' And finding that new level of thinking requires hard work."

"OK..."

"Struggle..." I pause, considering this carefully. "Struggle. Is what I've been doing for the last seven years."

I let that sit there for a second so that I can make sure he's hearing me.

"I've been hammering away at the same problems in the same way with the same kind of effort, not bothering to pay attention to the fact that all that struggling was getting me nowhere. And the worst part about it?" I take a breath, because this is the hard part to say. "The worst part is that I've been using Scotty as an excuse."

"What?" Tyler says. "No. Hey—"

I cut him off. "No. I have. And you have too. Both of us used Scotty as an excuse not to move on. To just keep struggling away at the *idea* that we were moving forward, but both of us still stuck in the past. And I'm done with that."

He nods, slowly, like this is the first time he's ever considered this. It's not the first time I've considered it. I've thought about it a lot over the years. It's just the first time I've voiced it.

"And so...?" he asks.

"And so, this is me doing something. Something that will help. That will, I dunno, have an impact on the world. And just as important, it'll put a nice, hard period at the end of this chapter of my life. And no matter how it plays out, I can close the book on it and actually move forward. Or that's my hope, anyway."

That's a word I haven't really used a lot over these years. Hope. But there ya go.

"OK, yeah. Fair enough," he says with resignation. "Hey, listen, I've got something for you."

He reaches into the duffel bag of clothes he's been keeping over here. "Clothes" is a stretch. It's really just a couple dozen t-shirts in different colors and an extra pair of jeans. I'm pretty sure that when he's done with them he just throws them out and buys more instead of doing laundry. Fuckin' weirdo.

"Here," he says, pulling out what looks like a cell phone and handing it to me.

"What's that?"

"It's a sat phone."

"Why do you have a sat phone?"

"It's for you," he says. "I picked it up at Sat Phones 'R' Us. It's right next to the Drone Store."

"What do you want me to do with it?"

"Um, I want you to keep it on you, and I want you to check in with me every night so that I know you're OK."

"No," I say, waving the phone away. "No way. It's too dangerous, and—"

"Too dangerous?" he shouts. "This whole fuckin' thing is too dangerous! At least this way you won't be some floating satellite that I can't find! And you'll have a way to reach me if shit gets out of hand. It's encrypted and dedicated and untraceable. I paid for the fancy stealth package."

"If they find a fucking sat phone on me…"

"They won't. And even if they do, you can tell them it's just a regular phone. They won't know the difference. It's top-of-the-line. Promise. Slayer told me."

I try not to smile at that, but I fail. And then he's smiling too. Sticking the phone in my hand.

"Take it. Please. OK? Just take it and promise that you'll call me or at least ping me every night so that I know you're OK."

"How do I do that?"

He shows me the features on the phone and how I can press a button to send him, like, Morse code and everything. And then he presses it into my palm and wraps my fingers around it.

"OK?" he asks. "Please?"

I nod reluctantly, because I'm not sure this is such a great idea, but I have to admit that it gives me some small measure of comfort to think that I'll be able to reach him.

"And take this," he says, taking off his watch.

"Why?"

"Because you don't have one, and because in case… I dunno. I just want you to have it."

I examine it. I've seen it on his wrist, but never really paid attention. I'm not a watch girl. But it looks expensive, which isn't surprising. It also looks like it's been to hell and back. Which it probably has.

"Nadir gave it to me," he says, looking at it.

"Nadir, your business partner? The translator guy?"

"Sure. Yeah. That's him. My *business partner*." He somehow mocks himself in saying the words back to me.

"It's nice," I say, studying it.

"Yeah," says Tyler. "It was a gift to him from a platoon he translated for before we met. I guess they gave it to him as a thank you."

"Why'd he give it to you?"

Tyler blows out a breath. "I dunno. Um... After we shook on partnering up on the bomb robot idea, he took it off and said, 'Tyler, please. You are doing a good thing. Please. Take this and always remember that I am grateful.'" He doesn't really get out the word "grateful" before his voice chokes off to a whisper. But I understand.

"Ty," I say, pushing the watch away. "No, you shouldn't—"

"I didn't do a good thing, Mads. I didn't do a *fucking* thing. He gave me that because he thought I was a good guy and was helping him. And what I did instead was get him killed and spend the next few years fucking around and blowing money that was partially his. You, on the other hand, are about to do something brave and courageous and basically... good. Trust me. If Nadir had met you, he would've wanted you to have it." He slides it on me. It dangles off my wrist.

"It's too big," I say. "You should—"

"I'll take a few links out." He cuts me off. "But just take it and promise to find some way to make contact with me at... I dunno... eleven o'clock every night. Please?"

"I... I'll try. It might get kinda suspicious if no matter what's happening, I steal away at eleven every night. Can we just say, 'before the morning?'"

His mouth tightens, and he rolls his head, shifts his feet back and forth, but finally he says, "Fine."

I give him a kiss and then go back to packing. Looking down at the sat phone in my hand, I'm struck by how small and compact it is. Not at all like the big, clunky one I used all those years ago when I was making calls to him when he was deployed. Calls that went unanswered. Just like the emails and letters.

And suddenly, a thought lands on me.

"I have something for you too," I say.

"Yeah? What?"

As I walk over to my closet, my heart starts beating fast. I never thought in a million years that he'd actually wind up seeing this after all this time. I certainly didn't think I'd be sitting in front of him when he did.

Reaching up to the top shelf, I fish around until my hand hits the shoe box. I swipe at it to bring it forward and it falls off the shelf into my grasp. I take a deep breath and turn around, placing the box on the bed.

"What's that?" he asks.

I remove the lid and inside are all the memories I've held onto. It makes me a little sad that every recollection, every reminiscence in my life that I've cared enough to keep can fit into a box small enough to hold just a pair of shoes. There's the business licenses from all the jobs I've failed to succeed at. There's a photo of me, Scotty, Mom and Dad at the waterpark when I was probably four.

There's another photo of Scotty, and Evan, and Tyler, all gathered around me, finishing singing Happy Birthday on my seventh birthday.

And there, at the bottom, buried under all the other memories I don't want to forget, I find it. I pull it out of the box, letting the other assorted images and papers fall away, and on one last puff of breath leaving my lungs...

I hand it to Tyler.

CHAPTER TEN

TYLER

I recognize it immediately.

The last letter I ever got from Maddie while I was deployed. The one I sent back unopened. The one with my handwriting on the back. *Please stop sending me letters.*

It's still sealed, the words she wrote entombed inside. I have some idea what's in here. She suggested a lot of things about it when she reminded me of its existence, the night we found out we're us.

My hands are shaking, and I can't pretend they're not because the jittering of the envelope betrays me. I flick at the paper with my middle finger, and I don't look up. Just keep staring at the hurtful and selfish thing I wrote, like if I stare hard enough the words themselves will start to mean something else.

"Shit," I manage.

"Yeah," she says.

After a moment I ask, "Should I open it?"

She shrugs. "Up to you."

I nod and chew at the inside of my mouth.

"But, like I told you back on Halloween," she says, "it's a good one."

She wears a half-smile that suggests she's as nervous about me reading it as I am.

I continue to flick at the corner of the envelope, nodding my head ever so slightly all the while, like someone standing on the edge of a high dive, looking down into the water, deciding how they're going to find the courage to jump.

And then, on a deep inhale—fuck it, I jump.

I slide my finger under the lip of the seal and rip a jagged tear along the seam. Looking up at Maddie, I can see no easily identifiable expression on her face. She's caught somewhere between telling me to stop and breaking into a fit of nervous laughter.

When I reach inside, the paper catches on the corner that I didn't completely sever with my finger and almost puts a rip in the letter itself. Which would be just fucking perfect. I stop tugging and reset my hands, like I'm performing delicate surgery. I rip away the rest of the offending corner and withdraw the contents, placing the envelope on the bed a foot from where Maddie sits, one leg crossed underneath her and the other dangling off the side.

It's folded in perfect thirds. Almost as if she used a ruler to create the folds. Which, knowing Maddie, she very well may have. I lift the top flap and see her handwriting staring at me, the words "Dear Tyler" at the top. And for the first time in my thirty years on earth, it lands on me the way I suppose it's intended. "Dear." "Tyler." Not "Hello, Tyler," or "'Sup, Tyler?" but "Dear Tyler." *My dear Tyler.* Huh. I never really processed that before.

I flip open the bottom third and then it's just there. Staring me in the face. A page of words, sent to me by a friend in need, that I never bothered to read. I'll bet these words never thought they'd see the light of day again. I'll bet that when they found themselves being stuffed inside that shoe box they were like, "Well, that sucks. We're good words. Somebody took the time to write us down and shit, and now here we are just being shoved in a dark fucking coffin never to get our shot at our job. Which is to make someone feel something."

Because that's all words are. Sounds that we put together to have an effect on another person. Like God/James Franco told me during the brief period I was in heaven: *They don't mean anything. Unless you give them meaning.*

I wonder what meaning these words will have on me now that they've been set free?

Only one way to find out…

Dear Tyler,

Hi. It's me. Maddie!

I hope that you're well and safe, and that the other soldiers are being nice to you.

So listen, I'm writing because—as I'm sure you're aware— we're coming up on Scotty's anniversary. That's a shitty thing to call it, I know, because an anniversary usually implies something happy that you want to celebrate, but I really don't have a better word for it. And I guess the idea that an anniversary has to be a happy thing is just something we made up anyway. People, I mean. Ugh. People. The worst. Amirite!? (LOL)

Anyway, I don't know if you've gotten all the other letters I sent, because I haven't heard back. It's fine if you didn't, they were mostly just, like, check-ins or updates about what's going on here and stuff. A couple of them had little things I made tucked inside. (I know you always LOVED the potholders that I would make. LOL. But seriously, you should actually try crocheting yourself. I mean it. It's super calming. It's really helped me a lot this year. No kidding.)

I hope, if nothing else, you got the package I sent with the chain. I found this gold chain (don't worry, it was fake, I paid like five bucks for it) that had a nametag on it that said, "Asshole." I thought of you the second I spotted it! (LOL) So anyway, I hope you got that at least.

I've tried to call a bunch too and sent emails and stuff, but I can't know for sure if you're getting the messages or if the emails are getting lost on some government email server or something. And if that's what's happening, or if the letters and packages I've sent aren't being delivered, I guess I'll never know, but I'm sending this one because... Because I'm not doing so good, Ty.

Now, I don't want you to freak out and come running back to Vegas on the next plane out of wherever you are right now just for me! (haha) I mean, I kind of do, of course, because it'd be awesome to see you, but I don't want you to like worry about me doing anything bad to myself or anything like that. Because that's not what I'm saying and that's not what I'm about.

I just feel... sad. Like all the time. And there's really nobody here who gets it or who I can talk to. You know how Mom and Dad are (they say hi, btw). They just kind of shove shit down and pretend everything's okay all the time. Which, don't get me wrong, I love them and I'm SO grateful they're here. I don't know what I'd do if they weren't. Sometimes I feel like they're the only thing keeping me together. So, I mean, I have them. Thank God. And that's great. But they're my parents, y'know? Not my friends.

And I don't have a lot of friends, Ty. Now, I'm not throwing a pity party. (OH, WOE IS MADDIE. haha) No. None of that. It's just true. I feel like I was starting to make a few friends in my first semester, but then... Y'know. And that kind of fucked all that up, so.

And it's okay not to have a lot of friends, right? I think you feel that way too probably. I've always kind of thought we were the same that way. You don't need a lot of friends when you've got one or two really good ones. Like how you and Scotty and Evan had each other. And, I guess, like how I had you guys too.

Because, I mean, that's the thing. I know you probably didn't feel this way because you're older and a guy and stuff, so I don't know if you ever noticed, but I always kind of saw myself as the fourth musketeer with you three. (Aramis or Porthos probably. I don't think I'm Athos and you're DEFINITELY D'Artagnan. LOL) But seriously, I don't know if you saw how much I followed you guys around, but I did. Mom and Dad used to give me a hard time about it. Did I ever tell you that? They did. I think Mom was worried I was a lesbian or something. That's why she was always shoving me in dresses and shit. I don't know if you remember the time I asked for a fire hat for Christmas because you guys all had them, and she got me a Barbie Dream House instead. I know Scotty would remember because we set it on fire. (The box said it was flame-retardant, so we decided to see. I blame the manufacturer. Don't claim that shit unless you can back it up.)

Anyway. I'm not a lesbian, btw! Like I am so totally not a lesbian. Not that it's a bad thing or whatever, just… I'm not one. I just want to make that clear. That's all.

Because…

Shit. I've tried to write this like three times and each time I scratch this part out and throw it in the trash. I'm only telling you that because my wrist is getting tired and I'm running out of stationery and I don't want to do it again, so I feel like maybe giving that disclaimer will help me just write it this time and not scratch it out or throw it away.

So.

Okay.

Here goes.

109

Because here's the thing…

And I know this will sound crazy! Okay!? Let's just get that out of the way right now! I'm not stupid! And I know that feelings are just feelings and they come and go and that you grow up and stuff and when you do things change and whatever. I know that.

But mine haven't. Changed, I mean. I'm nineteen now and I still feel exactly the same way I did when I was nine. And that's ten years. That's more than half my life. That's a long time. Half your life, I mean.

So the point is that when I say this, when I tell you what I'm about to tell you, don't think it's just because I'm feeling needy, or because I'm lonely, or because of what happened to Scotty, okay? Because I'm not. Okay? I'm not.

I'm really, really not. This is really how I feel and it's real.

I love you.

Like,   I   love   you,   Tyler. I always have. Ever since I was a little kid, and a then a middle-sized kid, and then a big kid, and now, as like, a grownup-type person.

I love you.

And I hope that doesn't weird you out or send you running. Because that's the last thing I want to do. THE LAST THING.

I just wanted you to know so that whenever it is you finally come back (you are coming back, right? haha)—whenever that is, I want you to know… I'll be here. I mean, I don't want to presume that you feel the same way or have you think that I expect anything of you, because I don't. I really don't. But I just needed you to know. Because it's been really, really hard this last almost year. And one of the things that's gotten me through is thinking I'll see you again.

And look, if this sounds crazy because it's been, y'know, like six years since we've seen each other… I get that. It sounds crazy to me too. But just because something's crazy doesn't mean it's not true. It's not a lie. It's just… a lot.

110

So.

I hope this letter finds you, and if it does, just know that it would mean THE WORLD *to me to hear from you. Anything. Just any small thing letting me know that you're okay and that you're keeping your head up. Because, even though it's hard—trust me, I know it's hard—that's where I'm keeping mine.*

I'll be looking for you.

Ever and always yours,
Maddie

CHAPTER ELEVEN

MADDIE & TYLER

MADDIE

I can't make out the look on his face as he's reading. His head is down. He sniffs out a laugh a couple times, which is nice. I don't remember what I wrote word for word, but I do remember trying to put some jokes in, because I thought he'd appreciate it, so I'm glad that he seems to.

It feels like it's taking a really long time for him to read the whole thing. And even though I want to ask him questions or say something to him, I force myself to sit there quietly until he finishes and looks up at me.

And then he does. And his eyes are glistening. He swallows. Shakes his head a tiny bit. Closes his eyes and smiles a bittersweet smile.

"I told you it was pretty good," I say.

He opens his eyes and suddenly he's on top of me, pressing my back against the bed and kissing me with the urgency of someone who's been stranded in the desert for days and just got handed a glass of water.

He takes the back of my head in his hands and presses his forehead to mine. He's gripping me tightly but at the same time pulling back, like he wants to squeeze me with all his strength, but knows that if he does, he'll crush my skull. Which I assume neither of us wants.

"I'm so, so sorry," he says, his voice quavering.

"I know," I say.

"No, you don't," he assures me. "I am sorrier than I will ever be able to explain."

"It's OK," I say, stroking his cheek.

"I should have been there."

"Yeah," I say. "That would've been nice. But you're here now."

"But when you needed me—"

I lean forward and shush him with a kiss. "Living in the past, babe," I say, and wink.

He pushes up off of me and sits next to me on the edge of the bed. I sit up and join him. He takes my hand. We don't talk, he just looks at my hand in his.

Finally, after a minute, I ask him, "What are you thinking about?"

And in true Tyler Morgan fashion, there's no way I can predict his answer.

TYLER

"Daniel Day Lewis."

That's what I tell her. That's what I'm thinking.

"What?" she asks. "Daniel... The actor? Why? Do I remind you of Daniel Day Lewis?"

"No." I laugh.

114

"OK. Good. Although he is very talented, so I suppose…"

"You ever see *The Last of The Mohicans*?"

"No," she says. Then adds, "I read the book."

"Pfft, book," I say with some scorn. "Reading. Blech."

She smiles and nods like she's tolerating me, silently asking me to go on.

"There's a famous quote from the movie where he goes, 'Stay alive. No matter what occurs. I will find you. No matter how long it takes. No matter how far. I will find you.'"

"Yeah, I know," she says. "It's also from the book."

"OK. Well, wherever it's from, it's all I can think of. It just keeps running through my head over and over."

I roll our interlaced fingers over so that I can see the back of her hand. It's strong, but delicate. Long fingers and white skin. Veins that tense with the clench of her grip. Freckles. Just a few light, faint, perfect freckles.

I have the same thought I had the other day. That I want to learn her. Her body. Every millimeter of her. I want it burned into my brain. I want to imprint her into my memory before she goes. I want to study her. I want to have a PhD in Maddie Clayton.

I let go of her hand and stand up, turn to face her and then kneel down.

"What are you doing?" she asks.

I don't say anything. She's not wearing shoes, so I start tugging at the toes of her socks and she giggles as I work them off her legs and then hold her precious feet in my hands, examining them. I stroke the bones that run along the top, ending at the tips of her toes, and I kiss each toe one by one.

I turn them over to inspect the scar I found the other day, and I give it a kiss. Then I spread her legs and slide in between them, popping my head up to give her a kiss on the lips, before I unbutton her jeans and draw down the zipper. She leans back, propping herself on her elbows, and shimmies her hips as I pull her pants down. They're so tight on her, so fitted, that they draw her underwear along with them as I pull, and then the pants are off her body and on the floor, and her bare calves, and knees, and thighs, and pussy are there for me to explore.

Still leaning back on her elbows, she tilts her head to the side, presses her lips together in a tight smile, and raises her eyebrows at me.

I lift one of her legs and place my face right next to it. Like an archaeologist exploring the contours of a priceless, ancient artifact.

Her smell. Her smell will be the thing that I know I will hold onto most. It's always been that way for me. Smell is the most potent sense I have when it comes to triggering memories. When I smell cinnamon, I remember my mom. Because she was baking when she collapsed that last time after chemo. And so that's the smell I choose to associate with my final memory of her, as opposed to the antiseptic smell of the hospital. Because that wasn't her anymore anyway. Mom stayed in the kitchen. Only the shell of her stuck around for a couple weeks more in the hospital bed.

Anyway.

Right now, Maddie smells like freshly cut grass. She's been packing and getting ready to leave all day, and it's been weirdly warm of late, so she's a little sweaty. And that smell—that pungent, dense, round smell of sweat on her skin that fills my nostrils—reminds me of summer. Which

I love. Because I suppose that means that for the rest of my life, there'll be an entire season where every day all I'll be able to think about is her. Even though I don't imagine needing a lot of prompts to steer my thoughts in her direction.

As I stroke my fingers along her leg, kissing as I go, and drinking in her scent with every breath, she drops down from her elbows, letting herself lie flat on her back, her legs dangling off the side of the bed. She traces her fingers up and down the line of her stomach, pushing her t-shirt up to the curve of her breasts as I continue my survey of her flesh.

I'm discovering things. Things that no one else on earth besides me will know.

Her right calf appears just infinitesimally stronger than her left. Her left knee is the teeniest bit knobbier than her right. And when I kiss her behind either of her knees, she shudders through her stomach, causing her toes to crinkle.

As I pass the bend in her knee, I draw my nose along the inside of her thigh. She wriggles a teeny bit as my beard moves along her soft skin. And then my mouth is right at the brink of her entrance. I take my thumb and run it along the pink folds and she lets out a "mmmmm." I tilt my head, studying my fingers as they massage her tender skin, and take note of what sound each gesture evokes from her.

Kissing tenderly on her opening causes her to growl from somewhere deep inside her throat. So I do. I kiss, and I let my warm breath signal my presence, but I don't want to penetrate her. Not this way. If she wants me to be inside her, I will happily oblige, but for now I just want to be here with her and hold her close.

And I will.

And I will hold her close in my thoughts every second that she's gone.

But more importantly...

I will hold her in my heart.

MADDIE

Some people search their whole life looking for that one place they belong. For that one person who gets them. Who brings them into their world, lets them fall easily into the pull of their gravity, and lets them just... be. Just exist. Quietly. Naturally. Freely. This is Tyler for me. The center of my universe. The man around whom I now orbit.

Not like a satellite, either. But like... like two things meant to be one. Like long ago something crashed into us, broke us into little pieces, and left us adrift. Floating in directionless space. Spinning wildly with no tether. And now we've been pulled back together. And we circle each other, still spinning, but with the purpose of joining. Of becoming one thing again. Not because of tragedy, the way I'd imagined when I sent that letter. It's not a lifeline of salvation connecting us now, but some force of nature we can't explain, or control, or bend to our will. Some law of the universe that dictates the fate of things.

We are connected by something more powerful than shared sorrow. And every moment we've spent apart has been valuable. Necessary. Critical.

His mouth between my legs feels wonderful. I could close my eyes and enjoy it. Let myself reach the heights of pleasure.

But alone?

No. I'm done doing things alone. We're connected now. And everything we do will be together.

So I whisper, "Tyler," as I caress his head. Run my fingers through his hair. Touch his shoulders. Slide my fingertips up and down the hills and valleys of his muscular arms.

He looks up at me, his eyes smiling even though they're half closed, even though his mouth is still working. His tongue still flicking against my pussy.

"Come up here," I say. "And kiss my mouth."

Now he smiles with his whole face. His hands plant on either side of my hips and he draws himself up to standing. He lifts his t-shirt over his head and undoes his jeans, letting them fall to the floor, and his nakedness reminds me that he has lived every single day of his time on this earth.

He leans onto the bed and eases forward. My legs open wider for him, welcome him between them as his cock—hard, and long, and ready—rests against my clit, making me want him.

If we stopped right now, if he just rested his chest on top of my breasts, became nothing more than heavy weight as he closed his eyes, relaxed, and fell asleep… I'd be content, happy, and satisfied.

And not because there'd be more chances to do this later. But because it's *him* I want. Not the sex.

He leans down, his hands on either side of my head now. Bending the mattress the way spacetime bends around a sun. And when his lips reach mine, my eyes are closed.

And I fall again.

I fall far, and long, and easily. The same way I drifted towards him. And as I drift, weightless, we kiss. But I'm still connected to him. Always next to him. Because this is what it feels like to fall *into* someone, not away.

This is not me slipping down the mountain.

This is not me losing my footing.

This is me finding myself. In him. In us.

So when I reach my hand between my legs and place him right where he needs to be, he enters me. And all those broken, spinning pieces come together to once again create the thing we were always meant to become.

Our bodies move together. Perfectly synchronized. Like the dance of stars in space. His body is hot, and my body is hot, and the heat we create between us doesn't burn like fire but rearranges us. Like the molecules of two metals mixing to form the strongest sword made of the very best steel.

Our lovemaking is slow. And perfect.

We reach the heights of pleasure together. As one. And it's the kind of climax that only happens once in a lifetime. The kind of release that means more than the way it makes you feel. It tells you who you are, and who you're with, and exactly where you fit in the grand scheme of things.

He says, "I love you, Madison."

And I say it back. "I love you, Tyler."

We mold ourselves into each other as we relax and grow sleepy. Our bodies back together. His arms around me. My back pressed against his chest.

Our hearts beating. Keeping time.

Becoming what we were always meant to be.

CHAPTER TWELVE

MADDIE

I see a lot staring out the window of Ricky's car as we drive south, towards Mexico. But then again, I see nothing. Because I'm picturing Tyler when I left him behind this morning. He tilted his head a little, like he was about to veto the whole thing. But I did this little headshake in response. A no. A soft one, but still a no.

It was hard to say goodbye, but we did it. I refused to cry because that wouldn't be fair to him. This was my decision, so I have to be strong no matter what. But I was sad, and he was sad. So…

I glance at the watch on my wrist. Tyler's watch. Nadir's watch. It's not lost on me that history is nothing more than the passage of time. And that we record time to give us some sense of our place in our own stories.

And now we've been driving for hours. In silence. Complete. Dead. Silence. Ricky and I haven't said one word to each other. Ricky is staying in character and I'm too paranoid that Carlos might have the car bugged. So I've been dwelling on my decision.

Was it really a decision? I mean, I guess I could've let Tyler pay the money, but would that've been the end of it? Would Carlos really have let me go?

No. There was never a decision to be made because it was made for me. Somehow, some way, I got Carlos Castillo's attention. And like Pete said, "You're in Castillo's orbit now. There's no getting out of it."

He was wrong though, wasn't he? He got out. Dead.

This thought gives me new strength as we drive straight through Mexicali. I know we're close to arriving, so my leg's been bouncing, and my hands are sweaty and my heart is racing... but Pete's words to me are just what I need to stay focused on this goal. I don't care if Logan killed him by accident. And I give no shits that Carlos didn't give the OK to kill Pete.

Pete is dead. You can't fix that. You can't take it back. There's no do-over.

So I'm gonna do my job.

More miles pass and then we're out in the countryside. It looks a little familiar from the last time. And pretty soon the roads turn to dirt and there's nothing but dust kicking up behind us when a large house appears off in the distance.

A fortress.

It's typical Spanish style. Stucco with arched windows and doorways. And the gate leading into the property is intricate metalwork and the walls surrounding it are solid and look impenetrable. There's lots of little outdoor walkways winding around the perimeter of the house that I never noticed before. All of them behind bars.

A prison, then.

When we approach there are guards with guns in a little building off to the side, who probably control the gate. But Ricky's car must be one they know because the gate opens for us and we pass through.

I let out a loud breath of air. And I can imagine Ricky's heart is beating as fast as mine, because his stake in this is as big as mine, even if he's not the person Carlos is interested in and I am.

He will be killed if his cover is blown. Brutally. Like… beheaded, maybe. Or hanged from a bridge and left there to decay in the sun as an example to the locals.

I want to say something to him. Make him say something to me. Something that builds my courage like, "We'll get him." Or something comforting like, "I won't let him touch you."

But he doesn't. And I don't either. Because we're past that now.

He needs to be Ricky and do his Ricky job. And I need to be Maddie and do my Maddie job.

The car stops too soon and then Ricky is out and my door opens, and a large man tells me to get out in Spanish.

I do. Swallowing down my fear. I'm wearing jeans and a t-shirt and sneakers just in case I need to run. I don't have any make-up on and my hair is pulled up in a ponytail because I'll be damned if I'm gonna make myself pretty for this murdering asshole.

The big guy takes the couple of small bags I brought with me, and my heart catches when I think of the sat phone and them finding it and keeping it, but I keep a blank, almost bored look on my face so that nobody gets to think I give a shit what they do.

I look around as the unfamiliar man beckons me toward the front door, which is open. Walking through it, I discover the inside decked out for Christmas, looking like something from a fairytale. Like a Brothers Grimm fairytale where somebody gets eaten by a wolf at the end. Holly adorns the grand staircase, ribbons and bobbles hang from everywhere, and on the far side of the hall is a Christmas tree that looks like it was stolen from the Rockefeller Center.

And, also dressed in festive holiday attire, the servants are once again all lined up, just like they were last time. Only this time it's only me arriving to greet them, not their master. So why the fuck are they doing that?

"Welcome, Madison."

I look to my right to see Carlos standing under an arched doorway that leads off to another part of the house. He's wearing a light-colored linen suit like he's on vacation in the tropics and we're going out for dinner. His tie is pale green, and the small sliver of pocket square I can see is red. Ho, ho, fucking ho.

Carlos Castillo isn't ugly. Or old. He's not handsome or young, either. He's something in between those things. He reaches for me, the gold ring on his right hand flashing in a sliver of sun that finds its way inside, until the massive front door creaks as it's closed up by a servant and the grand foyer goes dim with shadows.

I don't reach for him, but my hand ends up in his anyway.

He kisses it, which repulses me and for a second I try to withdraw it. But his grip tightens and I give up and do my Maddie job.

"Mr. Castillo," I say. Not cold, but cool enough.

He tsks his tongue, but smiles. "Please, call me Carlos. Unless you have a pet name for me already. Then call me that instead."

Ewww.

"How was the drive?" he asks.

I look around for Ricky, but he's gone. So's the other guy. Just me, the master, and his servants. They all look straight ahead, not at me. Just staring at the closed door like robots.

"Long." I sigh. "And hot. And boring. And silent."

"Well," Carlos says, placing my hand on his arm as he leads me forward into the interior rooms of the house. "Let's see if we can't improve conditions a little."

It is hot for December. Which is appropriate since I'm spending Christmas in hell.

We descend down several steps to a sunken living room and the temperature cools. There's ceiling fans and A/C, I'm sure of it. But the foyer was grand, and tall, a place that gathers heat. This room, which is tastefully furnished with overly large southwestern pieces, was meant to keep heat out, not trap it inside.

A servant, who's dressed like something out of the fucking *Nutcracker*, appears on my left, tray outstretched, glass of water on top. I take it automatically because my mouth is dry and tastes like paste. For a moment I wonder if maybe it's drugged. Like he's going to roofie me. But then I decide that's silly. Why would he? I came here on my own. So I drink it—all of it—and place it back on the tray, because that servant is still hovering, and then look at Carlos and sigh.

"Let's take care of the boring part now, shall we?"

Whatever. I nod. Force a small smile. And let him lead me through the house as he points out different rooms and special objects he has an affection for.

There's a lot of bedrooms. And two wings to the house, but our tour only covers one side. I soon realize the other side of the house is where I was last time. The prison side. This side is his personal residence. And by the time the tour makes it to the last of the bedrooms, I'm not surprised at the lack of bars on the windows.

He's pointed out paintings, pottery, rugs, and other pieces he's collected over the years. "This is my home, Madison," he says as we turn the corner and enter the master suite. "And now it's yours too."

Jesus Christ, he's fucking certifiable.

But I make myself smile. "It's lovely. Really."

He looks at the bed. Then back at me.

Fuck you, buddy. "We should swim," I say. "I'm still so hot."

This must be something agreeable to him because he draws in a breath. "You didn't bring very much luggage."

"No," I say. "I didn't. I figured you'd provide for me. I'm not wrong, am I?" I arch my eyebrow.

Which makes him beam for some stupid reason. "You're correct. You are mine now. And I will provide for you. That is what it means to be mine."

I nod. Smile. Say, "Yes. That's what it means."

He watches me carefully for a few moments, maybe trying to figure out if I'm sincere or this is all just bullshit.

He knows it's an act. He must. He's crazy, not stupid. But he doesn't address any suspicions he may have, and motions towards a set of double doors. The servant who's been following us around the entire tour jets out from behind us and opens them.

It's a closet. Huge. Something I'd die for if it was really mine and not an elaborate trap laid by an insane drug lord.

I take in the dresses. Gowns, some of them. The shirts, hung neatly from those fancy hangers you only see in movies. Or probably at Evan and Robert's. Pants, some folded on shelves, some clipped to hangers to keep them creased.

But it's the swimsuits I'm interested in.

I've thought about this first day and how we might spend it the entire drive down. When I wasn't missing Tyler, that is. Emily encouraged me to think of things that I might want to do that would please Carlos but simultaneously keep him at a distance. Use the fact that I have something he wants—that I *am* something he wants—to my advantage. And I came up with the idea of swimming to pass the hours. Luckily, the weather will allow for it, he can see me in a suit, and I can cool off in the pool, maybe sun myself. Pretend I'm on vacation. And hopefully, if I play it right, it will put him at ease and keep him from touching me at the same time.

Because I will not fuck Carlos Castillo. Not for Ricky, not for the DEA, not for my goddamned country. Not for anyone.

Carlos lets me move away from him, probably getting off on this moment. Seeing himself as some generous, benevolent king instead of some lowlife scum who needs to trap a girl to keep her.

I reach for the swimsuits hanging off to the side.

"There's two-pieces in the drawer down below," Carlos offers. As if I'd really choose a bikini when I have five one-pieces hanging in front of me.

Two of them are just strategically-placed strings. One *would be* fairly conservative… if it wasn't see-through mesh. One looks like something an Olympic swimmer might wear for a meet. And one is black, covers the most important parts, and shimmers with rhinestones.

I chose the bling-y one. I would choose the athletic one, but I have a plan, and that's not part of it.

"Do you like this one?" I ask, holding the suit up in front of my body by the hanger.

127

JA HUSS & JOHNATHAN McCLAIN

He stares at me. First my face, studying it carefully. Then his eyes track down, over the suit and my body, and he smiles. "I can't know for sure until you put it on."

"Some privacy?" I ask. Softly. Sweetly.

He nods his head, backs out of the closet, and closes the doors behind him.

I strip quickly, efficiently, kicking my own clothes into a heap at the edge of the ball gowns, and pull the swimsuit up, letting the straps snap against my skin as I adjust it.

There's a bazillion shoes to choose from. I scan the shelves, decide on a pair of bling-y black ones that kinda match the suit, then grab a white button-down shirt and pull it on over me. Sunglasses—all lined up neatly in a velvet-lined drawer—and a floppy cream-colored straw hat—sitting on a high shelf—complete my look.

So by the time Carlos gets antsy and knocks on the doors, calling out, "Madison?" I'm ready.

I open them up, find him about to knock again, then enjoy his pleasant surprise at my change.

Because I'm not Maddie Clayton right now. I'm Madison, civilian undercover for the DE fuckin' A. And I figure the quickest way to gain enough intel to take this asshole down and put him away for good is to assimilate.

"Is that what you're wearing out to the pool? Carlos," I say, taking his lapels in my fingertips and caressing the soft linen of his suit. "Go change. We can't play in the pool if you're wearing the wrong kind of suit."

He tilts his head at me, questioning my immediate surrender.

"What?" I ask. "What's wrong?"

He says nothing. Just stares at me.

"Look," I say, sighing, letting go of the false happiness and getting real. "I get it. Obviously, this is not the way I thought this was all going to go. And I've clearly not been very forthcoming before now. But I've thought about it all, and I've come to a brutal conclusion." He continues staring. "My life sucked, OK? I mean, I was a goddamned stripper, for fuck's sake. And not a very good one."

This makes him smile

"And I couldn't see a fucking way out of it, but this— all this—is an opportunity. My life's been going downhill for a long time, and this is a chance to be a little less miserable. Look, I know this isn't real. I know you don't really love me or anything. And you know I don't really love *you*. But I'm not gonna blow this, Carlos."

He squints his eyes at me. Confused. "Blow what?"

"This," I say, shrugging as I pan my arms wide to indicate the room. "All of this. I'm gonna enjoy it. I'm gonna eat your food and use your expensive soaps in the shower. And play in your pool, and sun myself, and probably drink too much. So there," I say, hands on hips. "What do you think of that?"

He chuckles.

I pray. *Don't kiss me. Please don't kiss me.*

"What else will you do?" he asks, his voice husky.

"Oh, you mean will I fuck you? No," I say, crossing my arms. "I might've been a stripper, but I'm not a whore. I can't be bought. If you want a whore, go get one. I'm your *companion*."

He does more than chuckle now. "You're what I want you to be, Madison."

"Yeah," I say, backing up one step. "And what's that? Do you want to force me? Do want me to pretend, Carlos?" He stares at me. I know I'm making him angry, but I push through it. "Or do you want me to give in? And be real? Because those two things are very different. And the way you get them is also very different."

"You just said you won't... fuck me."

I take a brief, secret breath and say, "If I come to like you, we can have sex. If I come to love you, I'll do anything you want. But I don't love you right now. I like your things. I like your money. I like your power. But I don't like *you*. In fact, I kinda fuckin' hate you. You think I owe you money when I don't. You sent your stupid nephew to threaten me."

Easy, Scarlett, Devil says. Because Carlos's face is turning red with anger. *Not sure this was part of the fucking strategy Emily taught you.*

Shut the fuck up, I tell him, silently.

I steel myself and say, "And you killed *my friend.*"

"I didn't order that," he says, coolly.

"Who cares?" I yell. "I'm mad about it. I'm mad as fucking hell, OK? And if you want to rape me... if you want to prove to me that you're the asshole I think you are right now, then I can't stop you, can I?"

We stare hard at each other now, neither of us willing to back down.

"But if you'd like to change my mind," I say, softening just a little, just enough, "show me another side of you, well... then I'll give you another chance. If you're patient with me, I'll be patient with you."

He looks down at his stupid expensive shoes. I catch him grinning like a dumbass teenager. And when he raises his eyes to meet mine again, I see that I've won.

Never underestimate the power of a woman.

CHAPTER THIRTEEN

I'm sitting on her bed, reading the letter she wrote me all those years ago for the fiftieth time since she left, when I hear the front door to the house open. I'm staring at the words 'I love you' when Caroline, carrying a Christmas tree, walks past the open bedroom door and sees me.

"Tyler?" she asks.

"Hey, Caroline," I say, pretty fucking mournfully.

"It's Diane," she says. (OK. Fine. Diane. Jesus.) Then she asks, "Where's Maddie?"

"Oh, she had to, uh, go out of town for a few days."

"Really? Where'd she go?"

Jesus Christ, I haven't seen Caroline and/or Diane in weeks and this is the day one of them chooses to come home and change their panties?

"Uh... Monaco," I blurt out.

"Monaco? Really? Why?"

"Parents," I say.

She looks concerned. And then she looks disgruntled. "Shit," she says. "She's not, like, moving there, is she? We already lost one roommate we're having to cover rent for. When will she be back?"

"Not sure," I say.

"Well. OK." Then she says, "Would've been nice for her to tell us she was going."

And suddenly, I find myself getting pissed. Which I don't want to get, but I don't think I have any choice in the matter.

"Yeah, Diane, it woulda been nice. A lotta things woulda been nice. Woulda been nice if she didn't have to live with a bunch of whores, but that didn't pan out either. We don't always get what we want in life though, do we? So you know what?" I stand and walk over to her. She takes a step back. "How 'bout this? How 'bout I run to a bank and get you, what, like, fifty grand? A hundred? However much you want. And you can shove that shit in your sock drawer for a rainy day and never have to worry about it again. All your problems will be solved! Everything in your life will be squared away! You'll never have to worry about shit again! You hear that? You'll never have to worry about anything ever again! Not Mookie! He's a rich man! He's a rich fuckin' man! He's a real Rockefeller!"

Without thinking, I've been walking her backwards. She's flat against the hallway wall now, cowering down a bit, the tree acting as a protective shield between the two of us. "Wh-wh-what?" she stammers out. "I don't understand. What is that? What are you saying?"

I leave my body for a second and see what this looks like from the outside. A massive, angry dude, towering over a scared woman who will clearly be spending Christmas in this small house in Vegas, and who didn't do anything wrong, and who's just worried about paying her bills. And I don't feel massive anymore at all. I feel like the smallest person in the world. And I am disappointed in myself for channeling my anger at Carlos and Logan and fucking everybody else involved in the shit show I find myself in at poor Diane. (Who I'm still not so sure isn't actually Caroline. But whatever.)

"Sorry," I say. "I'm sorry. It's from *Do the Right Thing*."

"What?" she asks, still scared.

"The quote. The Mookie stuff. It's from *Do the Right Thing*."

"The movie?" she asks, now scared *and* confused.

"Yeah, yeah. The Spike Lee joint," I say. "Sometimes I quote movies when I'm… Fuck. I'm sorry. I'm just having a bad fucking day. Not your fault. I apologize."

She nods a little. "Is there anything I can do?" she asks. She means it. Shit. And now I feel even worse.

"No, no. You're great. I'm the asshole. I'm in your house. Know what? Lemme get outta here and… Shit, I'm sorry."

I duck back into the bedroom to grab my duffel bag and the letter and turn to make my way past her. She steps back, still clearly afraid.

"I really am sorry," I say. "Listen, I wasn't kidding. If Maddie… doesn't come back for any reason—" I take a long pause to keep from going all misty on this kid. The last thing she needs is to take care of my trifling ass. Then I continue, "I got you. OK? I'll make sure you guys are both covered. Promise." She nods quickly and slightly. "I'm just… sad. That she's gone. And I'm, y'know, a dick. So I apologize again. It's not you. OK? You guys have been good friends to Maddie from what I can tell. You were better friends to her than I was for a long time and I, y'know, I appreciate it."

She takes a breath and nods a bit more fully. I give her a half smile and turn to leave. I'm almost at the front door when she stops me.

"Tyler?" she asks.

I turn. "Yeah?"

"Is she really visiting her parents?"

It's an odd thing for her to ask, but then it strikes me that maybe it's not. God knows what this girl has been through herself. What she's seen. What she understands. I don't know her. I don't know anything about her except that she's a girl who went to college with Maddie and now she's a prostitute. That's it. And I can make lots of assumptions about her based on that limited knowledge, but is that fair?

And I have this sudden urge to ask her lots of things about herself. Connect with her somehow. Open myself up and get to know her and let her know me and tell her what's happening with Maddie, even though I was told not to, and bring her on the inside. Because who knows? Maybe there's some unknown, unseen, impossible-to-foretell way that she could help this situation. Maybe she's been here, hanging in the background all this time, but she's actually the one person who could fix all of our problems.

Is that possible? Is that crazy? Is it just that when shit gets really, really bad and we feel adrift, we look for any possible, hidden shoreline to cling to? Or is it just that Maddie is alone right now? Maddie is in God knows what kind of situation as we speak. And my imagination is about to start racing toward places that I don't wanna let it.

"Tyler?" she interrupts my thoughts.

"Yeah? Sorry. What?"

"Is Maddie really visiting her parents?"

I stare at her for another second before saying, "Merry Christmas, Diane," and turn and walk out the door.

I keep looking at my wrist, but I don't have my watch. It won't be night for hours, so I won't have a chance to even know what's going on. But if I don't do something with myself I'm gonna crawl out of my skin.

Totally by accident, I drive by Pete's. Or what used to be Pete's. They've started to do the clean-up. There are a couple of dump trucks filled with the detritus, and it dawns on me that Pete is probably in one of them. Pete and Carolina. Mixed and mingled and together forever. Flesh into fire into ash into eternity.

Maybe some of their shared ashes will get blown into the wind and carried someplace nice. Someplace exotic. Fiji. Bora-Bora. Maybe they'll settle into the earth and become part of the soil there. Maybe a tree will grow from the place where they land, and maybe that tree will produce coconuts or bananas or some shit, and maybe one of the coconuts or bananas or whatever will then feed and nourish a kid who will eventually grow up to become a doctor who cures cancer.

Maybe.

I don't know if I believe in reincarnation, but if we never cease to be and our energy, our life force, just goes on and on and on, then that means that everyone who has ever lived is in us and we are a part of everyone else, and all of us are coconuts and all of us have the power to cure cancer.

And all of us are strippers. And all of us are sitting outside of Raven's house right now without being completely sure how we got here.

What?

Did I drive here? I must have. Fuck. Wasn't I just outside Pete's? Did I lose time? Like I was doing a while ago? Like I was a few… weeks? Ago? Or was it months? Or— Shit! Losing time is something I really thought that I was done with now.

I wish my watch was here.

Regardless, I'm sitting in front of Raven's house. I should go ring the bell, I suppose. She looks like she's home. There's a car in the driveway. What am I going to say if I ring the bell and she answers?

I decide to find out.

The cathedral chime finishes ding-donging, and no one comes to the door. I wonder whether I should be one of those assholes who peeks through windows and wanders around outside someone's house looking to see if they're inside. Or if I should be one of those assholes who rings a doorbell repeatedly even though it's a loud doorbell and if someone was inside, they clearly would've heard it. At the end of the day, I decide to just be the asshole I am naturally, and go.

I turn to leave, but only make it two steps down the walkway when the door opens behind me. "I swear to God, if you fuckin' carolers—" Raven is standing there in a short kimono thing, not dissimilar to the one she was wearing the night she came out to talk to me in the parking lot of Pete's. It may, in fact, be the same one.

"Tyler," she says. "Where's Maddie?"

Something about that makes me very happy. No. Not something. Everything. Because it implies that Maddie *should* be with me. It implies that Maddie and I are a package deal. And it also probably implies *what the fuck are you, a dude I don't really know, doing at my house without your lady friend?* Which you gotta respect.

"She's…" I start. "She had to leave town for a couple days."

"Yeah?" asks Raven, pulling her kimono tighter around her. "K. Whattayou need?"

"I… dunno," I admit. "Honestly, I didn't even really know I was coming here. Just sorta happened."

She squints at me and nods her head. "K. So, now that you're here, what's up?"

"Nothin'," I tell her. "Seriously, nothin'. I'm just… bored. Or something and thought—" And that's when I see a figure moving behind her in the open doorway. "Oh, shit, I'm sorry," I say. "I didn't know you were… I'll get going." And once again, I turn to start off down the walkway, and once again I'm stopped by someone calling out my name.

"Tyler?"

And when I turn around, I see…

Brandon.

"Uh, hey, dude," I sort of stutter out.

"You good?" he asks. "What're you doing here?"

Questions and information collide in my brain. Unless Brandon has been talking to the other guys at the station—and I know that isn't happening—he doesn't actually know about Maddie and the DEA. And also, why isn't Brandon wearing a shirt? And also, what the fuck is happening right now?

That question makes its way out of my mouth in the form of, "I didn't know you guys, uh… knew… each other."

Raven answers, "We met the night you guys came to the club the first time. You remember. It was the night Maddie sucked your cock."

That's so Raven.

"Oh," I say as nonchalantly as I can. "Yeah, well…"

"We exchanged numbers then," she says matter-of-factly.

"You did?" I'm shocked for like three reasons.

"Yeah," she says. "But shy boy here didn't do shit with it until I showed up the morning of the fire."

I look at Brandon, who shrugs.

Raven continues with, "I was surprised to see him. I didn't know he was a firefighter. But whattayou know? He is, and then, yadda, yadda, yadda. And now we're… friends."

I look at Brandon again and he shrugs again. *Nobody knows anybody. Not really.* That's what he said to me in the park. Well. That's clearly true, as it turns out.

"So, what do you need?" she asks. "You seriously just bored? What do you want? Come in and play Parcheesi or some shit?"

"No, no," I tell her. "No. I'm good. I'll amuse myself some other way."

"Yeah? Because we've got the board all set up!"

Ha. I really, really like Raven. And a huge part of me does want to come in and be a massive imposition, but not really. And I don't even wanna begin to try and imagine what exactly I'm interrupting. Because I have a wee bit of a glimpse into Brandon finally, but I know I'm still a long way from getting the whole story. And I don't wanna jump straight to whatever kinda freaky sex he and a ball-buster like Raven might be having.

"No. Thanks, I'm good. I'm just making the rounds, as it were." And suddenly, I'm overtaken with the urge to smile huge. And so I do.

"Fuck are you grinnin' at, shit-eater?" she snaps.

I shake my head. "Nothin'. You guys have a good Christmas."

"OK!" she says sarcastically. "You too!" And as she turns to head back inside, leaving Brandon there looking at me, he gives me a small half-wave/half-salute and for a second, I can almost swear the hint of a smile creeps onto his lips before he shuts the door.

I laugh to myself all the way back to the car. Until I sit in the driver's seat, close the door, and glance up to see the setting sun. The day is almost over. And from here on out the only thing I'm going to be able to think about until I get word that she's OK is what might be happening, at every second, to Maddie.

CHAPTER FOURTEEN

MADDIE

I'm disappointed in Carlos. Not for all the usual reasons, like he's a drug lord, or he's crazy, or he's lying about the money I don't owe him. It's because he's actually... kinda good-looking in his swim trunks. Like either Carlos had some surgery and works out daily with a personal trainer, or he's just one of those men who naturally gets better with age. Not that I've seen pictures of him young or anything, but...

Jesus Christ. I can't believe I'm having this internal monologue.

Just say it, Devil says. *He's kinda hot for an old guy.*

Angel pops up on my shoulder making gagging noises.

I brush them both away by waving my hands, which makes Carlos look over at me and smile. He's talking on the phone on the other side of the pool. There's a little waterfall dumping cold water into the hot tub just a few feet away from me, so I can't hear anything. Which is dumb. Because the whole point of pool day with the drug lord is to hear shit.

But I just sorta got him to trust me a little and if I ease into his private shit too soon, he's gonna figure out he's getting played. Ricky was right, Carlos is one paranoid motherfucker. He's always looking at the sky like bombs are about to rain down on us. So even though I think I did a kick-ass job at convincing him I'm just another money-grubbing bitch out to use him for his money and power, he's not really buying it. He's naturally suspicious. And there's a part of him that just knows this is all wrong.

I sold him a chance, that's all. A few days at most to feel each other out. I've already resigned myself to the fact that I'll be spending Christmas here. Which totally sucks because it would've been nice to have Christmas with someone I love, for the first time in years.

With Tyler, Angel says.

Yeah, with Tyler. I sigh, closing my eyes to stare up at the hot Mexican sun. But Christmas Eve is tomorrow and there's no fucking way in hell he's gonna trust me enough to get what I need by tomorrow.

The brightness shining down through my closed eyes dims from a shadow standing over me. I open them to find Carlos, no longer on the phone, standing directly in my rays, holding out his hand. "Swim with me, Madison."

It's fucking hot as hell out today. I mean, I know this is Mexico and all, but it's like almost a hundred degrees and sweat is pooling behind my back and under my legs so a swim would be refreshing.

It's just… getting wet and then getting out and then having him look at me…

"No, I'm good," I say.

Carlos snaps his fingers. Not at me, but some servant standing off to this left wearing full-on servant attire. Dark pants, white button-down shirt, Christmas tartan tie, and holiday festive sport coat. He must be dying in that uniform. "Miguel," Carlos says, "prepara el badminton."

I start to object because playing aquatic badminton with a drug lord is ridiculous. But so is everything about all of this. And Miguel snaps his fingers at some other servants and they're already jumping into the pool (fully clothed in the same uniform as Miguel) dragging a net across the center.

I really do want to get in the pool to cool off.

Well, I'd much rather go inside and sit in the AC, but somehow, I've convinced myself that it's less likely he'll want to fuck me outside. Dumb reasoning, I know. But I hold on to it anyway. I convinced him that he should be patient with me. Win me. And he agreed. But even though I don't know Carlos that well, I know him well enough to understand rules are made and broken on his whims.

So what if he agreed a few hours ago? That means nothing right now.

And then the net is up, Carlos is walking down the stairs into the water holding a badminton racket, and a servant is standing over me—sopping wet because he was one of the ones who had to jump in the pool—handing me a racket too.

I unstick myself from the lounge chair, stand up, take the racket and walk into the pool after Carlos.

It feels wonderful. The water isn't hot, but it's not cold either. It's just cool enough to be refreshing. And I'm not gonna lie, this, in combination with washing the sweat off me, improves my mood immediately.

He's already on the other side of the net. In the deep end. Which means he has to swim and swing his racket at the same time.

I wonder if I'm allowed to beat him? Is there some unwritten rule that says Carlos always gets to win?

Turns out I don't have to worry about that. Carlos serves the little shuttle at me and I miss, falling sideways into the water as I swing. And when I say, "Your point," he replies. "This isn't a competition, so we don't keep score."

So we just... play. Casually batting the little shuttle back and forth. He misses, I miss. He laughs, I try *not* to laugh.

And it's not even terrible. Which makes me feel super guilty. Because Tyler is probably at home worrying about me. Pacing the floor or something. Having one of those rambling conversations with himself, trying to remember why he let me do this in the first place...

And I'm here in Mexico, on a drug lord's compound that is a little too much like a resort, playing in the pool with him, almost enjoying myself.

You're a terrible person, Devil says.

But I realize that's not the Devil. It's me saying that to myself.

"What are you thinking so hard about, Madison?"

I throw the shuttle up in the air, bat it with my racket, and serve it over the net. He hits it back, and I have to scramble to keep the volley going, pretty much falling over sideways again, but manage to hit it back to him. Before I'm even fully upright, it's coming back at me, and I miss.

"I'm thinking about how much I suck at badminton," I say, pushing wet hair out of my eyes.

Carlos smiles. "You'll get better at it, don't worry."

I'll get better at it. Because I'm gonna be here forever so what choice do I have? What else will I get better at? Croquet? Golf?

"You look bored," Carlos says. "Are you hungry?"

I'm fucking starving. But I know this means we're going to have dinner together soon and then that means the day is over and it's gonna be night, and even though he tentatively agreed to my let's-be-patient-with-each-other plan, I'm not convinced he was serious, so I'm all stressed out about that.

"Come on," he says, swimming towards the net. "Let's change and have a nice dinner." He ducks under the water and resurfaces a few seconds later right in front of me. Standing up to his full height, water dripping down him as he gazes into my eyes.

Oh, God. He's gonna do it. He's gonna kiss me.

Both his hands land on my shoulders. I look away, over at the two servants who hooked up the net. They're still dripping wet from jumping in the pool, but I bet they're baking in the late afternoon sun.

Carlos tucks a stray strand of hair behind my ear and I wince. "You're never going to like me, are you, Madison?"

Shit.

I swallow hard and force myself to look him in the eyes. "Depends," I say.

"On what?"

I shrug. "If we become partners."

"Partners?" He laughs.

"Is that funny because I'm a woman? I'm a stranger? Or both?"

"Both," he says. "You're not here for me, Madison. You're here for you, remember?"

"I just said it a few hours ago. Of course I remember." It comes out a little testy, but I'm feeling very nervous right now. I want nothing more than to call up Tyler on that sat phone and hear his voice. He'd probably say something like, *Fuck this shit. I'm on my way to pull you out of there. Be there soon.* And even though I want to take this asshole down, I really do, I'd be so happy if that's what happened next.

That's not what happens next.

Carlos drops his racket in the pool as he leans in, both hands on my shoulders as his mouth makes its way to my neck.

I'm panicking. Like, my heart starts thumping wildly inside my chest. My jaw tightens. I move back just a step, but his grip on my shoulders tightens. Telling me in no uncertain terms that's not an option.

"Madison," he coos into my ear. "You're driving me crazy. And you're teasing me now. Wearing that suit. Jumping in the water. Your fire-red hair catching the afternoon sun. Your beautiful skin exposed and your nipples peaked up from the water so the only thing I can think about is getting you naked."

Shit. This is not going how I planned. At all.

"I will be patient, but you need to keep me satisfied in the meantime. I'm a man used to getting what he wants and I want you." He begins kissing my neck.

Think, Maddie. Think. Think. Think. What did Emily give you that gets you out of this shit show?

Yeah, Devil says. *You need a serious Plan B like right now… Because if you don't give him a good reason to stop, you're going to be sucking his cock under water in about five seconds.*

"You knew that Scotty died in a fire, right?" I blurt, both hands flat on his chest. Desperate to create some distance.

"What?" Carlos says, halting his kisses.

"My brother, Scotty," I say, taking a step back. This time his grip on my shoulders loosens instead of

146

tightening. "When you threatened me on Halloween. You said it'd be terrible if my parents lost another child. You clearly knew I had a brother who died. You must have known how it happened." I chance a look up at Carlos and find his face. Brow furrowed. Frowning. "Did you?" Carlos drops his hands to the water now. And that's all I could've hoped for. So I continue. "Did you know how badly he got burned? And that he lived?" I sigh. "I mean, he *survived*. He was not ever going to *live* again. Not like that."

And even though no one who wasn't there could really imagine what Scotty looked like in that hospital room, Carlos must have an idea. Because he says, "I'm sorry." And then, "I did not know the... particulars."

"Yeah," I say. "Well. Now you do. And when I found out that Pete, ya know... died in *a fire*... well, it hit me pretty hard."

"I didn't order that," Carlos says, defensive. "Logan was not supposed to kill Pete. I respected Pete. For standing up to me once. We agreed a long time ago that backing away from each other was in both our best interests. And so that's what we did."

"Until you didn't," I say. "If you gave Logan permission to burn down Pete's then you did this, Carlos. You killed Pete even if he wasn't supposed to be inside. It doesn't matter if Logan went off script or not," I say, shaking my head. "Because that fire happened. And Pete was burned alive, and it was your man—your *nephew*—who did it. I'm here. Yeah, I'm here. But when I said I kinda fuckin' hate you, Carlos, I meant it." I say that part softly. Without malice. Almost like I regret it. "And one afternoon playing in the pool won't change that. So if you try and kiss me again, you might as well rape me too.

Because I do not give you permission to kiss me. And I can't fight you. I can't stop you. So I'll let it happen. But if you do this... I will *never* love you, Carlos. Ever."

I expect shouting. Maybe a slap across the cheek or a strong hand pushing my face under the water until I drown.

But I get silence.

And when I stare up at Carlos I see... sorrow. Maybe.

He sighs, wades through the waist-high water around me, and says, "Get dressed for dinner, please," over his shoulder as he makes his way out of the pool. "We eat in an hour."

When I turn to get out I see Ricky, standing next to a servant handing Carlos a towel as he enters the house.

I want to catch his eye. I want him to send me some signal that things are going great. That he's got my back. That I won't be raped tonight when I go to bed. That Carlos Castillo won't kill me. That this is all going well...

But he doesn't.

He just turns his back to me and follows his boss inside.

Back in my closet, I stand there, looking at all the clothes and accessories. It's a custom-made closet, the kind with lots of shelving, and special cabinets just for shoes, and different levels of rods for hanging specific kinds of clothes. One corner is a jewelry cabinet. I mean, I thought it was for socks and underwear because the drawers are long and thin. But when I opened it I found what probably amounts to half a million dollars in jewels inside.

Those jewels represent the entire collection of dead Carlos Castillo girlfriends, Angel says.

Stuff it into your luggage, Devil says. *And take it with you when you leave.*

Which reminds me, the luggage I brought with me has appeared in my closet while I was at the pool. I checked to see if anyone had been rifling through it, but no. Not that I can tell. All my stuff is still neatly folded, just the way I placed it last night. Which is a relief, since the sat phone is hidden in a compartment beneath the snap-up handle in one side of the suitcase.

I'm not sure if I'm here as a prisoner or not. I can't quite figure it out. Like… if I wanted to take a car and go into Mexicali to shop, would Carlos let me? Am I allowed to walk out the gates that surround the breezeways and wander the property? Am I allowed to make phone calls? Like, could I call up Raven and just start shooting the shit with her?

I'm so confused, because on the one hand, I came here of my own free will. But on the other hand, Carlos made it pretty clear I had no choice. So… what am I?

Even if Carlos did find the sat phone, would that be so suspicious?

Are you fuckin' kidding me? Devil says.

What? I think that's a real question.

People don't have sat phones. That one you're carrying cost almost three grand.

Jesus. He's right. Maybe I would've been better off with just my regular phone?

No service down here, Devil says. *You're in Mexico. You better step up your game, Scarlett. Maybe you forgot that playtime in the pool was a ruse to stop Carlos from raping you.*

I wave him away with a hand. *I didn't forget, asshole.*

I have an urge to call Tyler, but I can't shake the feeling that Carlos has cameras in here. I don't see any, but isn't that the point of hidden cameras? And Ricky was paranoid of microphones in the car. So I'm pretty sure he's watching me. Listening, at the very least.

I can't call Tyler. Not until I figure out how safe I am.

I turn back to the closet and try and choose something to wear for dinner. I am pretty hungry. My stomach is growling because I didn't eat anything this morning before I left. Too nervous about, you know, giving myself to a drug lord instead of paying him money I never owed him.

The dresses are all summery. Which makes sense, since this is Mexico and it's hot as fuckin' hell out right now. Vegas is nice in December. Mild and sunny. And I know we're several hundred miles south of Vegas, but we might be breaking summer-high temperatures right now.

So... I end up in an ugly ruffle-y thing with a large-print flower pattern on it because it goes all the way to the floor and hides my shoulders. The swim suit was a risk. And I almost didn't make it out of that situation in the pool. So from now on, it's all about covering up.

I don't bother with make-up or jewelry. Just put my hair up in a ponytail and call it good. Outside my bedroom—which does seem to belong to me and isn't something Carlos and I will share, thank God—I can smell dinner and my stomach starts making demands.

Eat first, Maddie. That way if things go wrong, you'll at least be nourished.

I make my way down a hallway. There's men standing guard, maybe posted like sentries? I'm not sure. All I know is that they ignore me as I pass by and try to find the dining room. The home is traditional. Meaning all the rooms are separated by doors and hallways. And I suppose that's good if anyone ever came in here looking for Carlos. Lots of places to hide.

I stop, leaning forward a little to listen to soft voices up ahead.

Logan. That asshole. And Carlos. They're talking— no, *arguing*. But not loudly.

"She's playing you, Uncle," Logan says in Spanish.

"I think she's acclimating nicely," Carlos replies.

"Exactly," Logan says. "And you don't find that suspicious? Last month when you invited her to stay instead of paying off her debt, she would rather die. She's in love with that Tyler guy. I told you that. Why is she here when she loves him? It's Pete all over again."

What the fuck does that mean? And this fuckin' Logan asshole is going to ruin everything. He needs to just shut up.

"Pete didn't take Carolina from me," Carlos says. "I let her go. You know as well as anyone that no one lives if I decide it's time for them to die."

"That's what I'm telling you," Logan says. "So why are you lettin' this Tyler asshole live? Even if Madison is here for the money and the power, like she told you, why not just kill that guy and erase any temptation for another repeat of Carolina and Pete?"

Several seconds of silence hang in the air. I wonder if Carlos is glaring at Logan. Or maybe he's got a hand wrapped around his throat. I can only hope.

"There will be no repeat," Carlos finally says.

Just then a thug comes around the corner and sees me. "Qué estás hacienda?" he asks, pulling out a gun and pointing it at my head.

"What?" I say, feigning ignorance.

"Madison?" Carlos calls out from the other room. "Is that you?"

"It's me!" I say brightly. "Coming for dining as requested. Call off your dog. He looks trigger-happy!"

Carlos appears in the hallway, barking our orders to the thug, who holsters his weapon and walks away. "You look lovely," he says, taking my hand, bowing his head to kiss it.

It takes every ounce of self-control not to shudder with revulsion at that move. I have to dip into my special reserves to manage a smile when he rights himself and stares into my eyes.

"Thank you," I say. "I'm starving. And I smell dinner. Is it time to eat?"

Carlos just beams at me. Like a love-sick teenager. Which is kinda sad, but mostly creepy. "Yes, we've been waiting for you."

"We?" I ask as he leads me around the corner. "Oh," I say, pretending that I didn't realize Logan was with him. "Your nephew is here. How nice." And then I smile, because the Devil in me has something to say. "I guess you might be my nephew one day too, huh, Logan? How funny would that be? Will you call me Auntie Madison?"

He looks like he wants to rip my face off. But he can't. Because his uncle laughs, clearly pleased with my devil side, and says, "Are you asking to be my wife, Madison?"

It was a joke, you dumbass. Meant to piss your lowlife nephew off. But of course I don't say that. I just smile and sit down in the chair Carlos is holding out for me.

See, Angel says. *That's what you get for listening to the devil.*

"We were just talking about you," Logan says.

"Really?" I ask, unfolding my napkin and placing it in my lap. "I couldn't tell."

"How long were you hiding in the hallway?" Logan snaps. "Did you get any useful information about my uncle's business? That is why you're here, right?"

"What?" I ask. My heart is beating fast. They didn't even get to the useful information part. They were talking about me. But I can see from the look on Carlos' face that the idea of me eavesdropping on his private conversations is… upsetting.

Play it cool, Angel says. *Don't set him off.*

Fuck that, Devil chimes in. *Hit that Logan motherfucker back, pronto, and take him out. Carlos likes you. He wants to trust you. And hitting back is standard protocol. It's part of your charm.*

He's right. I can't afford to be weak. Fuckin' devil.

I smile at Carlos. He… doesn't quite smile back. Yeah, I'm losing him. And I almost had him before stupid Logan showed up. "Pete's funeral was last week," I say, just as the servers enter the dining room and start delivering plates of food.

"So fuckin' what?" Logan says.

But I'm not looking at him. I'm looking at Carlos. Who is looking at me.

So I continue. "And everyone was telling a story about him at his wake. You know? Like… a fond memory or something. And I didn't really know Pete so well. I'd only been there a little while, so I didn't tell one. But I should've told this one. Do you want to hear it?"

"No," Logan growls, stabbing at his food with his fork.

Carlos doesn't say anything. Just puts his silverware down and leans back. I take that as my cue to keep talking.

It's too bad Carlos is a psychotic drug lord. Because he's actually quite good at boyfriending. All the manners, the patience, the closet filled with clothes and jewelry… and now he's a listener too. Yeah, what a complete waste of relationship skills.

"Well, like I said. I didn't know Pete that well. But I figured a few things out about him."

"Yeah, that he's a piece of shit—"

"Shut up," Carlos barks at Logan. "And let her speak."

I offer Carlos a smile of gratitude and avoid looking at Logan. "I learned that he cares about us. You know, us girls. His strippers. Not in a creepy way, either. But like… a fatherly way, I guess. Someone who just looks out for others who can't look out for themselves."

Logan grunts as he shovels some food into his mouth, but that's it. Apparently, one warning from his uncle is enough to shut him up. Which gives me the courage to continue.

"So one day a guy comes into the bar. And he's threatening me, right?"

"What?" Carlos asks. "What kind of threat?"

"Apparently, I owe a drug lord money. And I was given a certain amount of time to pay it back." Carlos' face begins to turn red with anger. Logan stops eating, fork midway to his mouth. "But this drug lord's thug came in before my time was up and told me I owed him half. Like that day," I say, summoning up the proper amount of incredulousness. "And I was kinda having a bad day, if you know what I mean."

"Shut up, Scarlett," Logan growls, his eyes blazing with anger.

154

But Carlos backhands him right in the mouth with his ringed hand and says, "Continue, Madison," as Logan's split lip begins to bleed.

"And I was doing this little routine, right? Like I was wearing this devil costume." That seems to kind of turn him on, but I ignore that and keep going. "So I had a stage prop. A pitchfork, in fact. A real one. Made of steel and everything. So"—I put my hands up like I'm surrendering and stare at Carlos—"I just want to you know, I have a hot temper, OK? And sometimes when people push me too far, I lose it. And I know that's not an excuse for kicking your nephew's sorry punk ass, but—"

"You fucking bitch!" Logan says, standing up and flipping his plate over.

Carlos doesn't move this time. Doesn't have to. Because armed guards appear from nowhere and Logan takes a step back.

Yes, Devil whispers in my ear. *Keep going.*

"But he pushed me, Carlos. He wanted half the money. And that was not part of our deal. So I… I kicked his ass with my pitchfork. And basically just went a little crazy."

"I thought this was about Pete," Carlos says. Calm. Cool.

"It is," I say. "Because Pete pulled me off Logan. Saved his life, I think. Because I was done at that point. Done with him and his threats. Done with him showing up at my work to watch me strip and offer me money to show him my pussy."

Yeah… bingo. Carlos stands up and overturns his plate too.

But then he just stands there. Huffing air. Glaring at his nephew. If he was a cartoon steam would be coming out his ears.

"And I was gonna kill him," I continue, because why the fuck not? The Devil was right. Gotta be real or he'll see through me. "So I have to apologize for that. And thank Pete for taking control of me. Otherwise you'd probably have killed *me*, right? I mean, offing your nephew would be bad, I get it. So I owe Pete my life, I guess."

Dead. Silence. Everyone. Logan huffing and puffing. Carlos staring at nothing in particular. The armed guards unsure what to do.

"I should've told that story at his wake," I say. "But it feels good to at least tell it now, so thank you."

I smile a sweet smile right at Logan.

There's another thick moment in which nobody moves.

And then the entire room erupts in violence.

Evan and Robert are having a fucking tree-trimming party. If there's ever a time when I wish that I hadn't burned down my apartment, it's now. Not that I'm against tree-trimming, or parties, or wassailing, or any of that shit, but it's making it very hard to focus on what I'm currently focusing on, which is hitting refresh on my computer over and over and over again to see if the GPS tracking on Maddie's sat phone tells me if it's moved at all. (I had to pay a preposterous premium for that feature, but who the fuck thought I wouldn't?)

It hasn't. Moved, that is. It's still in the same place in what appears to be a massive goddamn compound somewhere in Mexicali. I don't have a live satellite shot, which pisses me off, but I can sort of make out the contours of where she is, using my maps app.

Out in the other room, _Deck the Halls_ is being butchered by all the guys who clearly could not make it into the Las Vegas Men's Chorus. Phone says it's eleven-forty-three PM. Computer says the same thing. So I guess it is. Fuck. I asked her to call at eleven.

It's OK. It's OK. She brought up a good point. It might be suspicious if she called right at eleven every night. I don't want to put her in an impossible position. We agreed that she would just make sure to reach out sometime before the night is over. All good. No problem.

Refresh, refresh, refresh. Sat phone is still at its same location. Refresh, refresh, refresh. Still at its same location. *Deck the halls!* Refresh, refresh, refresh. Same location. *With boughs of holly!* Refresh, refresh, refresh. Same location. *Fa la la la la la la la la!* Fuck! What was that?

"Dude…?" Oh. It was Evan knocking on the bedroom door. Now he's poking his head in. Shit, why even bother knocking?

I assault him with the question. "Shit! Why even bother knocking, bro?"

"You OK?" he asks.

"Why? Do I not seem OK?"

He stares at me. And those eyes of his don't betray shit. If this was a staring contest, I'd lose. Then, finally, he says, "No."

"Well, shit, man. What the fuck do you expect? Maddie's somewhere in Mexico with a fucking drug lord doing God knows what."

"The guy is with her though, right?"

"Who? Which guy? Friggin' Ricky? Yeah, I don't trust that dick-box to do shit."

"Why?" he asks, stepping into the room with an extra glass of eggnog, which he hands me, and which I pound back. He knows I fuckin' love eggnog.

Wiping my mouth, I tell him, "Because. He's got his own agenda. And he's clearly an opportunist. And because I never found out why an Army Ranger knocked him out. But if you've been hit hard enough to be knocked out twice in your life, there is clearly something wrong with you."

"Really? How many times have you been hit that hard?"

"Hard enough to be knocked out? I dunno. Like a dozen. But it's not a fair question because I don't get knocked out. You know that. But if I did, that would just prove my point! Would *you* trust the man *you* love to be left in a fucking life-and-death situation with this dick-box?" I point both thumbs at myself to emphasize that I'm referring to me. (Who's got two thumbs and is a total dick-box? This guy.)

"You already know the answer," Evan says. "Of course I would." He lets that land like an anvil and it kind of takes the wind out of the sails that are propelling my angst.

"Yeah, well, whatever. You love me. I don't love good old Ricky. I don't even know the guy!" I flop back onto the bed where I've been sitting and throw my arms above my head. I couldn't be more of a teenage girl right now if I tried.

"Listen," he says in his infuriatingly calm tone, "she's got the phone, yeah?"

"Yeah." I pout.

"And the Ricky guy knows how to get hold of you too, right?"

"Yeah," I grudgingly acknowledge.

"So, look, if she doesn't reach out to you by the morning, then you can freak out. But she said she would, and my bet is that she will. Give her a little credit. You know her. Worrying like this isn't helping her and it sure as hell isn't helping you."

I prop myself up on my elbows and watch my best friend, appointed in grey flannel trousers and the most well-tailored white cashmere turtleneck sweater I've ever seen, unflinchingly sip his eggnog. He looks like the headmaster at the fancy boys' school who all the moms, and some of the dads, want to fuck.

"Give her credit, huh?" I ask.

He nods, swallows some nog, and says, "Yep."

"She's a total fucking badass, isn't she?"

"Always has been, and I see no evidence to suggest that's changed."

I pick my phone up and turn it over and over in my hand. "I just want to know she's OK. I love her, man."

"I know. I love her too." I open my mouth to start, but he says, "Different. Obvs, bro. But I do. And I'm worried about her too. We lost Scotty. And then we lost her for a long time. And now that we have her back, the last thing I want is to lose her again." He finishes off his eggnog and turns the empty glass around and around in his hand.

After a moment's rumination I say, "If she doesn't check in before morning…"

"She will. I feel it in my gut. But if she doesn't… You're tracking her? You know where she is?"

I nod. "Roughly. Yeah. More or less."

"Then I'm right there with you when we fucking roll in to get her back."

I've been looking down at my phone, but that snaps my attention up quick.

"Dude," he says, "it's been a long time since I've mixed it up with anyone. I don't wanna get soft just because I'm settled down. Besides, Robert would never admit it, but he'd think it was hot as shit if I went on some pre-dawn raid on a Mexican drug fortress or whatever the hell it is. Marriage, bro. Gotta keep it spicy." He winks.

I sniff and shake my head. "Yeah. OK. Look, man, you get back to your party."

"What are you gonna do?"

"I dunno. Sit here and keep hitting refresh to make sure the phone hasn't moved."

"Nope," he says, stepping over to grab me by the arm and tug at me.

"What are you doing? Stop pulling," I say. (Seriously. I might as well be fifteen and named Britney right now.)

"Get up, bitch," he says. "Come out. There's a shitload more nog and Rodney keeps asking about you."

"The fuck's Rodney?"

"You met him at Thanksgiving. Owns the salon?"

"Oh. You mean Mustache?" I ask.

"Yeah, that's him. He's obsessed with you."

"He knows I'm straight, right?"

"What's that got to do with anything?"

I take a moment to consider that. "Fair question."

"Come on, man. She'll connect with you soon. I promise," Evan says.

I put my hands on my knees and push myself up to head into the party with him, seeing if there's any way possible I can stop worrying about Maddie for maybe five minutes. I mean, the answer is a resounding no, but I'm nothing if not game.

"You don't think Rodney just wants me for my beard, do you?" I ask.

"I think he wants you in spite of it, man." Evan claps me on the shoulder and we head into the living room where now we are on to, *Five gold rings!*

Please call, Maddie. Please call soon.

161

The clock on my phone says four-forty-five AM. I'm lying on my back in my bedroom. The phone is on my chest, staring at me. Mocking me. Toying with me.

The last of the revelers left over two hours ago. Robert and Evan crawled into bed and Evan told me that I should let him know if Maddie hadn't called by the time the sun was up. Well, the sun is coming up in a little over an hour and she still hasn't made contact. I should wait. I should wait one more hour. I should…

Fuck it.

I spring out of bed, grab my boots, and lace them up without turning the light on. It's now officially the morning of Christmas Eve and the late December moonlight streaming in through the window gives me enough visibility to get ready for what I have to do. I grab up my computer. Refresh. Phone's still there. OK. Good. But not good.

This is bad. This is very bad. It's day fucking one and she hasn't reached out like we talked about. That means one of only two things: One. She's in a situation where she *can't* make contact. Like they've got eyes on her twenty-four-seven, or worse, they've got her locked down somehow. Or two. They found the phone and also see reason number one.

There is a third reason why she wouldn't have called by now, but I won't even let myself go there. I will not.

I shove my own phone in my pocket and grab my car keys. And I suddenly wish I still had a gun. I gave the gun I had, Logan's gun, back to Pete. And Pete took Logan's other one. Both of them burned up in the fire, presumably. I'm not a big gun guy. I hate them, ironically. But I'd rather have a gun and not need it than need a gun and not have it. (That's a line from *True Romance* by Quentin Tarantino. I mean, probably other people have said it too, but Christian Slater says it in that movie right before the whole fucking film turns into one big blood bath. Which, even though I'm hoping this situation won't... You never know. Shit. Rambling.)

But I do feel like I need backup. Something that gives me an edge. What I'm about to do is head to an unknown location, without any recon, and no idea of how many hostiles might be fortifying it, to try and confirm the safety of an asset. Shit, no I'm not. Let's be honest. I'm going on a retrieval mission. Once I get down there and confirm she's OK (because she has to be), there's no way I'm leaving without her. So I wish I had a gun. That's all.

Because even though I appreciate the offer, I'm not bringing Evan. I can't. He's married, and he already puts his life on the line every day. Every day when he goes to work, his husband has no idea of whether Evan will return home at night. And while that's true for all of us all the time—it's a dangerous world—that shit is *conscious* for Evan and Robert. I can't go into his room and drag him out of his warm bed to go on what might be a very fucked-up mission. I can't. I won't. I love him too much.

And I love Maddie too much not to go.

But I barely even like myself most of the time, so if one person's gonna fucking buy the farm in this equation, I vote for me.

Still... it would be nice to have some kind of backup. Some way of at least knowing what the hell kind of mayhem I might be wandering into.

And then all of a sudden I realize...

There is.

163

CHAPTER SIXTEEN

MADDIE

When I wake up the next morning Carlos is staring at me.

Not in bed with me, thank God. But sitting in the chair in front of the window. In the same suit he was wearing last night. In the same position as when I closed my eyes after he walked me to my room and waited for me to change into one of the many nighties in the closet. After he pulled the covers back and watched, hungrily, as I got under them. After he tucked me in, or whatever.

He didn't touch me. But this man staring at me the entire night was almost worse.

"Happy Christmas Eve, Madison," he says.

Oh, right. Yeah. Happy, happy.

"Jesus, didn't you sleep at all?" I ask.

He just smiles, his face backlit by the rising sun behind him. "I was too... wound up."

He's referring to the ass-kicking he gave Logan last night at dinner. Beat the ever-loving shit out of him right in front of me. I cannot even imagine what Logan looks like today. Both eyes were already swollen shut last night by the time Ricky pulled Carlos off him. After that all the thugs disappeared, Ricky holding Logan up as he helped him stumble away to wherever one goes after Carlos loses his temper on you. And it was just the two of us. Servants came, cleared the debris as Carlos and I had drinks. They bustled around us like we weren't even there and set the table again, brought new food.

And we ate. Like nothing happened.

Carlos talked about what we'd do today. I offered up the pool as a possibility, since that's the only thing I'm familiar with and I was shaking so bad after witnessing the extent of his temper, I just said the first thing that came to mind.

That was his *nephew*. What would he do to me? Or Ricky? If he knew why we're really here?

"And then I was too enthralled by your sleeping face," he continues. "You're so beautiful. I didn't want to close my eyes. Couldn't close my eyes," he adds.

"How sweet," I say, sitting up in bed. *In a very disturbing, psychotic way,* I don't add.

But, with any luck, I won't have to worry about Logan anymore. He wouldn't dare touch me now. Not after... *that.*

Shit. I didn't get a chance to call Tyler and he's going to be going out of his mind with worry. I mean, my first night and I didn't check in. All kinds of bad things are probably running through his head.

Rightly so. Since all kinds of bad things have already happened.

You think this is bad, Devil says. *Wait a few minutes. I'm sure there's another shit storm coming.*

Yeah, Angel says. *This is just the beginning. And you asked for it, so now you gotta deal with it.*

You know you made a serious mistake when both your angel and your devil agree that you're stupid.

"Are you hungry?" Carlos asks.

No. I'm most definitely not hungry. I'm still sick from having to eat food last night, Logan's bloody face still fresh in my mind. But there are already servants in the room. Probably what woke me up. And they're setting up a table next to Carlos with plates and plates of food.

I tossed and turned for hours after getting into bed. But finally, I was so exhausted, the day's happenings too much for me, there's no way I couldn't sleep.

So… "Yeah," I say. "Starving."

Assimilation is my goal, right? I've been here one day. Less than one day, actually. And I've had enough. What have I done? What have I agreed to? I just want to get the fuck out of here. Get away from this crazy psycho and put him away for good. But I can't do that unless he trusts me enough to slip up and give me the information Ricky needs.

Breakfast it is.

I do not want to get out of bed wearing this sexy nightie, but what choice do I have? Besides, bad-ass Madison is a stripper. And Carlos' Madison wouldn't care about showing her sexy off in front of him.

So I force myself to get up. Let him look at my legs. My breasts. As I walk slowly to the closet and get a silk robe I saw hanging in there yesterday, and put it on, cinching the sliver of a belt tight around my waist.

I join Carlos at the table, thankful for the coffee at least, and start picking at my eggs and bacon.

Carlos eats with enthusiasm. And I start thinking, like really thinking this whole plan through for the first time, and realize this is all normal for him. Beating his nephew to within an inch of his life is just standard practice. You piss off Carlos Castillo and he doesn't forgive you. No matter who you are.

Which gets me thinking...

"You know," I say. "I have a question for you. But it's really none of my business."

"Ask," Carlos says, still busy eating his breakfast. "The worst that can happen is that I say nothing."

"Is it?" I ask. "Is that the worst that can happen? I mean... you got pretty mean with Logan last night."

Carlos stops eating. Fork midway to his mouth. And looks at me.

Shit.

"You wanted me to get mean with Logan, Madison. That's why you told your little story."

"OK," I say, letting out a long breath of air. "Maybe that's true. But your... your reaction took me by surprise."

"He disrespected you," Carlos growls. "And he lied to me about that day you beat him. He said Pete's men did that. And then he used that lie for revenge. He used *me*."

"So this is my question," I say, swallowing down my fear. "If Pete took a woman you loved, then why did you let him live? Why did you let *her* live? If... if you don't mind my asking."

Carlos places his fork down on the table. Wipes his mouth with his napkin. Takes a sip of water. Then places both hands on the table, leaning in as he stares at me.

My stomach does this flip thing. That feeling you get when things are about to go terribly wrong. That feeling you get when you realize you've made a mistake and nothing good is gonna happen ever again, because this is a major fuckup.

But I force myself to stare back at him.

"Because I loved her. And I wanted to keep her safe. And back then... I was young. And stupid. And took too many risks. Pete loved her too, and she loved him. And I realized..." He sits back in his chair, maybe relaxing a little, and takes a deep breath. "I realized... if she stayed with me she'd die. Someone would kill her if she was with me then. I was not yet... the man I am today. So I let her go."

"And me?" I ask. "You're not worried about someone killing me?"

He smiles. It's a very evil, drug-lord smile. "No one can touch me now, Madison. You're perfectly safe."

I force myself to sigh with feigned relief. And then I smile. A fake smile that does its job and makes him smile back. Makes him relax even more. And I begin to eat.

He eats too. And we say nothing for a little bit. Me thinking about all the ways in which he's gonna kill me when he figures out why I'm here. Him probably planning our wedding. Which is ironic, since he only met me because I was his daughter's wedding planner. Fucking hilarious. Or not.

"One more question," I ask, something else suddenly bothering me.

"Yes?" Carlos says, finished eating now. Opening up the morning newspaper.

"Your daughter..."

He glances up at me over the paper but says nothing.

"I mean, she..." I swallow hard.

Don't say it, Angel says.

Yeah, Devil agrees. *This is a very bad idea.*

But I do anyway. Because I need to know. "She disrespected you too. Didn't she? Much worse than Logan. So... I just..."

169

JA HUSS & JOHNATHAN McCLAIN

He clears his throat. "Did I kill her?" he deadpans.

I nod, afraid of his answer.

He stares at me. Smiles the creepiest, most unnerving smile I've ever seen. And then he folds his paper and stands up. "You wanted to play in the pool again today? Get changed and I'll meet you out there in a little bit."

And then he turns away, walking towards the door.

"Madison," he says. I turn my head to look at him. His hand on the doorknob. His back to me.

"Yes," I say, almost a whisper.

"You came here of your own free will. And yes, you like my money and my power, but you're honest with me. And I like *that*." He glances over his shoulder, his eyes meeting mine. "As long as you're honest with me, you have nothing to worry about."

I nod as he opens the door.

But he stops again and says, "Wear a bikini today. I want to see your body." And then he leaves, closing the door softly behind him.

I force myself not to freak out. Like… I cannot afford to freak out. But when I get in the closet and see my suitcase, it takes every ounce of willpower I have not to grab that sat phone, call Tyler, and beg him to get me out of here right the fuck now.

Two things stop me. One. I am sure there's cameras in here. Positive. And two, I can't bring Tyler into this. No way am I getting him killed.

So I deal. I suck it up and deal. I put on the skimpiest bikini in the drawer, the highest stripper shoes on the shelf, and don't even bother with the cover-up this time.

I need that information, and I need it fast. Maybe he was a good man once upon a time. Maybe he let Carolina go. But he said it himself. He's not the same man he was back then.

He's worse.

When I get out to the pool, I'm surprised that there's a bunch of men sitting with Carlos around the patio table. And when I walk past, meeting Carlos' appreciative gaze as he checks me out, I wonder if maybe they're business associates. Possibly? Nobody else is around. Not Ricky, or servants, or anyone. It's like a secret cabal. Could this be a chance to get the information I'm here for? I should see how far I can insert myself into his business. I have to try. Otherwise, what's the point?

So I try to sit in his lap, but even though Carlos' hands are all over me saying one thing, his mouth says something completely different. "Get in the pool, Madison. And swim around so I can watch you."

I nod and obey, walking into the water, fear replacing the refreshing feeling I had yesterday. I swim laps. Back and forth, back and forth for what seems like hours, but they never talk loud enough for me to hear anything. And their Spanish is a lot of slang that I don't really understand.

After a while I get tired and start to get out, until Carlos says, "Keep swimming, Madison."

So I swim some more, all the while he has his important meeting just twenty yards away and I get no information out of it.

I will have to stay here for God knows how long. Despite Emily's insistence that we cap the amount of time I can be here... she's not here now. Ricky is. And it's clear that Ricky is ready to let me spend the rest of my life here if that's what it takes.

How stupid was I? How naïve was I? To think I could get what I need in one day? That I could stop him from fucking me? That I had any control over this situation at all?

Hours go by and I eat lunch alone, sitting at a separate table across the pool from Carlos and his pals. All the while I'm sure they're talking about things I could use. Things that could get me out of here. Things that could save my life.

When I finally get back in the pool, after waiting the required thirty minutes after eating—which I forced myself to do, since, you know, that's what people who aren't planning to bring down the drug lord in residence would do—it's afternoon and I'm starting to worry about tonight.

Will he get in bed with me this time? Will he take my clothes off? Rape me?

Yes. The answer to all those questions is yes.

Just then the meeting breaks up. All the men stand, clapping each other on the back and wishing each other Feliz Navidad. They ate too, and drank a bit, so they're happy, and probably a little bit drunk. Even Carlos, who's been sipping scotch from a cut-crystal glass since this morning.

And then… and then I get the lucky break I've been so patiently waiting for.

They go inside. All of them. And leave me alone.

I climb out of the pool, wrapping myself in a towel. Slowly. Lazily. Like I'm in no rush at all. And while I do that, I look around for guards. There's a bunch of them all around the perimeter, along the edges of the property. But they're all facing away from me, looking out towards the desert, on watch for things guards watch for, I suppose.

Not looking at me is the only thing I care about.

I walk around the pool towards the table where they were sitting, and I'm stunned by what I see. I don't know if it's because they got a little drunk, or because the holiday spirit overtook them, but…

There's a map.

A map?

It's crude and awkwardly drawn, but there's some writing in Spanish along the edges. The handwriting is awful, but I think it says… transport? Maybe?

Is it possible? Jesus Christ. Could it be? There's no way. This is too good to be true. It's almost too easy. Might I really have just stumbled into the very thing I'm here to find?

It's a Christmas miracle! the angel shouts.

Bah fucking humbug, the devil grouses.

And just as I'm about to swat both of them off my shoulders yet again, I hear it. A hum, up in the sky. And when I look up, I see…

A drone coming towards me. Its wings tipping from side to side, erratically, like the person in control has no idea what he's doing. Like the person in control is known for flying drones badly. When it does a nosedive, a dogfight move straight out of World War II—or something—and pulls out of it just in time to avoid crashing into the pool, I smile.

And that's when all hell breaks loose.

CHAPTER SEVENTEEN

Why is this thing so fucking hard to control?

Seriously. It's not like I've never flown a drone before. But this thing is impossible. It's imbalanced or something. Fucking Slade. Dude definitely sold her a bum, stolen drone. 'Drone store.' Jesus. (Or I just suck. Could go either way.)

The sat phone has led me here. About two football fields' distance from what looks like a fucking comic-book version of a bad guy house. Or I suppose it's possible that the reason we think bad guy houses look the way they do is because bad guys build them that way, but that's a real chicken-egg contemplation that I can worry about later.

Right now, I'm just trying to keep the fucking drone steady so that I can survey the terrain here and get a sense of what I might be up against when I go charging in there like Rambo. And I hope, unlike Rambo, I don't wind up captured and tortured, strapped to an electrocution bed or some shit.

And not because I'm afraid of dying. I'm not. Not even a little bit. I've done it before and it's not that big of a deal. Honestly, I'm not even that afraid of being tortured in and of itself, because, y'know, I don't really feel pain.

But it totally looks like it sucks and is also the kind of thing that might encourage someone to test the boundaries of how much I can endure. And I gotta believe that there's a point at which I *would* feel a lot of pain, and I'm not keen to discover what that point is.

But what does scare me is anything happening to Maddie. And if I get caught and tortured, that means Maddie will probably get tortured too. So that really only leaves me with one choice here, and that's to get her out of the stupid fucking setup that she's in right now, and that I still can't believe is really happening... and save her.

So that's my plan.

And if I see her and one freckle on her body looks to me like it's out of place, then I hope everyone inside has been to confession before midnight mass tonight, because it'll be *The Magnificent Seven* up in this bitch.

OK, so watching the monitor, I can see what looks like muscle around the perimeter. A not insignificant amount of it. Super. All right, that looks like the main entrance, and shit, the thing just sprawls out forever. I know that there's a way to get 3D imaging of what's happening inside, I just don't know how to work it. There's gotta be a way to get at least a heat signature, for Christ's sake.

I'm playing with the settings on the touch screen to see how I can activate any of these features, which *have to exist*, when I spot what looks like a pool. And standing next to the pool is a body. A sexy body, in a sexy bikini, topped with sexy, unmistakable red hair. *Shit. Yes. She's there. She's here. She's OK. Thank you, baby Jesus. Happy birthday to you.*

But I have to make sure she's actually safe. I don't see anyone near her, but I gotta be sure. So, I'm just gonna zooooooom in, real careful and... Fuck! That's not the zoom! Shit! I think I'm—Ach! I'm dive-bombing. This is not stealth. Good Lord. But it's her! The look on her face is one of shocked confusion, which is a look she gives me a lot, so I know she knows it's me. *Hi, Mads!*

I wonder if this thing has a speaker or microphone. I mean, the plan wasn't to walk right up to the front door and knock. It was most definitely supposed to be more clandestine than things are currently going, but since I'm blowing my cover anyway, I may as well say hi. But it looks like I'm actually about to ditch this thing in the pool, so I have to pull up. Shit. And right as I'm pulling up, on the screen I see...

One of the strapped-up perimeter guards has spotted me. I know, because on the monitor I see him pointing directly at the drone and shouting. I'm too far, hidden where I am out in the brush, to hear him, but shouting looks unmistakably like shouting whether you can hear it or not.

I'm working as hard as I can to pull the drone up and away, but it's not moving vertically very well or swiftly enough in any direction. And now other strapped-up goons are gathering around the first strapped-up goon, and all of them are pointing and shouting. I can see Maddie kind of drifting into the shadows, trying to make herself scarce. And then Carlos comes running out poolside.

I have never actually seen Carlos Castillo. I saw a couple of hazy pictures of him on the internet, but I've never seen him in person. Maddie and I haven't even really talked that much about him apart from Maddie's situation. But this is undeniably him. There is an aura of power and influence that bleeds out of the guy, up into the atmosphere, and all the way through the screen of the drone monitor.

He looks to his muscle to see where they're pointing and then he turns his head and he sees... me.

Oh. There's the zoom. Shit.

I press down on the zoom-in feature and the camera settles right on Carlos's eyes. And I know he can't see me. Obviously. Obviously, I know that. But it sure doesn't feel like it the way his glare seems to land right on my shitty-drone-flying ass. There's a brief moment where it all has the impression of a standoff between the two of us. A Mexican standoff. Literally. Ha. That's funny.

And then he points, says something. And that's when the shooting begins. I see it before I hear it. The sound has to travel to where I'm hiding, but the bullets only have to reach the camera and blast the drone out of the sky. The screen goes dark and I snap my head in time to see the black, metallic bird drop from the sky like... well, like a 900XZ black-market military drone that's just been shot to shit.

Son. Of. A. Bitch.

My instinct is to run. Not away. Toward. In fact, I have to stop myself from breaking into a sprint straight for the reinforced metal gate that protects the driveway. I don't have the urge to run because I'm brave. It's because I'm stupid. But Maddie's alive and she smiled when she saw the drone, so that means she's at least in a place where she can smile, so the last thing I need to do is fuck that up any more than I maybe already have. Carlos was inside when Maddie and I made eye-to-camera contact, so there's a chance he wouldn't necessarily, immediately assume that the drone was here *because* of Maddie.

Right?

178

I'm kicking this around in my addled brain when I think to reach in my rucksack and grab the field binoculars I had the good sense to bring. I hit the dusty carpet of the desert floor, put the binoculars up to my eyes, and a wave of memory comes crashing down. Not the good kind.

It's not that this reminds me of any one moment in particular, it's a patchwork of moments from my time in the military all stitched together. Belly down on the sandy, dusty deck of the earth, glassing the enemy through binoculars, trying to get a read on an unreadable situation. My fingers stiffen and my arms start shaking, causing the 'nocs to judder and bounce against the bridge of my nose. I can't see much through the gate and down the driveway anyway, but what I can see looks like it's being shaken in a blender.

My breathing is shallow and I'm having trouble swallowing. I really don't need this. Not now. I need to figure out what my next move is. I need to find a way to still my nervous system and either get the fuck out of here or charge the castle. And then, while I'm trying keep my brain from sneaking out of my head and crawling across the desert, reality snaps me back.

Through the shaky lens, I see several of the perimeter guards come charging out the front, weapons drawn, in a semi-circle formation, like a human shield, and in the middle of the shielded safe area is Carlos. His head is down, but he's easy to ID because I just saw him when he directed these jokers to shoot down my drone. They're sweeping their weapons back and forth looking for... what?

You know why he won't fly? It's not because he has some innate fear of flying, it's because he thinks the US government will shoot him down. Ricky DEA's words come back to me. Jesus.

179

Does Castillo think this is the government coming after him? Maybe. He must. Because this is a wildly disproportionate response to a little drone action, if you ask me.

Suddenly a black Mercedes pulls into view, flanked by two big, black SUVs. The human shield forces Castillo into the back of the Benz and half of the guys jump into one of the SUVs which takes off first, with the Mercedes following, and then the rest of the guys jump into the other SUV and it peels out on the Benz's six. It's tactical. Precise. Efficient. Like they've run this drill many times in preparation for whatever they think this is that's happening.

And then, like a lightning bolt, it occurs to me… Maddie wasn't with him. They just shoved Carlos into the car. Alone. So where the hell is Maddie? Is she still inside? And if she is, who's in there with her? Are there any more armed assholes? And if so, how many? Do I risk it? Is now my chance?

Fuck it. I don't see where I have a choice.

So I jump up and I start running. I cut wide left because I saw from the drone, before it was so rudely dispensed with, that there was another point of entry along the side of the perimeter wall. Smaller. Looked like maybe it was a servants' entry gate or the grounds crew's gate or something. Because God forbid anyone should sully up the main gate with their proletariat existence. And suddenly, in addition to all the other reasons that I have feelings of hostility towards Carlos Castillo, I can now add income and class inequality to the list. Which is probably hypocritical coming from a rich asshole like me, but fuck it. It's how I feel. As if I needed another reason to want to bury this prick.

I've covered half the distance and am probably a hundred yards away when I stop, because the gate that I'm running for begins to open. Again, I hit the deck. Again, that wash of bad memory spills onto my shore. And again, I force it away and bring the binoculars up to my eyes.

A raggedy old Ford pickup truck rumbles out through the opening gate and through the 'nocs I can see Ricky fuckin' DEA driving. In the passenger seat, I can almost make out Logan. But like, a really fucked up and battered Logan. But it's gotta be him. The scowl is unmistakable. I wonder how he got all bloodied up? I wonder if Maddie did that to him again. Or maybe it was someone else. Oh, well. Poor Unlucky Logan. Ha. Asshole.

Why are Logan and Ricky heading out the side exit in a busted old junker of a pickup? And where are they going? And what do I do? Follow them, follow Carlos, or keep on motoring inside for Maddie?

And before I have to decide, my decision is made for me. From the bed of the pickup truck, I see a spark of bright red hair. There's a tarp over it, but the hair flashes from underneath, and then a second later, so does Maddie. Still in the bikini I saw her wearing. She looks pissed, and then I see why.

Carlos, who is wearing gardener gear now, and who has been lying flat, pops up and draws a protesting Maddie back down on top of him, pulling the tarp over them both.

That cocksucker.

I have to give him credit, though. The diversion he ran with the decoy motorcade ushering whoever was dressed in his clothes into the car and out the front with such noisy fanfare was pretty well executed. Had me fooled. But then again, I'm stupid. I don't know if it would fool whoever

Carlos thinks is after him right now. Because it sure as hell ain't me that he imagines is coming for him.

But faint praise for his escape plan aside, I'm pretty fucking heated at seeing him using Maddie as a human shield. Because that's what he's doing. I assume that part was improvised. Or maybe there's some housekeeper or somebody who's supposed to be the one to protect Carlos with their body in the event they have to make a getaway, and Maddie's a convenient and more appealing substitute. But the idea of her bikini-clad body pressing up against that asshole in the back of that truck is pissing me off.

I sprint back to the Defender, which I have parked where I was doing my surveying before, back at my original distance from the house, and I am struck by the toll that a dozen years of booze, drugs, and getting blown to smithereens a few times has on a body. I ain't in basketball shape no more, that's apparent. It feels like my heart's gonna cave in on itself, if I don't throw it up first. Fuck. I gotta get to a gym soon.

But it's incredible what adrenaline can do, and I power through the pain and into the driver's seat. I hit the ignition button and peel off, fishtailing like a motherfucker in the desert sand. Ironic, I think. Fish. Desert. Whatever. Not the time.

As my car plows in the direction in which they split, I grab my phone and thumb up the sat tracking app. It says that the phone is still where it was. The blinking icon tells me its location is staying behind as I drive forward. Shit. She doesn't have it on her anymore. Which means I can't afford to lose them.

The trail of dust from the pickup gives me enough of an arrow to start, and now I just have to catch them and stay far enough back that they don't see me but not so far that I lose them. My one hope is that if Ricky DEA spots me in his rearview, he'll be cool about it. Which seems like a real fucking stretch to imagine right now, but I've got to hope. Which I will.

Because, shit. I'm nothing if not a goddamn, motherfucking, cock-licking optimist.

Everybody fuckin' says so.

CHAPTER EIGHTEEN

MADDIE

I've been shooting before. I've handled guns. I'm familiar. I met this prepper chick a few years back at one of my many martial arts classes and ended up at her family bunker out in the desert one weekend where she let me shoot all the guns I wanted at their homemade range.

So I know what gunfire sounds like. It's louder than you can imagine. Real-life gunfire isn't anything like what you hear in the movies. There's just no way to replicate that when watching a film. You can't feel the soundwaves hitting your body, or smell the gunpowder filtering up into your nose, or see the clear air change to hazy smoke before your eyes.

The preppers out at that desert bunker were a crazy bunch, no doubt. But what happens in Carlos Castillo's compound is something right out of *Narcos*. And I just… stand there, paralyzed with fear.

The drone explodes and people start shouting, "Get down! Get down!" Bullets spit out of long-barreled assault rifles in short, staccato bursts. Someone grabs me by the arm and pulls me inside, where Carlos is crawling across the floor towards me, barking orders for one of his men to go outside and grab the map. At which point the guy looks outside and thinks about this order for maybe two seconds before looking back at Carlos with an expression that quite clearly says, *No fuckin' way, ese.*

Carlos shoots him in the head and there's no two-second hesitation on his part. Minion's brains just splat a red blob on the peach-colored plaster wall behind him and yeah… game over. The gun goes off so close to my ear, it's still ringing five minutes later.

Now I'm stuck in a closet. The doors are just those louvered things that look like shutters, so I can sorta see what's happening in the room. Carlos is changing into some old baggy jeans and a sweat-stained t-shirt. It takes me a moment to realize he's actually trading clothes with the gardener. And the gardener—once I get a glimpse of him through the thin slits of wood—looks like he's about to shit his pants. Because he is now the decoy. If anyone else gets killed today, it will be him.

I don't want him to get killed. I mean, I get it, he works for Carlos Castillo so he should've known what he was getting himself into. But that was *my* drone. And the only person who can fly my drone that badly is Tyler. And I know Tyler was just worried about me and he's not like… gonna storm the place. He'd never do that.

Right? *Right?*

"Tyler," I whisper softly, closing my eyes. The barrage of yelling and gunfire is still happening all over the compound. "Do not get yourself killed because you're worried about me. Because if you do, I will hunt you down in heaven and kill you again myself."

The closet doors open, startling me so I stumble backward into the hanging clothes, and Carlos is standing two inches away, glaring down at me. "What?" he barks over the compound commotion. "What did you say?"

Holy fuckin' shit! How the hell did he hear me? "Hail Mary, full of grace," I stammer, trying my best to remember the prayer.

Carlos squints his eyes at me and for a moment I swear to God, I think he's gonna shoot me in the head too. But then his eyes soften and he places his hand on my cheek and says, "Don't worry. We're getting out of here."

And then he leans in and kisses me. Right on the lips.

I don't kiss him back, but he doesn't have a chance to notice, because Logan is behind him, yelling, "Let's go, let's go, let's go!" in Spanish. And it strikes that this all seems like a massively disproportional reaction to seeing a drone. But then I also remember that drones drop bombs on people sometimes, so…

And then Ricky is there, grabbing me roughly by the arm. I try to catch his gaze, but he refuses to look at me as he drags me behind Carlos and Logan and we make our way through the house just as all the gunfire ceases.

Things go quiet—like unearthly still—as I'm forced to follow them down hallways and through rooms until we finally make our way outside and through a courtyard to a small building where inside a little pick-up truck is waiting.

"Get in," Logan says in Spanish. Not pointing to the cab of the truck, but to the bed.

I frown. "What?"

Carlos leans into my ear and says, "We have to hide you under the tarp until things are safe. Don't worry, there's a mattress to keep you comfortable." And then he throws back the tarp to reveal an old, stained, lumpy piece of shit that looks very much like something that *used* to be a mattress like… fifty years ago.

Well, that's fuckin' wonderful. And I almost hesitate, but then I replay the whole head-splatting-against-the-plaster-wall scene and decide to do what I'm told.

I'm still wearing the stupid stringy bikini, so I do not—like absolutely *do not*—want to crawl into that bed, giving them all a view of my ass. But I have no choice. I do it. I climb in and crawl across the mattress, and to my horror, Carlos climbs in next to me. His arms automatically reaching around my waist, he pulls me close to his body as Ricky throws the tarp over both of us. I catch Ricky's gaze for one second, but then the tarp covers us, and everything goes dark.

It's eerily quiet for a few seconds. No gunfire, no shouting, no nothing. Just the sound of my own heartbeat thumping in my chest and then… "Shhh," Carlos whispers in my ear. Just before the truck doors slam in unison and the engine starts up. "We'll be fine. Logan won't let them get us. He'll die before he lets that happen."

Will he? I mean, Carlos beat the ever-loving shit out of Logan last night. His face is swollen and purple. I don't even think he can see out of one eye, that's how puffy it is. So will he? Really? I just don't believe it. There's a part of me that wonders if Logan isn't here to do exactly the same thing Ricky and I are doing. Not for the same reasons, of course. But family or not, underlings sometimes have grand ambitions. And Logan definitely strikes me as that type of nephew. Maybe he's just biding his time? Waiting on Carlos to get himself killed so he can take over. And if that happens I think… I think I'm just a piece of property that Logan would inherit.

What have you started, Tyler?

Carlos pets my head, snapping me back to the reality of this current situation. And the only thing that keeps me

188

from gagging in revulsion at that disgusting display of affection is the fact that one hand is no longer pressing on my lower belly.

The truck is on the move now. Heading God knows where. My heart begins to flutter with panic. The dirty roads around here are bumpy, so of course we hit a pothole going around a corner and my body goes flying up in the air, which gives Carlos an opportunity to pull me closer and when I stop flopping from the bumpy road, his hand slips right between my legs. The bikini is so skimpy, his fingertips actually flitter across my clit. And I do not care who the fuck he is right now. I don't care if he's goddamned Scarface incarnate. I break free of his grasp, throw the tarp off of me, and I'm ready to jump out of this stupid truck and run.

"Madison!" he barks. "Get back under the tarp!"

He grabs me by the arm so hard, there's no getting away. And a moment later, I'm back under, pretty much on top of him now, and his hands are all over my ass. Caressing me, like this is supposed to make me feel better.

"Carlos Castillo," I growl, trying to find his eyes in the hazy darkness. I'm so pissed off.

Easy there, Red, Devil says. *Play it cool, bitch.*

So I close my eyes for the count of one, take a deep breath, and in my calmest Scarlett voice I say, "This is not my idea of a glamorous getaway. You should have an airstrip. A private plane ready to take me to a yacht. I mean, what kind of bullshit is this? I actually think I'm getting bit by something. Does this mattress have fleas? Were there goats sleeping on this disgusting bag of filth before today? Because I'll tell you what. You'd better not so much as scowl at me when you see all the bedbug bites I have when we get to wherever we're going. And you better have antibiotics waiting for me too. After all I've been through in my life I refuse—*refuse*—to die of typhoid, or tetanus, or some equally third-world bullshit just because you're afraid to fly!"

There's like... five or six seconds of silence. Just the rumble of the engine in this old-ass truck and the wind flapping against the heavy canvas tarp as we race away to parts unknown.

Oh, shit, Angel says. *Now you've done it.*

And I might've. Ricky's right. I really do have a temper problem. Because I think Carlos is holding his breath. And now I'm holding my breath and I'm pretty sure he's gonna pull out a knife or a gun and cut my heart out or shoot me in the head.

He laughs so loud I startle. And he laughs so long, I figure he's actually gone insane. I brace myself for the violence. For the sharp pain as he sticks a knife in my ribs. Or the crack of a gun as he blows my brains out.

But instead his long laugh devolves into a chuckle and he kisses me on the lips again. "I love your spirit. I have been right all along! You're the perfect woman for me."

"I... I am?" I stammer, unsure where this is going. Thoroughly disgusted at the second kiss, but too afraid to say so.

"You know what you want and go after it. I love that about you."

OK, Devil says. *Lay down the ground rules*, chica. *This is your only chance. Scarface respects you. Time to remind him of your deal.*

"We had a deal, right?" I say, finding his eyes and staring him down. "You be patient with me, I'll be patient with you. And that means you do not take advantage of me because we're in this dangerous situation. You keep

your hands away from my pussy, Mr. Castillo. Or I'll…
I'll…"

"Or you'll what?" he asks, but not angrily. Kinda…
playfully. Which is revolting. "Tell me what you'll do if I
don't respect you, Madison Clayton."

Make it good, Angel says. *God helps those who help themselves.*

I want to punch her. But she's right. Carlos expects
some classic Maddie right now. So I pull myself together,
take a deep breath, and say, "I'll make you weak with want.
I'll give you just enough to make you crave more, and then
withhold all the very best parts of me. I'll be with you, but
never truly *with* you, Carlos Castillo. I'll be yours, but you'll
still be alone. Because we made a deal and if you break
your promise to me on day two, then how could I ever
trust you with my heart?"

He blinks. Three times in a sliver of sunshine filtering
its way through a crack in the tarp. But says nothing.

"I couldn't. Trust you, I mean. And relationships are
built on trust, Carlos. Trust is earned, so if you want me,
truly want me, then we have to do it right and build that
trust together."

Angel and Devil stand united on my right shoulder,
high-fiving each other.

Nailed it, Devil says after their hands slap.

But Carlos remains silent.

Shit.

Don't. Say. A. Word. Angel whispers. *Let him come to you.*

The seconds tick off and I start counting. One-one-
thousand, two-one-thousand… and when I get to eight-
one-thousand he says, "You… are the only woman I want.
We can do it your way."

191

I smile. I even force it to reach my eyes. Place a hand on his cheek and gaze lovingly into his hard gaze—a move that might've won me an Academy Award if I was an actress—and say, "One day, Carlos... I think we'll look back on this moment and think this was the moment when we redefined our future. And I will kiss you on the lips as we replay it in our minds, and say, 'This was the beginning of everything that came next.'"

I kiss him now. Force myself to do it. To make him believe. To remind myself *why* I'm doing it. It's awful, but I do it.

It's the forced cohesion of two like ends of a magnet.

Parts of a whole that are decidedly repulsive. Entirely repellent.

And what comes next, when he kisses me back, isn't the explosive fever of love, but the inevitable combustion of two volatile chemicals.

His kiss is an agreement to be patient. Mine, nothing but the promise of payback.

Our truce is tentative. Like that moment when a match is being held over a puddle of gasoline. Right before the fingers holding it let go and it falls, like angels fall from Heaven, and Carlos and I are there together.

This is going to end badly... but revenge always has a price.

And I'm willing to pay it.

CHAPTER NINETEEN

We're headed west. The winter sun is already starting to set and it's not even five o'clock. I don't think. I don't have a watch and the battery on my fucking phone is dead. There's a clock in the Defender but I tried to change it when Daylight Savings Time ended, and I think I managed to set it to Tokyo time somehow.

Fancy fuckin' car.

But I'm pretty good about tracking time, and I've been counting in my head to keep myself focused, and it feels like we've been driving just about three hours or so. It would seem that I've been doing a good enough job of keeping my distance from the truck that I haven't called attention to myself. Or, if I have, Ricky DEA has chosen to ignore it. No way to know which, I guess. There was one moment where it sped up a little, which made me think they might be trying to lose me, but then it pulled over at a gas station and Logan hopped out and ran to the little boys' room.

The whole time, there was no movement in the back. I kept willing Maddie to throw the tarp off and jump out and then I'd grab her and we'd make a break for it, but there's no way for her to know that I'm still here, I suppose. The idea of her pressed up against this Carlos fuckweed for all this time has got me seething, but I'm keeping it together. He must really be scared of whoever he thinks is after him if he's willing to lie in the back of that busted-ass ride for this long. Of course, Maddie is there cushioning the trip for him, but... Nope. Not gonna fucking go there. Stop. Head in the game.

Speaking of gas stations, I hope to hell we get where we're going soon, otherwise I might just run dry. The gauge is sitting right on fucking empty. All in, I've driven damn near seven hours today. I'm actually impressed I'm still going. It's a nice car and all, but it ain't no hybrid, that's for damn sure.

There's a sign just up ahead. *Ensenada.*

And now I can see a huge Mexican flag coming into view right at the edge of the water where the final streaks of light from the setting sun are being cast off the ocean.

The flag is gigantic. Towering over the city like a watchman. There's a harbor and a cruise ship all decorated with Christmas lights. Maybe it's just because I was in the Navy and I have a "been there, done that" attitude about being on the sea, but I hate cruise ships. And I really can't imagine going on a fucking cruise for a holiday vacation, stuck with a bunch of jerkoffs in madras shorts, being coerced into forced frivolity. But right now, comparatively, I'd take Maddie, a piña colada, and shuffleboard in a second over the bullshit we're into.

The truck turns left up ahead, and I follow. It's dark enough now that I should turn on my headlights, but I don't know if that'd call more attention to me, so I leave them off. The whole time my eyes are fixed on the gas gauge. The mileage meter told me that I was going to run out of fuel about fifteen miles ago and I don't know how much of a reserve this thing has built in, so I'm just keeping my nuts crossed that we're almost to wherever 'there' is. And then, mercifully, once again, as if willed by the Christmas gods, unto me is delivered news of great motherfucking joy.

The truck pulls up to a guard gate right along the beach. There's a long, tall, brick wall that runs parallel to the ocean, spanning easily a mile or more in either direction from the guard station. Looks like a fancy gated community. A private beach probably, only for the rich assholes who live beyond its walls.

I don't know why I'm so hung up all of a sudden on the fact that Carlos is rich. Because who cares? But it's not that he's got money that's bothering me. It's how he got it and what he does with it and how he uses his money and power to serve himself only.

I guess it bugs me because in some ways he reminds me of another selfish, rich asshole I know.

And as soon as we're out of this clusterfuck, I want to talk to Maddie about doing something good too. Something that means something. Just like how she signed onto this because it was important for her to do something meaningful so she can move forward with her life, I want to do that also. And I want us to do it together.

And I'm fully aware that there's a chance she'll be pissed as all hell at me for showing up here in the first place (*I'm not a kid, Tyler! I had everything under control!*) but there are other ways she can move forward and still do good. Ways that don't involve imminent mortal peril. She's sacrificed enough if you ask me. And, while I have zero idea how I can contribute value to the world, I'm sure there are ways.

But I want us to figure out what those things are as a unit, as a team, because I never want her to be away from me like this again. Not if there's another option. New Year's is right around the corner, and even though I've never made a resolution before—because I've always known I was just gonna break them, so why bother?—this year it feels like it's worth it to try. And even though I realize that resolving to be a better person than a murdering drug trafficker is a pretty low bar… you gotta start somewhere.

This is what's running through my head as the Defender's engine whines and gasps, trying to force one more drop of gasoline to combust into forward-moving energy. But it can't. There's no more left. The car wheezes and coughs one last time, and then sputters finally to a stop.

It's pretty well dark now, and there aren't really any other cars that I can see. Presumably, most people are home with their families putting presents under trees and lying to their kids about Santa Claus and shit. But I can't risk someone coming along and finding me or it, so I need to get it off the road. I throw it in neutral, hop out, and push this heavy bastard into the overgrowth on the other side of the street. It's harder than I thought it'd be. That roll cage adds some serious weight. Fuckin' roll cage.

Now. How best to breach the wall that protects whatever's on the other side? I could try and scale it, but it's tall, it's stone, and I'm not Batman. So that's out. I could also try and survey how far it runs along each side and determine if there are any possible access points, but the shit seriously looks like it goes on forever and I also risk exposing myself.

Think. Think.

And that's when I hear the ticking sound of the Defender's cooling and exhausted engine, and I have an idea. It's not the best idea I've ever had. It's dangerous, unpredictable, arguably excessive, and could very well make things worse. But unless I figure out how to get inside there, I won't know how bad things are for Maddie over that wall, and not knowing or being able to do anything about it seems worse. So. Fuck it.

I grab my rucksack out of the back and pull out the t-shirts I have stuffed in there. I toss them onto the front seat. Then I gather up some dried palm branches and other foliage that's laying around on the ground and throw that on top of the shirts.

I have an eerie moment of déjà vu, thinking back to Halloween. The night I set my apartment on fire. This is different, of course. I was a bit out of my mind then and I had just discovered that Maddie was Maddie and that she pretty much hated my guts, and it seemed like my life was ending and so I kind of went insane. Setting my place on fire was a *re*action to everything that was happening that night.

This, on the other hand, is a *decisive action* that I'm taking to rescue Maddie now that we've declared our love for each other and we plan to be together. Because that's what lovers do. Shit, that's just what decent friends do. They show up for the other no matter what, and they're there when they're needed. When the time comes, they're the one person you can count on. The one who has your back. I've had that illuminated for me over these last couple of months with startling, hi-def clarity.

And that's what this is that I'm doing now. It's decent. It's romantic. It's needed. And it's totally, *totally* sane.

Right?

Anyway.

I go to the back of the car again and lift the mat that covers the spare tire and roadside emergency kit. I grab up the kit, open it, and pull out the two road flares that are inside. I take a breath, looking at my car. There's a moment of wistful nostalgia. A few weeks ago I didn't even want a car, but now I'm kind of attached to it. Not because of the car itself, but because… because it's one of the first things Maddie and I talked about, back when she was Scarlett and I was just jabbering to her. Because it's what I was driving the night I found her running from Logan and Ricky in the alley behind Pete's. Because… shit, because of the thing Raven said to me when she was giving me advice about how to handle my situation with Maddie. *Your car,* she said. *It's a Defender, right?*

But, hell. Now Pete's is gone. And so is Pete, for that matter. And Maddie's Maddie, not Scarlett. And I'm me, not fuckin' Ford Aston. (Heh. I still chuckle every time I think about the fact that *that's* the name I came up with. "Ford Aston." Ha. As if.) And the simple truth is that nobody gets what they want in life without paying a price. Everything comes at a cost.

It's been that way since the beginning of time. Adam and Eve wanted to eat the apple, but the price they had to pay is that paradise was taken from them. And if that myth is true (and hell, it's Christmas Eve, so if we're gonna buy into a friggin' virgin birth, then Adam and Eve is no more implausible) then we've all been paying for their fuck-up ever since. And that is an expensive goddamn toll to ante up for.

So, I guess if—in order to get Maddie back in my arms—I gotta torch a Land Rover Defender that I paid five hundred thousand dollars for… Well. While it stings a little, it really ain't nothing compared to all that other shit.

I pop the top off one road flare, ignite it, toss into the car, and then do the same with the other.

If you set it right, a car can go up in flames pretty goddamn fast. They don't really explode though. When I see that in a movie, I usually roll my eyes. Because it just ain't likely to happen. Unless, of course, there's a flammable metal or some other explosive component involved. Like magnesium. If a car has magnesium components, boom. Huh. I don't know if mine does, when I stop to think of it. This could turn into a much bigger deal than I'm anticipating. But... only one way to find out.

What's guaranteed is that the dampeners that hold the hood and tailgates and stuff will absolutely explode and blow shit off the car. The wheels will explode too. And that's what I'm expecting to happen first.

After I toss the flares, I throw on my pack and hoof it out of the way as fast as I can, trying to position myself where I can see the guards. I'm maybe a thousand feet away at this point. Just under a quarter of a mile or so. And when they hear the gunshot-like sound of the tires exploding, they should come running. Again, this plan is unpredictable, dangerous, possibly excessive, and may not result in anyone being pulled away from a guard gate to investigate shit. I have no idea. But I'm fucking in it now. So I wait.

The interior goes up in flames really fast, as expected. Leather burns quickly. It's just skin, after all. And skin burns pretty fast when it's all lit up.

I know.

There's a nice, toasty, marshmallow-roast-sized inferno baking away when I see that the flames have spread up inside the interior panel, because I can clock smoke and a hint of fire peeking out from under the hood now.

And in under a minute…

Pow. The hood supports blow and the hood slams up, cracking the windshield. And that actually seems to have been loud enough to draw some attention. Two guys who I guess are community guards, even though they're not dressed in uniforms or anything, step out to the road and crane their necks to see what's going on. This is encouraging.

And then the tires explode.

Holy shit!

I was not expecting it to be that loud. Nor was I expecting the Defender crashing down to make the squealing noise it does. But it sure as shit gets the job done. The two guys come running in the direction of the fire, which is now burning enough to be seen from where they are. One of them grabs up a walkie-talkie and shouts something in Spanish and suddenly two more guys are running out in the direction of the fire, too.

Looking through the binoculars, I can see no one manning the gate anymore, so I decide this is my shot. I gotta get in there and see if I can find the truck and hopefully find Maddie. But when I go to take my first step, I find it hard to will my legs to move. *Fuck. Please, not again. Not now. Don't do this to me.* I have no idea how long these dudes will be away before they run back to get a fire extinguisher or call for reinforcements or whatever. I have to go now.

So I close my eyes and I think of Maddie's face. Underneath me. Smiling. Telling me she loves me. And in a second, that image gives way to an almost too-soon forgotten lifetime of memories. Scotty, Maddie, me. All jumbling together and cascading over one another.

And I take that first step.

It feels like I'm running through molasses or quicksand, but I'm moving. And as the memories tumble past, faster and faster, my gait gets faster too. And before I know it, I'm in a full sprint and tearing past the unmanned gate at the entrance to see...

Are you kidding me?

Wow. It's not a private community.

I mean it *is*, but...

Jesus.

Fucking Carlos Castillo.

CHAPTER TWENTY

What a way to spend Christmas Eve. I mean really. You'd think God would cut me a break or something.

The drive is pure torture. I'm talking I'd rather strip for the devil in eternal damnation than spend one more goddamned minute listening to Carlos whisper his grand plans for our future together in my ear.

I want to throw up.

And we're on the run from... whatever he thinks we're on the run from. But all he keeps talking about is *us*. What the hell have I gotten myself into?

I'm freezing, hungry, and there's a cramp in my leg that's been burning for hours. And no matter how I try to change positions, I can't make it go away. Plus, every time I move to try and get more comfortable, Carlos's hands are there, pulling my body back next to his.

I can't deny needing his body heat. It's been hot as hell out, and I'm sure it still is, but I can't feel it. I feel the cold. Maybe it's fear and I don't know it. Or maybe it's that I'm wearing an outfit that's nothing but strings and strips of fabric.

I've had enough. Several hours ago.

Finally, well after dark, the engine finally cuts off and there's the sound of many sets of feet as they rush over to the truck. The tarp is pulled back to reveal a perfectly dark, starlit night above my head. I squint up at it as Logan helps Carlos out of the bed. Then Ricky has my arm, pulling on me to follow.

"Where are we?" I ask Ricky. But he says nothing, just hands me off to Carlos, who takes my arm and begins walking towards a... house? Mansion? Hotel? I plant my feet, making Carlos stop, and say, "Where *the fuck* are we?" Only this time, it's loud. And ragey. Because I've had enough. I need some fucking reality right now.

"You don't need to worry about where we are—" Logan starts.

But Carlos cuts him off with one raised hand. "We're home. I don't normally spend a lot of time here. I prefer the open desert. I've had a deal with the Federales. I stay out of Ensenada, they let me live in peace." He stares down at me, his dark eyes suddenly blazing with anger. "But they broke our deal today."

And that's when something explodes outside the compound.

Men start shouting in Spanish. Everyone, and I do mean everyone, in my sight has a gun out. Half a dozen armed men are rushing towards the front gates.

Carlos points to Logan and says, "Llévala a mis apartamentos. Now!"

Logan grabs my arm—not roughly, but not gently either—and starts pulling me away.

"Wait!" I say, resisting. "Where will you be?" I'm happy to be out of that truck and I'm delighted that Carlos is no longer touching me... but Logan. I do not want to be alone with Logan. I'm the reason his face looks like pulp today.

"I have work to do," Carlos snaps back. Like I'm sorta stupid if I can't figure out that an explosion outside his safe house trumps my needs. "We'll have dinner soon. Take a bath and dress so you're ready when I call for you." Dinner? A bath? What the fuck?

And then Logan stops pretending to be gentle and yanks on my arm. I look back over my shoulder to see if Carlos caught that, but he's already walking away, talking in hushed whispers to other men as a stream of black smoke fills the air above the concrete block walls around this new compound.

The only good news is that Ricky follows Logan. That is my first lucky break today. He stays well behind us, but at least he's nearby. I need to get him alone. I need to know what the hell is happening. I need to know if that really was Tyler flying my drone and I need to make sure he's OK. I mean, I know it was Tyler. I've seen his drone moves. And then the memory of our date night out at the Hoover Dam comes to mind and I smile.

"What the fuck are you smiling at?" Logan barks, pulling hard on my arm again.

"Your uncle," I say, letting him pull me along the outside of the—house? Mansion? Hotel? It's huge, just like the compound. But this new place is very different than the last one. It looks and feels more like a small town than a residence.

"Why is this place so big?" I ask, trying to take it all in. It's pretty dark, but there's lots street lamps as Logan drags me down a sidewalk towards a group of buildings away from the main one where we parked.

205

"Because," Logan says. "My uncle needs to keep our smugglers happy and close to work. And this place is how he does that."

"Oh," I say. *Good to know, Logan. Thank you very much for the first real piece of intel all day!*

But Logan stops abruptly and tightens his grip on my arm. Squeezes it hard enough for me to feel a bruise forming in real time.

"What are you doing?"

"You speak Spanish?" he growls.

And that's when I realize Logan just made that impromptu confession in *Spanish*, not English. And I just gave myself away. Not that I was hiding the fact that I understood them or anything. But I certainly never let on that I understood to anyone but Ricky. And he's on my side, so…

"Everyone speaks Spanish," I snap, trying to pull out of his grip.

But he holds tight, his fingernails digging into my flesh. "Does my uncle know this?"

"Know what?"

"That you're spying on him?"

"I'm not fucking spying on him, you idiot. Like I said, everyone knows Spanish."

But Logan grins. It looks painful too. His left eye is swollen completely shut now. So it's more like a sinister wink than a smile. But it gets the job done. Because my stomach flips with fear.

"Oye, vamos," Ricky says, coming up behind us. "Es Nochebuena y quiero llamar a mi novia antes de ir a la cama."

I stare at Logan, not even daring to look at Ricky, even though I want nothing more than to see his familiar face and know that he's got my back. Because I think I might've really fucked things up here.

"What did he say?" Logan asks, nodding his head to Ricky.

I shrug. "I dunno. Something about calling his friend before bed."

Logan glares at me. "Mentira pequeña perra."

I force myself to laugh. "Now that, I understood. And I'm going to tell your uncle you just called me a lying little bitch."

"Go ahead," Logan says, pulling me along the sidewalk again.

We walk past what looks to be a private gas station where dozens of trucks are lined up for fuel. I bet this really is the staging point for Carlos Castillo's drug-running route. I mean, it sure looks the part. And it's all hidden behind massive concrete block walls. In fact, now that I look around a little, I notice a lot more too. Dozens of people. All rushing around looking very fucking busy. And it's Christmas Eve. Maybe this is like the biggest night of the drug-running year? Like... all the US border agents are busy being festive and shit, so no one's minding the store.

"Tell him, puta," Logan growls. "He's gonna be very interested in your new skillset as a translator."

You better up your game, Angel says, popping up on my shoulder. *Because shit is getting real. This is the major league, Scarlett. Not schoolyard kickball.*

It suddenly pisses me off that she's referring to me as Scarlett. Because Scarlett has retired and fuck Angel for bringing her back from the dead. I'm goddamned Maddie Clayton now and forever.

But I don't have time to respond to her. Not when I need to respond to Logan. Because she's right. He's out to get me. If I fail and get myself killed for being a DEA informant, it'll be because Logan turns Carlos against me.

So I swing for the fuckin' bleachers and say, "And I'll tell him you slipped up and sold him out. Told me all about his business. And we all know what he does to people who disobey him, right? I can only imagine what he does to traitors. So you better be very careful about spreading rumors. Your uncle loves me. He wants to marry me. Wants me to have his babies. And I love him back just as much. I can't wait to give him sons. Sons who will one day take over his business." I have to choke that last part out. But I do it. Because a guy like Logan wouldn't put up with the abuse Carlos hands out if he didn't think he was gonna get something big in the end.

"Puta," he spits.

"Hijo de mil putas," I spit back.

"OK, OK," Ricky says, coming between us. "Vamos a dejarla, Logan. Tenemos trabajo para hacer esta noche."

"Yeah, vamos, Logan. You've got work to do. Don't want to piss your uncle off again. You don't have another eye to spare."

"Cállate, perra!" Ricky shouts. It's so loud I startle backwards.

"Fuck you!" I yell back. "Fuck both of you!"

Ricky takes my arm and drags me away, calling over his shoulder, "I'll handle this whore. Meet me at the house." Except he says all that in Spanish.

I don't look to see if Logan follows us or not, but he must take off and leave me to Ricky, because a few seconds later Ricky leans into my ear and says, "What the fuck do you think you're doing?" in English.

"Fuck that asshole. I'm not gonna let him get me killed, OK?"

"You're doing a very good job of that yourself. Just shut your fucking mouth for once and let things go!" He whisper-shouts that last part.

"He called me a slut," I seethe.

"And you called him the son of a thousand whores. Nice way to escalate a battle you can't win."

"What the fuck is going on?" I ask. "Where the fuck is Tyler?"

"I thought that was him I saw. Son of a bitch. I can only hope he's still back in Mexicali, where he was not supposed to be in the first place. Fuckin' asshole. The two of you are an undercover agent's nightmare, you know that? This whole thing is FUBAR. I'm getting you out of here tonight, you understand?" And then he takes my hand and slips something into it.

"What's that?" I ask.

"It'll knock Carlos out cold. Slip it into his drink at dinner and be ready for evacuation at three AM, got it?"

"Oh, OK. Fuckin' James Bond," I say.

"Don't screw with me, Maddie. Just do it."

"Fuck that!" I say. And now I'm the one whisper-yelling. "I didn't just spend most of a day pressed up against his disgusting body listening to him daydream about all the babies I'm gonna give him for nothing! I'm not leaving until he's dead."

Ricky's lips tighten, but he doesn't say anything else. Just keeps me moving along. We finally make our way to Carlos' apartments and stop in front of a large double door guarded by two gigantic men with assault rifles at the ready.

Ricky says, "She's to stay inside and not leave, understand?" in Spanish.

They nod their affirmation, and Ricky opens the door, shoving me inside so hard, I fall to my knees on the floor. "Keep your fuckin' mouth shut and do as you're told." Again, in Spanish.

I'm about to tell him where he can stick his orders, but he slams the doors closed and I hear the unmistakable sound of a key turning in a lock.

"Asshole!"

I shower and pick a dress out of the fully stocked closet. One with a pocket, where I stash the pill Ricky gave me. Whose clothes are these, anyway? I force myself not to think about it. Instead I pace the room for what seems like hours. It's already ten o'clock and there's no way I'm leaving at three AM with Ricky if the job isn't done. It's goddamned Christmas Eve and Santa's bringing baby a present. Carlos Castillo in handcuffs and Logan whatever-his-last-name-is dead.

Which means, Devil says, *you just gotta get the job done before then, right?*

Don't be stupid, Maddie. I smirk at Angel's change in nomenclature. But yeah. Fuckin' right I'm not Scarlett anymore. *Put the drug in his drink and get out of here. Your Christmas present is living to see another day.*

I'm just about to answer her back when the locks on the door disengage and it swings open.

Carlos walks in, slams the doors behind him, and lets out a long breath of air as he stares at me.

Oh, shit. Logan told him and he's pissed.

But then he smiles. "Madison," he says, coming towards me, arms outstretched. "You look lovely tonight."

I force a smile back and say, "Thank you," relieved that my threats to Logan actually worked. "But I've been waiting forever, Carlos. And I'm starving. Are we having dinner yet? I'm so hungry."

That's not even a lie. I *am* starving. But I just want to be taken to the dining room so I can slip the drug in his drink and then go scout out the property. I need to find something to bring this whole operation down before whatever Ricky has planned comes into play.

"I have more work to do. It's a big night. We have lots of business happening."

"But it's Christmas Eve," I whine. It's a stupid girly whine that makes me feel stupid, but I don't care. I need to get this shit on the road. "We're just starting our new life together"—funny how it's getting easier to lie about this fake future we're not planning together—"and we need to celebrate it properly."

"Oh, we will, darling," he says, petting my hair. And then he claps his hands and the doors swing open again. This time a staff of servers come in carrying platters and plates with silver domes covering them. They head into the dining room and one produces a tablecloth, snapping it into submission as it's laid out on the table. After that it's a whirlwind of glassware, and dishes, and bottles of champagne.

Fuck yeah. We're having drinks. Fizzy ones, which are perfect for dissolving pills. Now I just need a chance to plop it in.

When all the table-setting fanfare is over, Carlos pulls out a chair for me. I smile politely and say, "Thank you," as I take my seat.

He sits across from me, grinning like a boy as he opens his napkin and places it in his lap. Servants remove the silver domes over the plates and platters, revealing a proper Mexican Christmas feast.

"Delicious," I say, biting my lip a little to entice him to soften up and forget about work.

Champagne is poured and then Carlos orders the servants to leave us alone.

"A toast," he says, raising his glass. "To our first night together."

I raise mine too but tilt my head at him a little. "Yes, well, technically it's our *second* night."

"But it's our first night as a couple."

"No," I say, correcting him again. "We're still in the getting-to-know-each-other phase, right? I mean, we did agree."

"I've been thinking about that," he says, putting his drink down. "You want a courtship? Yes?"

Courtship. Jesus Christ, this guy. He's so delusional. "Yes," I say. "Exactly. A courtship."

Carlos smiles. It's kind of a... sneaky smile, if I had to put a name to it. A sly smile. A cunning smile. Like he's got a trick or two up his sleeve that I never thought of yet. Like a cat on the prowl after a mouse, where he's the cat and I'm the mouse and I just walked right into his trap.

"Well," he says, getting up from the table to walk around behind me. He takes my hair in his hands, plays with it, his fingertips brushing against the back of my neck, making the little hairs stand up on end. And not in a good way.

Something is wrong here.

He leans down, his lips pressing against my ear in a soft kiss. "Well, that means we are… dating, mi amor. And people who date do other things while they get to know each other. So you're going to stay with me now. Every night in my bed, starting tonight. What do you think of that?"

I'm holding my breath, my chest tight, my mind racing with what this means. "Other things?"

"Si," he purrs into my ear, kissing my neck now, his hands on my shoulders. I didn't pick a revealing dress, but they were all strappy. He slides the straps down my arms now, his hand moving forward to caress my breasts.

It takes every ounce of self-control not to elbow him in the mouth. Every bit of willpower to let him touch me like this.

I let that breath out. Slowly. Silently. And say, "Where are the tamales?"

"What?" He laughs. But it stops him. Stops his kiss. Stops his hands.

"Tamales?" I say. "I love tamales. The sweet ones. But I don't see any on the table. Don't you have any tamales?" I turn in my chair to look up at him. "Please? Can you ask someone to get me some?"

He starts playing with my hair, a hungry look on his face, and not for the food on the table. "Dessert comes later. And tamales weren't the sweet ending I had in mind."

I will remain calm. I will think critically. I will win this game by being smart, and strong and—

Fuck it.

"Please, please, *please*," I beg him, standing up in my chair and turning, so we're face to face. I place both hands on his cheeks. Gaze lovingly into his eyes. Then take one more for the team, lean in, and kiss him on the lips.

He grabs at me, pawing at the straps on my dress like he's going to take me right now. His kiss is forceful. Hard and overly demanding.

I will not let my revulsion fuck this up. I won't.

So I kiss him back. And just as he's about to lose control, I pull away and say, "Please," again. "Can you get me some tamales? I promise to thank you for it later."

He hesitates, and I stop to consider that he may be crazy, he may think he's in love with me—hell, he may actually *be* in love with me—but this tamale gambit is still pretty goddamned thin. But I'm in it now and so I keep playing the game.

"Or I can thank you now, if you prefer." And I wink at him. Because I just need him to turn his back so I can slip the drug into his champagne. Once he does that, I can deal with whatever comes next. I will have to. He'll pass out soon. I just need to get the damn drug in his glass or there's no way he's not gonna fuck me tonight.

His grin grows. Then he lets out a hearty laugh. "Very well. Give me a moment."

"Take your time," I say.

He turns away and walks over to the large double doors, opening them wide, looks over his shoulder once, again with the hungry look, and then starts speaking to the guards.

I whirl into action. I have the pill over the top of his glass in one blink. It plops into the fizzing champagne and begins to bubble.

Carlos is still talking when I look over my shoulder to check. But when I look back at the glass, the pill is still clearly visible.

Jesus. Fuck. Leave it to Ricky to give me an insoluble drug! I stick my finger in the glass and give it a swirl real fast, still looking over my shoulder at Carlos's shoulders between the two half-open doors.

I look back at the pill. Still there!

I hear Carlos say, "Gracias."

Oh, my God. I'm so busted.

My finger comes out, I sit back down, and reach down to pick up my napkin on the floor where it fell when I stood up.

A hand on my shoulder makes me gasp. "What are you doing?" Carlos asks.

"Waiting for you to deliver dessert," I say back, adding a coy smile to my play. "What else?"

He stares at me. Then his gaze begins to wander around the table. Looking for something out of place...

Shit. Shit. Shit.

I'm sure he's just about to spot the pill in his glass—sure I'm about to be raped, then killed—when shouting and a hard knock at the door pulls his attention in another direction.

I exhale the breath I was holding.

The doors burst open and a man is standing there, talking so fast in Spanish, I can't keep up with the conversation. Something about a truck, and a blockade near the border...

Carlos turns back to me and says, "I have to go. But I'll see you later when I come to bed for the night." He strokes my cheek, looks at me with real affection, and I let myself feel a little relief.

I won't be raped and killed.

Not yet, anyway.

215

"It's fine," I say, my voice slightly shaky. "I'll be here."
But then I get another idea. "But before you go…"

"Yes?" Carlos asks, already walking towards the door
to deal with whatever drug-lord emergency he's having.

"Do you mind…? I mean, it's Christmas Eve and all.
And I'm all alone. Do you mind if I take a walk out near
the beach? I haven't seen it yet. I promise not to go in the
water. I'll just walk on the sand."

He's shaking his head no before I even finish. "It's not
safe, Madison. Not tonight, I'm sorry."

"But… But you have guards, right? Like everywhere?
Right? Surely, it's safe. I know it is. You control the whole
place. No one can get in here. I mean, you brought me
here to keep me safe. And there's walls and—"

"I said no, Madison." He looks a little angry at having
to tell me twice.

I only have one trick left. So I do the only thing I can.
I cry.

Not sobs or anything. Just a tear. Just one. I let it leak
out of my eye. Let it fall down my face. He's transfixed at
the whole display. And when I say, "OK," in the smallest,
weakest, meekest voice possible…

He sighs.

"Fine. But only the beach right in front of the house."

"Thank you," I say, standing up. I finger the lapels of
his suit. Smile up at him. Kiss him gently on the chin. And
say, "I feel so much safer knowing your guards are
watching. I'll be right on the beach."

He kisses me. Good God, how many times do I have
to let him do that?

As many as it takes to keep breathing, Devil says.

Truth.

Carlos leaves, pulling the doors closed behind him.

And I bolt towards the sliding glass doors, opening them up just enough to slip through.

I force myself to walk, looking over my shoulder at the guards. But they're congregating together, heads pressed in tight. Talking. Then shouting begins on the other side of the wall around Carlos's private dwelling and they scatter in several directions to see what new fresh hell the devil has conjured up.

I take my chance and run.

Because fuck this. Tyler was right. I'm gonna get myself killed. And the way it's going, that's gonna happen before morning.

I figure he can't own the entire coastline, right? So I can just dart up the beach until I get far enough away to slip through some other rich drug lord's compound. Or whatever.

There's not much cover, but there's little shrubby bushes and lots of hilly dunes. I climb one, slip down the other side, and look back to see if anyone's coming after me.

Nope.

I smile, sure I'm gonna get away. Sure I'm gonna be on my way home soon, back to my fucked-up life that's looking not so fucked up right now…

And that's when a large man in black jumps out from behind a dune, cups his hand over my mouth to make sure I can't scream, and tackles me to the ground.

TYLER & MADDIE

TYLER

The balls.

That's where she knees me.

Right in the balls.

And I'm not gonna lie, it feels pretty good.

"Maddie!" I stage-whisper. (Which is a term I learned back in good old Speech and Debate.) "Maddie, stop thrashing! It's me."

She stops flailing but I can feel her still shaking underneath me, her coiled energy causing her to vibrate. She is what in Sanskrit is called Kundalini and what is represented in imagery by a female serpent.

Yeah. That sounds about right.

"What the fuck are you doing here?" she shout-whispers back.

"Helping!" I say. "Saving you from whatever the fuck! You didn't check in. You were supposed to check in. You didn't check in. So I'm here. This should not be surprising."

"I'm not surprised!" she says. "I'm…" I wait for it but get no more words. She just stares at me.

Finally, "What?" I say.

And then she grabs my face and kisses me on the mouth. Hard. And I know it's been less than forty-eight hours since she last pressed her lips to mine, but it may as well have been since time before time. Because I think I'm gonna start fucking crying.

Grabbing her face in return, I kiss her hard back, and then my hands are fumbling down her sides, reaching for her ass. She grinds her hips into me as I claw at the bottom of her dress, dragging the material up her legs and digging my fingers into her skin.

"Stop," she says. "Stop."

"No. Why?" I pant, still kissing.

"Uh…" She gestures outward with a we're-in-the-middle-of-a-beach-out-in-the-open-with-drug-lords-and-armed-guards-and-shit-all-around-us look on her face. And, I can't deny it, she makes a good point.

But still.

So I shrug and keep kissing her, letting my hand find its way up the inside of her thigh, under the hem of her dress, pushing her panties aside and discovering that she's already wet.

"Doesn't seem like you think it's *that* bad of an idea," I murmur, still nibbling at her red, pouty lips.

"We. Could. Get. Killed," she grunts out in between gasps of breath as my fingers slide inside her.

"Yeah, well, this is how I'd want to die," I tell her.

"Uh-huh," she whines, and nods her head. And then she's seizing my belt, unfastening it, and working my pants down my hips. She uses her feet to push them all the way down to my ankles so that our lips don't have to separate as we continue recklessly, wantonly, foolishly consuming each other's life force.

Because she's right. This moment—this here, this expression of passion and love for each other—could get us killed.

So we may as well make it fucking count.

MADDIE

This is a bad, bad idea. Bad? No. Catastrophic. But I don't give a shit. I want him so much that I don't care if we get annihilated in a meteor shower of bullets. Or in an actual meteor shower, for that matter. Or if the sea decides to become angry and swallow us whole, dragging us both into the briny unknown. I just don't care. I want him.

I want him to purge me of the feeling of Carlos. Of Carlos's body against mine. Of his lips on mine. Of his fingers touching my skin. I want to feel Tyler inside me instead and, in this most ridiculously unsafe of situations, feel safe.

I take his cock in my hand even as he pulls my underwear down. He has to contort himself to draw my legs free of the fabric, but I won't let him go. His dick is throbbing so fast. It feels like I'm holding his heart.

With my dress hiked up and my bare ass resting on the sandy beach, I can close my eyes and pretend that we're somewhere else. On some island vacation somewhere. Maybe twenty, thirty years from now. Still hot for each other. Still ready to fuck any time, any place.

It's so weird. I'm not a schmaltzy chick. All that destined-to-be-together crap that people believe in, I don't. Not usually. But after all this time and all that I've been through and all that he's been through, the fact that we're here now, together, well… I mean there are seven billion people on the planet, and yet here we are.

So maybe this was all supposed to be. Maybe everything's gonna turn out OK.

I wonder if he's thinking the same thing. I wonder if he's as scared as I am, but willing to put it aside for this chance to hold each other this way. I don't know for sure if he feels the way I do, but I do know that just in case everything doesn't all turn out OK…

We may as well make it fucking count.

TYLER

I press my lips to hers again as I thrust my hips forward and enter her. She throws her head back and moans, but just as she does, I hear some shouting in Spanish off to my left. I know she hears it too because she stops moaning and we both freeze for a second. We try to stop our breathing, but both of us gasp in and out in short, sharp bursts. But we manage to still ourselves, me resting inside her.

After a moment the voices disappear off into the other direction and I lift my head to see if I can spot anything. I see nothing but beach and sea and the lights of the— whatever the hell it is. City?—that Carlos has built for himself here. And then my eyes are back on her.

This whole thing is so totally over the top that I can't help but find it funny. I tap her on the nose with my index finger and she looks at me oddly.

"What?" she asks.

"I love your fucking nose," I say.

"Yeah?" she responds, beginning to move her hips again.

I swallow and manage to croak out, "Yeah," before I lose interest in speaking and grind along with her.

She's holding my ass now. Her fingers pressing into my skin. Pushing me into her deeper. Her eyes are closed tightly and the expression on her face is caught somewhere between joy, pain, and that look people have when they're dreaming and to them, in that moment, the dream is real.

My hands are on her hips and I hadn't noticed before, but they wrap almost all the way around her. I have large hands. I can palm a basketball no problem. But even still, it strikes me just how fragile and malleable her flesh is under my touch.

Pulling her back and forth under me causes her to want to make noise, but she knows she can't, so she's stuffing it down. When she comes, all that pent-up energy has to go somewhere though, so I'm bracing for the pornographic air-raid siren that's likely to echo out of her when she lets go.

To counter the fact that she's trying not to scream, she digs her fingers into to me harder and harder. As if all that noise has found its way into her limbs and is trying to escape. I can feel her nails digging into my ass cheeks and the sensation of it make me harder. And as my cock stiffens even more, it fills her up entirely, pressing against her pussy walls, consuming all the space inside.

She's biting her lip, trying not to make any noise. "Goddamn it," she whispers, turning her head to the side. Unfortunately, I'm not helping matters because everything she does is driving me crazy and it makes me fuck her that much more enthusiastically.

The puffs of air leaving her nose let me know that she's close. There's the hint of a whimper along with her breathing and I'm gasping now too. But just then...

More voices. Again in Spanish. Shit.

I lift my head to see if I can spy anyone, but Maddie doesn't care if anyone's there. She just wants me. She wants my attention. I know, because what she does now gets it back on her in a hurry.

MADDIE

As my finger finds its way inside his asshole, I'm not sure how he'll react. I've actually never done it to a guy before, I don't think. But in my understanding, it can go either very, very well, or very, very badly. And I didn't know I was going to do it. It just happened.

I was already clinging to his ass for dear life and then when he took his gaze up and away, I... I dunno. I panicked or something. I don't want it to be over just yet. I know that we need to hurry and get out of here, but I want us to be the ones to decide we're ready to go. Not be forced to stop what we're doing just because we might get killed. I mean, hell, people die every day, right? But what's happening between us now happens... well... never.

As my middle finger slides in between his ass cheeks and finds the opening inside, his head snaps back to face me. His eyes are wide. Not in surprise exactly. It's something else. I think it's... delight. In fact, I know it is. Because he's got a little smile. And the smile turns me on so much that I push harder. Just a bit. Seeing how far he'll let me go.

The smile spreads and he nods a tiny nod that says, *It's OK.* I can feel myself biting my bottom lip as I press my finger deeper and a noise comes out of him, from the back of his throat, like a stifled groan. Like he wants to moan and say dirty shit to me, but he knows he can't, so he stuffs it down and it's just a squeak.

And he's pounding into me now. I feel that he wants to be as far into me as I am into him. And he takes one hand off my hip and works it between our bellies so that he can land his thumb on my clit. I shake my head at him because I don't know if I can take it. But he smiles and nods his head at me as he begins rubbing me savagely.

If we are to die tonight, let it happen now.

I know that's a morbid thought, but it's the one that lands on me.

I'm not a dumb person. I'm not a naïve person. There are many, many people who have suffered immeasurably more than I have. I've seen it. And there are those who have suffered more than I can imagine, who I've never seen. But my pain is mine. It happened to me. And even though it may make no sense, I held onto it because to share it would make it less mine.

But now I have. Shared it. I've shared everything. With the one person in the world who could've abated it sooner and didn't. The same person I blamed for compounding it. And the only person who could have ever really understood it. And it doesn't feel like it's less mine. It feels like it's just... ours.

And so, if we are to be taken away from each other in this world, I'd rather it happen while we are totally, completely joined than not. In French, orgasms are known as le petit mort. The little death. So hell. Let's just go fucking all in.

My lips press together and I nod at him, trying to let him know that I'm about to come. But his eyes are closed and his expression is contorted, which I think is him trying *not* to come yet. What a gentleman. So I do what I have to do to get his attention. I slap him across the face with my free hand.

His eyes pop open like he forgot where he was, but he never lets up on the churning energy that propels him in and out. And when my eyes widen and I nod, he gives me a tiny, urgent nod in return. His thumb strums at my clit. My finger drives deeper into his ass. My hips make tiny circles under him as his back arches and crashes down with each penetrating thrust. And at the moment I come, he does too. Both of us struggling not to make a noise as the tiny grim reaper waves his sickle and we die in and around each other in exquisite anguish as our mute desire gives way to the sound of crashing waves.

TYLER

When I was ten, they demolished the Aladdin Hotel and Casino on the Strip. Scotty, Evan, and I skipped school to watch it in person. It was an implosion. Four floors of dynamite that went boom and brought the entire thing down on itself. Implosions are deceptive, because they just look like a collapse. Like it seems less messy and violent than an explosion.

They may be less messy in that they consolidate the debris to a more manageable space, but they are no less violent. The power, the force that's required to bring a building down is just as severe as that required to blow it up. Entropy. Chaos. All that science shit. But when all is said and done, the only thing that matters is that something extremely fucking major is happening to a physical object.

Without the ability to scream, or moan, or shout, "Oh, fuck yeah!" what Maddie and I experience is something akin to an implosion. All that force. All that shared energy. All that power between us. It just causes us to collapse into each other.

Her body goes limp beneath me, drained of all its strength, and I fall limp on top of her, equally spent. It's not that we fucked so hard. We've fucked harder. It's that we were both revving at an insanely high acceleration when we crashed into each other. And now we should be allowed to rest.

But we can't.

I pull out of her, and it's the loneliest my cock has felt in a long, long time. Probably ever. The look on her face when I exit makes me wanna murder somebody. I mean, the truth is it makes me wanna cry, but I can't afford to do that right now, so I convert that sorrow into anger.

Because as I pull my pants up and she cleans herself off, I am reminded of where we are. I almost forgot. Hidden behind this dune, bathed in the wash of a Christmas moon, it felt for a second like we were actually living the life I wished for us when she was packing in her bedroom. In some hidden locale, stashed away in paradise, living out our days off the grid and all alone.

But yet again, I hear shouting in Spanish from down the beach and remember, yeah, we ain't there just yet.

I grab her panties when she's not looking and stick them in my pocket. I don't know why I do it. I just want to keep this moment with me for longer or something. It's weird, I suppose. Or else it makes all the sense in the world. I dunno.

And then, leaning close to her, I whisper, "Hey. So, what happened? Why didn't you check in?"

"I couldn't," she says, straightening out her dress and sitting up next to me to also look and see if anyone might be coming.

"Why? Did he, like, fucking tie you up or something?" I want the answer to be 'no,' but a small part of me wants it to be 'yes,' so that before getting out of here I can feel justified in killing this motherfucker.

"No. No, we had dinner and then he watched me sleep."

"He *watched you sleep?*"

"I think so."

"Jesus." Then I amend with, "I mean, he's not wrong to want to do that, but still... Fucking weirdo."

"Yeah. Tyler?" she says, with more concern than makes me comfortable.

"Yeah?" I stroke her cheek.

"What the fuck were you thinking?" Huh. That is not what I expected to come out of her mouth next.

"Whattayou mean?"

"I mean... I mean, yeah, I know I didn't call, but shit, dude. I had it under control."

"Well, I didn't fuckin' know. And we had a deal."

"Fair enough, but the deal didn't include you starting a full-scale war with the guy."

The phrase "full-scale war" lands on me hard. "Shit. I am Rambo," I mutter.

"What?"

"Nothing. Look, I'm fuckin' sorry, but I don't care what kind of warranty you got when you bought that drone. Shit's defective."

"Or you can't fly it."

I'm not arguing this point right now. "Hey! All I could think was that something fucking awful had happened to you and I had to come get you. If I had done it my way, I would've just crashed through the front door and started looking to make sure you were all right. I thought I owed it to *you* to be a little more tactical."

"So you're saying this is my fault?"

"Yeah. Maybe? Little bit?"

She looks at me like she can't fucking believe my gall. And she shouldn't. But then she laughs. She laughs the laugh of a person you've known your whole life but who still manages to surprise you. She laughs the laugh that you laugh when you're infuriated and scared, but when you step back to look at everything, it's just too ridiculous not to laugh. She laughs the laugh of a person who loves you.

Me.

Who loves me.

She loves me.

And that's all that matters in the world.

Well, that and the distant shouting I continue to hear that reminds me we still have to get the fuck out of here alive somehow.

"What's with all this?" she asks, referring to my dark clothes.

"Tactical night operations. I slipped it on when this went from a daytime raid to an evening affair."

"An evening affair," she repeats.

"Yeah. Sorry I didn't bring a tux. This'll have to do. But look, while I could chat fashion choices—you look great, by the way—all night, we gotta get the fuck outta here."

"No shit. Where's your car?"

You know those moments in life when someone asks you a question that you know the answer to, but your brain just malfunctions and it's like they're speaking, I dunno, Basque or some shit?

I do.

"What's that?" I ask, like I didn't hear her.

"Where's your car? Can we make it there from here without being seen?"

Again, it's like she's talking Zulu.

"My car... Yeah. Um. So..."

This is not a moment when you want to be slowing down the forward momentum of a situation by explaining a lot of shit, so in this second, I'm figuring out how to explain clearly but still efficiently. Her mouth is open in a way that suggests maybe if she prompts me to speak, she'll somehow plant the words in mine.

Just like when I went to tail Logan into the strip club the day he got his ass kicked by Maddie and I found myself playing checkers instead of chess, not thinking two moves ahead... Boy, do I have egg on my face now.

And then something either fortunate or unfortunate happens, depending on how you look at it.

It's fortunate inasmuch as I am spared the embarrassment of explaining to Maddie what happened to Chocolate Thunder. (That's what I named the Defender. So dubbed after my favorite basketball player of all time, the great Darryl Dawkins, who played on the Philadelphia 76ers with Dr. J. Before my time, but in clips I've seen, dude was a savage on the rim. RIP, Double D. Wow. So not the time to be thinking about this...)

It is deeply *un*fortunate in that apparently even thinking about Unlucky Logan has summoned him into being. Because from behind us, in the total opposite direction from which we've been looking, I hear what feels to my ear like the bolt of a Kalashnikov rifle being cocked, followed by, "Tyler. My amigo. So good to see you again."

I close my eyes, take a breath, open them and see Maddie looking terrified, before I turn to—sure enough—see good old Logan strolling up with his fucked-up face and his AK-47. Shit. Unlucky Tyler doesn't have the same ring, but it's what I am at the moment. Or maybe just Stupid fuckin' Tyler. But. I gotta be me. So…

"Logan! Oh, shit! Are *you* my Secret Santa? Well, color me surprised."

Logan smiles a little and nods. It looks like it hurts him to smile, with his busted chops and all, and that makes me happy. Ricky, who is on Logan's six, and who looks incredibly unsettled, does not smile. Eh. Fuck him. I know it was a solid joke.

In reference to Ricky, I say, "Hey, look! It's your girlfriend! I haven't seen the two of you together since I fucked him up in the alley that time. Wow… Logan. I gotta say, he looks like he's healed up from that beating. You? Buddy. Did Maddie have another go at you?"

I like that move for a couple reasons. One: It lets Ricky know that I'm not stupid enough to blow his cover. I can tell he appreciates it because his body language shifts ever so subtly. And two: It pisses Logan off.

On the other hand, Maddie is looking at me like I'm out of my mind. Which, I mean, shit, I am. She shouldn't be that shocked. She knows me pretty good. Anyway.

Logan keeps smiling and nodding. I swear to fuck, it's like the guy went to cartoon villain school or some shit. So silly. But, sadly, whether it's silly and cliché or not, when the butt of an AK smacks you in the chops, it stings a bit. Even me.

231

My head snaps back and I black out for just the tiniest of seconds. I can feel my knees get weak and I almost think I might actually go down, but then my nervous system rallies, everything comes back into view, and I shake the lights back on.

I smile and ask, "That wasn't my present, was it? 'Cause honestly, it's kind of a shitty gift."

I can tell he's a little confused by the fact that I'm still standing, and he winds back like he's gonna give it another try, but when I lean my face toward him and point at the spot on my cheek where I suggest he aim next, he grabs Maddie by the arm instead. Fuck. Shit. Goddamn it. Did my fucking wise-ass behavior just make life worse for Maddie? Son of a bitch.

He shouts something to Ricky in Spanish as he's dragging Maddie away and Ricky comes up next to me and punches me as hard as he can (I'm guessing) in the ribs. And no kidding, it's the best punch I've ever been hit with. He nails it perfectly. Right in the soft spot just below the rib cage. Not quite a kidney punch, which I'm supposing he avoided on purpose, but in a pretty tender location and with enough force that I feel it. I'm impressed. I'll have to remember to compliment him later.

As Maddie's being dragged off, she looks over her shoulder at me, her red hair being blown about in the night sky, the urgent confusion and pleading in her eyes. I tense to go charging for her immediately. Ricky grabs my arm and pulls me back.

"You will fucking die," he whispers to me.

"Yeah? And?" I ask him.

"And so will Maddie." Fuck. He's right. "I can help her, but you gotta let me. Don't fuck me here more than you already have."

232

I glance at him. He means it. I can tell. I nod and shout toward Maddie, "I'll see you later, babe! We'll unwrap presents and roast chestnuts and shit!"

Ricky steps in front of me, gets right in my face. "What the fuck is wrong with you? The both of you?"

I contemplate the answer to that. There's so much to unpack in the question, I don't even know where to start. So, I just shrug and say, "You don't find us charming? That's weird. We're super fucking charming. Everybody says so."

And when he grabs my arm and starts leading me toward whatever the fuck is waiting for me inside, I swear to God, he cracks the hint of a smile.

CHAPTER TWENTY-TWO

MADDIE

There's no talking as Logan pulls me along by the arm. No threats. No dramatic declarations. Nothing. The bedlam that was going on before, with everyone running around all frantic, has calmed and the lapping of waves on the shore is the only sound. It's possible that from somewhere I might hear the playing of *Carol of the Bells*, but it might also just be my imagination. I've always loved that song.

I'm tempted to speak, but what the hell am I going to say? There's no explaining I can do. Nothing I can offer to get myself out of this. I can only assume he saw me and Tyler fucking. Or, at least I hope he did. I hope he saw it and it made him furious. I hope he saw my ass pressing into the sand and Tyler's big cock sliding in and out. And I hope it made him hard and lonely.

Fuck him.

Once we're inside, he drags me back to the room where I was before. The one that's set up for dinner. The one with the champagne flute that has the pill in it. Had. *Had* the pill in it. The flute is still there, the champagne is still filling it, but the pill has disappeared. Has it dissolved finally? Did someone see the pill sitting in the bubbly liquid and pull it out? Where did it go? If it's the former,

JA HUSS & JOHNATHAN McCLAIN

then maybe there's still a chance Carlos will drink it and knock himself out? If it's the latter... I'm screwed. More screwed. Whatever. Who gives a shit?

Carlos is sitting at the table smoking a cigar. The hazy, grey-white smoke hovers in the space like a misty morning fog. The smell is rich and round and reminds me of Pete a little bit. I take a breath and close my eyes for a moment.

"Madison," Carlos says. "How was your stroll?" He takes a long puff off his cigar, throws his head back, blows the smoke out.

I don't say anything. Again, I see no point.

Logan shoves me further into the room, toward Carlos. "She was with *him*," he says.

Carlos nods, pursing his lips. He tilts his head back again, like he's contemplating something. He takes another puff off his cigar and asks, "Which *him*, exactly?"

"The Tyler him. He's here. He's the one."

"I see," says Carlos. "And what were they doing? The two of them?"

I look at Logan. He looks at me. To hell with it.

"We were fucking," I say. "I fucked him. He fucked me. We fucked. He's my boyfriend. I missed him. That's what you do."

Logan's bad eye is still too swollen for me to gauge an expression, but his good eye goes as wide as it can. Carlos's expression, on the other hand, doesn't change.

"And where is this Tyler now?" Carlos asks.

"Ricky has him. I'm going to go talk with him myself," says Logan.

Carlos takes another puff, then rests his cigar on an ashtray sitting right by that still barely bubbling glass of champagne. He stands. "Very good. But please, before

236

you kill him, find out exactly from whom he got his hands on one of my drones."

There are two things inside those eighteen words that snap my attention up to Carlos real, real hard and cause my breath to catch in my throat.

Logan nods, gives me a shit-eating grin, and goes, closing the door behind him and leaving me and Carlos alone. Carlos taps his fingers on the table twice and then clicks his tongue against the roof of his mouth five times. I find myself acutely aware of the specifics of everything happening at the moment.

He picks up a champagne glass and takes a sip. Not *the* champagne glass. *A* champagne glass. What was intended to be *my* champagne glass. Shit. Then he wanders over to the tray of tamales I requested, which have appeared in my absence, and picks one up. He smells it.

"They are very good. You are right to enjoy them. That is assuming you actually do."

He cocks his head, as if he's asking me a question. I say nothing. He keeps the tamale in his hand as he wanders over to me.

"Oh, my sweet Madison. It is very hard to be me. I know, I know, what could be hard about it? Right? I have money. I have power. But that all comes at a great cost. Responsibility. Heavy is the head that wears the crown, as they say."

He's circling me now. Like a shark. At least as far as I understand the way sharks behave. Or it could be like a vulture circling an animal, waiting for it to die. Either way, it's not a comforting feeling.

"People think I am crazy. I know this. Which is good. Because it means that all the work I have done to make people believe I am is working. Can I ask you… Do *you* think I am crazy?" He's behind me, leaning over my shoulder, pulling my hair back to whisper the question into my ear. "Or perhaps you just think I am stupid. Love. Sick. Controlled by my…" He presses his crotch into my ass. My ass that is only covered by this thin dress, since I don't have any panties on. I saw Tyler take them. Weirdo.

I close my eyes and try to keep breathing.

"You know," Carlos goes on, "when I hired you to plan my daughter's wedding, I liked you immediately. You did not seem intimidated by me. And I appreciated that. Very much. So many people work so hard to please me that when I meet someone who seems like they are strong and have the courage of their convictions, I like that. Especially in a woman. You, in particular, reminded me of another woman I felt that way about once."

Oh, Jesus. Please don't say—

"Carolina. You know about Carolina, yes? You know who she was? I assume you do, since you talked about her the other night."

I don't nod. I don't say yes. I continue standing still as he circles around the front of me, holding that goddamned tamale. The combination of the tamale smell with the cigar smoke is making me want to throw up. Or maybe it's just the fear that I can't deny is creeping in now.

"When I discovered that you had begun working for Peter Flanagan, I was… surprised? Shocked? I do not know the word. But I could not believe that you, this woman who reminds me so much of a woman I once knew, would find herself associated with the same man. That is quite a coincidence. Don't you think that's quite a coincidence?"

He's inches from my face. I can smell the cigar and champagne on his breath.

238

"Pete," I summon the will to say.

"I'm sorry?"

"His name wasn't Peter. It was just Pete. As far as I know."

There is a pause as he looks at me curiously, then smiles.

"Ah. Yes. Very good. So, tell me... How is it that you came to work for *Pete*? After you and I met, and you spent all my money—"

I open my mouth to speak, but he puts his tobacco-stained finger against my lips.

"Shh, shhh, shhhhh. You did spend my money. Whether or not it is 'your fault' is beside the point. You did, in fact, spend it. So. How did you come to work at Pete's? Exactly? Where did the idea come to you from?"

There is a shiver running down my spine now. Moments ago, he told Logan to find out where Tyler got hold of one of *Carlos's* drones, and now he's asking me questions about how I came to work at Pete's. Which, as I told Tyler, was because of the flyer I saw at the drone store. Or warehouse. Or whatever the fuck.

"Why?" I summon the voice to ask.

"Because," has says, pressing his face directly into mine, "I want to know *precisely* how long you've been working for the Drug Enforcement Administration of the United States of America."

The crashing of waves is all I hear.

Then, "Madison? You don't look well. Oh, I'm sorry. Forgive me. You still haven't eaten. And from what you say, you had quite the workout. So here, please, please. I want you to eat."

He holds up the fucking tamale.

I try to lick my lips, but there's no saliva. So, raspy and barely audible, I eke out, "I'm not—"

"Eat!" he screams. Right before he squeezes my cheeks, forcing my jaws open, and shoves the sweet, mushy corn husk violently into my mouth.

The first thing I notice about the room Ricky leads me into is what it doesn't have. Furniture. At all. It appears to be pretty much empty. But that also means it isn't outfitted with any kind of electrified torture bed like they strapped Stallone to in *Rambo, First Blood Part II*, so I'm feeling pretty good about things right now. Although I was curious how I would take having electrodes and shit strapped to my junk. Maybe Maddie and I can find out if we make it out of this.

"You're a piece of fucking work, man. You know that?" Ricky says, as he closes the door behind us and tosses my rucksack on the floor.

"Thanks. I'll take that as a compliment. Hey, I don't really give a shit what happens to me, so do me a favor, would you, and go fucking find Maddie?"

"Orders are for me to wait with you until Logan gets here. I'll go as soon as I can."

"If that motherfucker hurts her, I will rip his spine out through his fucking dick hole."

"Man," Ricky says, shaking his head, "will you just fucking dial it back for a second?"

"No. I really wish I could. Believe me. But I don't think I have the switch for that."

He sighs. "What the fuck were you thinking, coming down here?"

"We had a deal. I gave her a sat phone. She didn't call like she was supposed to."

He nods. "You don't trust me, do you?"

"Gee. Is it obvious?"

"Well," he says, rubbing his hand over his mouth, "that's fine and all, but if something happens to Maddie tonight, know that you did this shit."

We stare at each other for a long beat as my fingers tighten into fists. Not because he said it, but because—fuck—I know he's right.

And then the door opens and in walks good old Logan, carrying his AK in one hand and a fucking baseball bat in the other. Which is just adorable.

"You guys got a league?" I ask. "Shit. I didn't bring my mitt."

Logan looks at Ricky and gestures with his chin to the wall behind me, which is when I notice, for the first time, the handcuffs bolted there. Ricky grabs me, marches me over, and locks my arms above my head into the metal bracelets. As he's backing away he gives me a look that's half "I'm sorry," and half "Don't fuck me here."

"Wow," I say, as he steps back, leaving me hanging there. Literally. "Logan. I know we don't know each other that well, but I had no clue you were into the kinky shit."

Logan rests his rifle against the wall where he's standing. Ricky makes for the door—I hope to fuck to go find Maddie—but Logan stops him with something that sounds to my ear like, "No. Quedarse." Ricky says some other shit to him in Spanish I don't understand and Logan answers back. Ricky again tries to leave, but now Logan shouts, "Quedarse!" Which causes Ricky to put his hands up and step back into the corner. He looks at me with a tilt to his head that suggests an apology, and one raised eyebrow that says, *I fuckin' tried.* And even though there are a thousand other things that should be on my mind at present, the only thought I have just now is *I wonder if he can raise both eyebrows or just the one?*

And then it dawns on me: If he's not leaving this room, then who the fuck *is* going to protect Maddie?

Logan walks over to me now, baseball bat propped on his shoulder. It's kind of hard to take him seriously with his face all fucked up and him sauntering like a little leaguer who just got called to the plate. But it makes it a tad bit easier to take him seriously the moment after the bat crashes into my ribs.

He smiles just before the wind-up, and, swinging with all his force, he lands the boom stick in more or less the same area where Ricky punched me. I'm crediting the fact that it knocks the wind out of me more to Ricky having already tenderized my flesh and less to the mighty power that is Lame-Ass Logan. Which I've decided is his new nickname.

But no matter the reason, it does smart a teeny bit, and I wince. My knees buckle, and I feel the tug of the cuffs on my wrists as they pull at my skin and keep me from collapsing. It's a simple, but effective way to torture a person, I have to admit. You can beat on them all you want, but they can't retreat. They're totally exposed. And when they finally do break down, the cuffs rip and tear the flesh of their wrists and threaten to pull their shoulders out of their sockets. Solid. And way less messy than cutting somebody up with a chainsaw.

243

Anyway.

"Strike one," I manage to cough out.

"OK," Logan says, nodding and backing up to stare at me. "So my uncle is chatting with Maddie, and you and I are gonna have a little talk too, and then we'll see if everybody's stories line up. How's that sound?"

"Like you pulled that question out of a Steven Seagal movie from the nineties, but whatever. Continue."

He closes his eyes and takes a breath. "Where did you get the drone?" he asks.

"What drone? I ain't got no drone."

"Man, just... don't!" He slams the bat against the floor. It's a wood floor and a wood bat, and the sound reverberates through the room with a rich, tribal tone that causes me to think of a Kodo drum from Japan.

There's a reason I allow my mind to wander. For a long time, I thought I couldn't control it. I actually think I probably could if I wanted to. But I don't, because then I would have to be present. And for years, being present meant being present in a shitty situation that I hated. Or caused pain. Or both. I've been finding lately that with Maddie, my mind doesn't wander as much. Because when I'm with her, where I am is exactly where I want to be. But here, now? A situation like this? I got no problem letting my brain saunter off. It's what's going to keep me from giving my power away to the fact that, in theory, I should be intimidated. Because I won't be. Not by this fuckbucket.

Logan continues talking. "We know that the guy we were buying our drones from was working for the DEA. And we know that they were tagging our own fucking drones to see if they could figure out the shit they were too stupid to figure out any other way. Which is why we stopped using them. And then, lo and fuckin' behold, Maddie shows up and then *the very next day* a drone that we confirmed from the serial number was one of ours, from a shipment we never picked up because we fucking figured out what was going on, shows up dive-bombing my uncle's house."

I glance at Ricky, who shakes his head a tiny bit and looks to the ground. Logan doesn't see the exchange, I don't think, and continues. "So, my question is: Who is it who supplied you with the fucking drone? I mean, I know *you* aren't fuckin' DEA. So, how'd you get it?"

Fuckin' Ricky. Piece-of-shit, lying cocksucker. Was Maddie right? Was she somehow fucking dragged into this thing before it even began? Ricky's looking at me with a tight grimace now. Is he worried I'm gonna blow his cover? He goddamn well should be.

Fuck you, bro.

I take a breath and say, "I dunno what the fuck you're talking about. It's Maddie's. She bought it. She didn't know I was coming down here. I just didn't like the idea of your uncle and his shriveled old fucking cocaine dick near her, so I borrowed it to make sure she was OK."

I know there's no way he'll believe me. Why would he? It's the truth.

With a lunge that shows a level of spry agility I have heretofore not seen from Lame-Ass, he cracks me again in the same spot. This one I feel. It runs through my stomach and into my back like... well, like fire. Which sucks. But I can't help it. I burst out laughing. "Oh! Oh, shit! Nice try, bro! But strike two!"

Logan is huffing a little, partially from the labor and partially from his anger. I'm coughing and laughing at the same time, stomping my feet to shake off the burn, and then I throw my head back and howl at the ceiling. "This is, bar none, the best Christmas ever!" I scream. I'm not actually going crazy, I just want him to think I am.

Or I might actually just be going crazy. It's hard to tell.

I glance again at Ricky with a (I'm guessing) maniacal smile on my face. He looks pained. Good. He should. It's nothing compared to the pain he's gonna feel if I get out of this shit. I wonder how far he's willing to let Logan beat on me to keep from blowing his cover. I have a feeling we won't have to wait too long to find out.

"Shut up!" Logan shouts over my howling and carrying on, and he winds up for another swing.

"Stop!" That's me. "Stop! OK. OK. I'll tell you what you want to know." Logan lowers the bat and steps back again. "It's me. OK? It's me. I'm the DEA agent. Maddie doesn't know. I've been gone for a long time, but I knew her when we were kids, and when I started working for the DEA, I discovered that she had this relationship with Castillo, so I've been using her to try and get close to your organization. OK? It's me. It's my fucking drone. She's my informant. It's all me." Christ. I wonder if that story sounds as stupid to Logan as it does to me.

Logan gets an impish grin, which is pretty macabre on his busted kisser, huffs out a half-laugh, and says, "You're no fucking DEA agent."

"No? I'm not?"

He shakes his head. "Nope."

"Yeah? You're sure?"

He nods. "Yeah. I'm sure. I know *exactly* who you are."

Hm. I'm super curious what that means. "Oh. Do ya? Well, OK, Agatha Christie. Then please, by all means. Tell me what you think you know."

He grins and says, "Senior EOD Technician Petty Officer First Class Tyler Hudson Morgan. Birthdate, March fifteenth. Born to Jack Edwin and Barbara Anne Morgan. Power forward for his high school basketball team. Rejected the receipt of the Purple Heart for injuries sustained in combat and released from the Navy under a disability discharge. Owner of the patent for the "blast seeker" artificial intelligence augmentation currently utilized by the US government, a dozen private corporations, and in negotiation for use by half a dozen other tech and research companies as well. Technology *actually* created by Nadir Al Madani, now deceased. At present, the proclaimed boyfriend of Madison Clayton, chained to a wall in Ensenada, Mexico, and in a world of fucking trouble." He gets right up in my face and echoes back to me some shit I jokingly said to him the first time we met. "Dude. I know *everything* about you."

I am never. *Ever*. Speechless. I don't always speak, but I am *never* at a loss for words.

"Hey. Look at that. Logan has the internet."

And I'm not at a loss now either. Fuck this asshole.

"WHERE'D YOU GET THE FUCKING DRONE!?" he shouts.

"I told you the truth the first time, man. It's hers. She intended to buy it to fucking do the wedding planning shit. Probably for you assholes."

"So you're telling me that she just *happened* to be working for Pete. And she just *happened* to buy a drone that was tagged by the DEA to track back to us."

I glance at Ricky with a clenched jaw. "Yeah. I know. It's hard for me to believe it too, but that's how it happened."

"So you don't know nothing about the cops, or the Federales, or the DEA, or none of that shit. You're just some lovesick asshole spying on your woman."

"Yup. Pretty much. Can I ask you a question?"

"You wanna ask me a question?"

"I do."

He sizes me up. What the fuck he's looking to determine with me hanging here, I'm not sure, but he eyeballs me for a long moment before saying, "OK. What?"

"Logan. That's not a very Mexican name. Are you his nephew by marriage or were you like, adopted, or—?"

But that's as far as I get before Logan grabs up the bat and rears back, clearly going to swing for my head this time. Oh, boy. This is gonna smart, I have a feeling. And out of some primal instinct, I close my eyes, readying to absorb the blow, when I hear…

Click.

And for the second time tonight, there is the sound of a Kalashnikov rifle being cocked.

I open my eyes and the question I had about how far Ricky would let Logan go before blowing his cover is answered. Logan snaps his head around to find Ricky there, weapon drawn, Logan scoped the fuck out with nowhere to run.

"Strike three," I say. Probably unnecessarily.

Logan stares at Ricky for a second and then just drops the bat.

In the movies there's always lots of talking and explaining in a situation like this.

Ricky? What the hell are you doing?

Don't move, Logan! Richard Martinez! DEA! You're done!

Ricky! You bastard! You betrayed me!

And shit like that.

But in the real world, like now, Logan knows he's been played, he knows who's DEA and who ain't, and he knows he stands a way better chance of beating some kind of drug rap in court than he does of dealing with the blowback from trying to kill a fucking undercover DEA agent. Beyond that, he knows that there's a fucking assault rifle like five feet from his chest and making a thing of it right now isn't gonna help him a whole, whole lot.

Ricky pulls a key from his pocket and hands it to Logan, keeping the gun drawn on him the whole time. He says something to him in Spanish (Which is odd to me, it's like… Dude, you've blown your cover. Just drop the shit and talk in a way everybody here can understand already) and Logan comes over to uncuff me from the wall.

"Dude," I whisper in Logan's face. "I'm gonna say this just to say it. If Maddie's not exactly the way she was when I last saw her, I'm gonna rip your uncle's head off his shoulders and then bring it back in here to beat you to death with it."

Logan doesn't say anything. Which is fine. I mean, really, what do you say to something like that? So, once he releases my wrists, we finish the drill. I spin him around, lock *him* up—which looks a little more painful because he's shorter than I am so the cuffs stretch him out a little further (Hey. Not my fault)—and then turn to Ricky and ask, "Why the fuck are we still standing here?"

"Because there are men all over the fucking place. You have to stay here with him."

"What? Shut the front door, fucker. No way. You stay."

"You will get shot if you go out there alone."

"They don't know who the fuck I am."

JA HUSS & JOHNATHAN McCLAIN

"Which is exactly the point."

Touché.

"Well, tough shit," I say. "I'm going with you." Ricky screws his mouth up like he's about to protest more, but he's met me. He knows he's not gonna win this argument. He nods in acquiescence. "Hand me my bag," I say. He does. I open it up and start riffling through.

"What are you looking for?" he asks.

I don't answer. Just keep searching. I'm looking for something to shove in Logan's mouth to keep him from shouting once we're both gone and he's here all chained up. I find the roll of duct tape that I have in there, but I need something else. It never works just to slap tape on a person's mouth. Another fallacy of the movies. You can use your tongue to eventually work it free. If you want to gag someone properly, you have to stuff something else in their mouth first.

Unfortunately, all the t-shirts I had got burned up with Chocolate Thunder, and the only other stuff I have in the sack is, like, rope, a couple of MREs, a flashlight—you know, survival shit. I had some gauze in the car, but I forgot to pull it out and now it's burned up too. And then I realize... I do have the perfect thing to stuff in his ugly maw.

I pull Maddie's panties out of my pocket, grab up the duct tape and get right in Logan's face again. "Honestly, man, you don't even deserve the privilege of having Maddie's dried pussy juice in your mouth, but since it's Christmas and all..."

Once Maddie's panties are safely taped up inside Logan's cake-hole and I'm sure that the gagging and snuffling he's doing is just him being a baby and not him actually choking to death (although I could give a shit

250

really, but Ricky's being a bitch about it), I turn to Ricky and say, "I'll fuck you up later. Where is she?"

"She's likely with Carlos. And you need to calm the fuck down. Jesus. You two are exactly alike."

"Again, I'll take that as a compliment. And *calm the fuck down*? Dude, I *know* that you set Maddie up!"

"What are you talking about?"

"You've been using her this whole time?"

"I've... what?" Ricky asks. Either genuinely confused or genuinely faking it.

"What dick-sniffer said!" I point at Logan, in case there was any ambiguity about who "dick-sniffer" is. "You fuckers were selling drones and shit and you roped her in?"

"That doesn't even make sense."

"Doesn't it?" (Does it? Shit. Now he's got me confused.)

"Brother," Ricky says, which again ruffles my feathers, but whatever, "yeah, we were trying to get intel from setting up the drone op, but the fact that Maddie happened to be drone shopping while we were running it is just bad luck."

"She was *working* for Castillo when she stumbled in there."

"I know, man. But that's just the way it goes. That wasn't us."

"She started working at Pete's because she saw a flyer IN THE FUCKING DRONE PLACE."

"Again, man. I know. Probably some intel about Carlos's history with Pete. That's a lead we were following. But, also again, just a coincidence."

"So when the fuck did *you* find out about her?"

251

"First time I ever heard about Maddie Clayton was the night you and I met. That was the first time I got sent on a run with him." He lifts his chin to Logan. "That was when I knew I had finally earned some fuckin' trust in the organization. But honestly? Now that I've met you and Maddie? I wish it had taken me a little longer. Because then I might still be able to do my job instead of having the last year and a half of work blown the fuck up."

Yeah. Well. That's what I do. I make shit explode. Ironically.

I shake my head a little. "No. No. There's no way that—"

"That all this shit that's happening is just fucked-up, bad luck?" He takes a deep breath. Lets it out. "I know. But it is. I dunno what to tell you, man. Not everything always happens for a reason. Sometimes things just... happen."

I don't know how many times and in how many different ways the universe is going to conspire to teach me the same damn lesson. But it sure keeps fucking trying.

"C'mon, man," he says after a beat. "Let's go get Maddie."

I snap out of my brief stupor, nod, and head for the door. He stops me. "Hold up." He grabs me and pulls me to his side. "It needs to look like I'm bringing you to Carlos or we won't make it five feet."

I nod and let him take me by the arm. And then it occurs to me to say, "Hey." He looks at me. "I'm sorry I blew your cover."

He laughs a little and shakes his head. "You didn't. I did. I had to. I knew you'd let Logan fucking beat you to death before you'd say anything."

"Yeah, well. What can I tell ya? I'm kinda stupid."

He opens the door and pushes me out into the hall as he laughs and says, "Yeah. I know… Everybody says so."

CHAPTER TWENTY-FOUR

I'm shaking. Physically. I don't know if it's anger or terror, but it's probably both. Carlos is touching my chin, moving my mouth up and down.

"Yes, that's right. Chew. Chew every bite. Don't want you to choke."

Fucking sadist.

And all of the sudden I'm thinking about his daughter. Where is she? Why isn't she here? Why wasn't she at his other house? It's Christmas. And I realize that when I asked him if he killed her because of the way she betrayed his trust, he never answered me. And although it's almost unthinkable, I am. Thinking it.

Oh, Jesus Christ.

"Madison, Madison, Madison," he says, now moving back to the table. "What are we going to do?" I don't respond. "I mean, on the one hand, I do like you. I like you very, very much. I appreciated that you were—I thought—truthful with me. You did not throw yourself into my arms and profess to love me. You made it... what's the word? Plausible. Yes. It was plausible. I believed that you were here because you wanted a chance to escape your life. That terrible life of yours." He stands

JA HUSS & JOHNATHAN McCLAIN

by the champagne glass that may or may not have a dissolved knockout drug in it. "Your brother, dead. Your family, gone. Your every attempt at a success, nothing but failure. A twenty-five-year-old girl taking off her clothes for money and still not able to get by. It seemed that no matter what you tried, you could not help yourself. So it made sense to me that you would want someone strong who could take care of you."

He picks up the flute. Oh, shit. Is he going to drink it? Is the pill dissolved in it? Will it knock him out? Shit. I guess I'll find out soon.

"But the truth is, you were just allowing yourself to be used as a pawn in another way. Honestly, that would not have bothered me. If I had found out that you had been manipulated by the DEA, that would not surprise me. Despite your show of strength, you are weak. And they are powerful. It is not your fault. You are a woman. Women are simply weaker than men. And it is so easy to bend a weak woman's will. So if it was only that you had been cooperating with the DEA all this time—"

"But I wasn—"

"SHUT! UP!" When someone who is generally quiet screams… it's not nice. In this brief time with him, it's easy to see how he became as powerful as he is. He's unpredictable. And if unpredictability doesn't get you killed, it makes you strong. Which is why I'm not even attempting to correct him with all the "weak woman" shit. Because he should think that as much as he likes.

I am confused about the DEA thing, however. He obviously doesn't know what he thinks he knows or Ricky would be dead right now. And then I realize… I don't know that he's not. I don't know that Tyler's not either. And I have no idea what's going to happen next, but I know for sure that someone in this room is going to die tonight. And I plan to do everything in my power to see to it that it's not me.

"But it is not just that you were lying to me." He stands in front of me with the glass of champagne. "It's that you… fucked… someone else. As you said. Here. At my home. Under my nose, while I waited for you to come to me. I will be honest with you…" He pokes me in the forehead with his index finger to punctuate each word of the following. "That. Does. Not. Sit. Well." He grabs my face and squeezes my cheeks. Again. "Not well at all." And then he lifts the glass of champagne…

And he drinks it.

Jesus Christ.

Well, I'm going to go ahead and assume the pill dissolved and didn't magically rescue itself from the champagne glass. We'll find out, I suppose.

He throws the empty champagne flute onto the floor and it smashes at my feet. I don't jump. "So! What are we to do now?" he asks, walking away, turning back to look at me when I don't immediately answer.

"About what?"

"About you and me. The truth is that we have your *boyfriend*." He says it pointedly. "The drone pilot. He is the one we want the information from, so I don't really need you, do I?" I say nothing. "I mean… I could see what it is you might be able to tell me, but… Truthfully, knowing you as I do, I would have to torture you to get anything out of you. And I don't want to do that…" He comes back toward me, bends down and lifts my dress, drawing his hand up my leg and along my thigh as he does. And again, I'm still not wearing fucking underwear.

257

He stands and lands his cheek against mine, putting his mouth by my ear. The base of his palm is resting against the edge of my pussy.

"Everything I have said to you, I have meant. I have not felt about a woman the way I feel about you in thirty-five years. If we can get the information we need from your Tyler, then it is possible that you and I can discuss options that allow you to live. Otherwise, I'm afraid that, even though I don't want to hurt you, you may force me to. Isn't it funny? You and I are always having to negotiate new terms when our original contracts are broken."

And he wraps his mouth around my earlobe as his fingers clumsily fumble between my legs. Shit. I close my eyes and stiffen up my entire body as tautly as I can in preparation for engaging in the deadly martial art known as being Maddie Clayton.

And then…

Wham!

Carlos's body hits the floor.

Holy. Fucking. Shit.

It worked. Thank you, Ricky double-oh-seven! Jesus Christ. Jesus Christ. OK. OK. Now think. Think. I can't just waltz out of here. I had one shot to do that and they found me and brought me back. No doubt this whole fucking mini-city is going to be on the lookout for me. Think. What to do? What to do?

On the other side of the room is a fireplace. It's all lit up and roaring. All holiday festive. And as I stare into the fire, I think of Pete. And I think of firefighter Jeff.

And I think of Scotty.

And I also think this may be my one shot to get out of here.

I snap into action, pulling the tablecloth off the table and letting all the dishes go crashing to the floor. Shit. I should be more careful. But this place is so massive, presumably nobody can hear me. Or maybe they'll just think it's reindeer or something.

Grabbing up the cloth, I dip it into the fire and it goes up almost immediately. Must be silk or some shit. Keeping the flame as far from me as possible, I run to touch it to the area rugs and the tapestries hanging from the walls. Anything I can find that's flammable. Fuck, I hope this works.

And just as I toss the burning cloth onto one of the lush, upholstered side chairs, the door creaks open and I hear, "Jefe?" Goddamn it.

"Help! Help!" I shout. "Someone's here! Someone came in and—Tyler?"

"Hey, Mads," he says, poking his head in. "Um. Looks like you got a little fire in here."

Ricky pushes Tyler into the room. He's holding a gun. He looks around and says, "Je. Sus. Christ. What the fuck did you do?"

"I dunno! I was trying to get the place evacuated. Or create a distraction. Or. I thought… I dunno! I'm a little freaked out. And honestly? WHO FUCKING CARES? CAN WE GO??"

Tyler looks down and sees Carlos. "Is that Castillo? What did you do to him, babe? Did you fuck him up?" He asks this with far too much glee, I think.

"He"—I nod at Ricky—"gave me some kind of partially insoluble fucking knockout drug. Thanks for that, by the way. Woulda been nice to have a heads up that the shit would take like a month to dissolve."

"Jesus," says Ricky. "OK. Look. Grab him and let's just get the fuck out of here."

"Fuck that," says Tyler. "Leave him. Let the fucker burn."

"My job is to bring the bad guys in, not burn them the fuck up."

I reach out and touch Tyler's arm. "Ty…" He looks at me. "He's right. We can't. Not like this." I gesture to the spreading flames. Which are really spreading now. We seriously need to get the hell out of here.

Tyler still seems unsure. Ricky says, "Hey, if it makes you feel better, I'll never get you two past the gate without him. At this point, our best shot is to use him to keep us safe."

"You mean a human shield," Tyler says.

"I was thinking more like a negotiating tool, but sure. Know what? Let's just at least get the hell out this burning room!"

Ricky goes to lift Carlos, but Tyler pushes him away and grabs Carlos up over his shoulders into a fireman's carry. And then he does something I've never seen him do. He winces. Like he's in pain. One hand grabs at his ribs.

"Babe?" I say. "You okay?"

"Yep," he grunts. "Too good." Then he winks and says to Ricky, "Lead the way."

CHAPTER TWENTY-FIVE

TYLER

Either this son of a bitch is heavier than he looks, or else Logan really did manage to put some work in on my ribs. Shit hurts. But no rest for the weary, as some asshole once said.

I feel like old Saint Nick himself, carrying a present for all the good girls and boys of the DEA. I realize that Maddie has yet to get any active intel that helps shut down the operation, but if Carlos is in custody, then that leaves Logan to run things and with that taint-griddler in charge, I imagine they can bring down this show in about five minutes.

Saint Nick. Hm. I wonder if that makes me Saint Tyler. I like the ring of that, but the Claus notwithstanding, most motherfuckers only achieve sainthood posthumously, so I don't know if I should be gunning for it so enthusiastically.

Regardless, these are the thoughts running through my head to keep my mind off the amount of unexpected pain I'm in at the moment.

We approach the first corner in the hallway and Ricky peeks around to make sure the coast is clear. Just as a fire alarm goes off loud as fuck from wherever.

"Shit," says Ricky. And looking back, I see smoke billowing out of the room Maddie lit up. I'm half-stunned that she did it and half-super proud of her. But both of those feelings are overtaken by a much stronger one. Paralysis.

Something about the smoke and the alarm and hauling this body...

Nadir.

The explosion that killed Nadir and the other guys wasn't the one that got me. I mean, it was, but not exactly. It was like a chain event. Nadir and the other guys caught the first blast, and when I grabbed him and threw him over my shoulders to haul him out of the combat zone to a dustoff location, that's when I triggered the blast that nailed me.

No one has ever come right out and said it, but I know that the reason I survived is because I was carrying him. His body acted as a mini-blast wall and absorbed enough of the discharge that no heavy shrapnel hit my vital organs. I just know it. I was pinned down though. Held there for however long. I don't know. Just what they told me. It wasn't the blast itself that fucked me up so much as the fire, I guess. Nadir's charred body and whatever other burning shit was lying on me.

I don't plan to ever tell Maddie that stuff.

And then, as if waking from a deep sleep, I hear the far-off sound of, "Tyler?" Maddie's voice. And I blink myself back.

"Are you OK?" she asks. The concerned look on her face breaks my heart.

"Yeah. Yeah, fucking killing it. Locked, cocked, and ready to rock. Where's the party?" And shit like that. I'm not sure how many tired, macho, war-time clichés I spew, but finally she just smiles, stands on her toes and kisses my cheek.

And then we're on the move again.

Once we round the corner, Ricky throws his fist up. I am more than familiar with the signal to halt progress. Maddie, not so much, and because she's glancing worriedly back at me, she kind of rams into Ricky.

"Why are we—?" she starts, but stops when she sees what Ricky sees. Four armed guards up ahead, all talking in Spanish and pointing in different directions. They haven't seen us yet. The alarm is blaring all over the place, but the fire appears to still be contained to the room. Although, at the rate it was spreading, that won't be true for long. Fuck, Carlos is getting heavy. I bounce to adjust him over my shoulders and I can feel my ribs pinch. I try not to let it show on my face.

The house/hotel/village/wherever-the-fuck-we-are looks like a Mediterranean architect partied too hard with a Spanish-style interior designer and they threw up everywhere. So there's arches and alcoves and shit all over the place. Ricky pushes us inside one such alcove and says, "Stay here."

We step back, just out of eyesight from the hallway, and when Maddie presses against me, it makes me forget for a second about all the pain, and the weight of carrying Carlos, and all of it... And Chuckie Stiff says hi.

"Are you kidding me right now?" Maddie asks in response to the sensation of feeling my throbbing hard-on pressing against her ass. I shrug a "what're you gonna do?" shrug, and she rolls her eyes. Fuck, I love her so much.

I slide past her so I can peer around the edge of the alcove and down the hall, and what I see is... well. It's some shit all right.

Ricky approaches the four dudes, speaking Spanish to them, and then points back to where we are. I pull my head back into the shadows as they all look this way but manage to keep one eye on the five of them. And what that one eye sees is some fucking next-level super-soldier nonsense.

Ricky laughs and bends down like he's tying his boots, and when he pops back up, he's holding a fucking bush knife he pulled from an ankle sheath. He slices the throats of the two dudes standing next to him with one sweeping motion, stabs the next guy in the chest—twice—before he can move, then breaks the fourth dude's arm, pins him to the ground, and steps on his neck and snaps it.

I can't believe I fucking knocked this guy out. Holy shit.

He looks back, giving me the sign for "don't fuckin' move," runs out of sight for like twenty seconds, and then comes running back down the hall to where we are.

"OK," he says, not even fucking winded. "What you did may have worked." He addresses that to Maddie.

"Whattayou mean?" she asks.

"I told the primary strike team that you and Carlos are missing and that this wing is on fire. I directed half of them to go look for you and the rest to deal with the fire."

"But then—" she starts.

Ricky shakes his head. "I directed them to run around the long way. Told 'em this way was getting blocked off."

"Jesus," I say. "That's pretty fucking thin."

"Yeah?" says Mr. Super Soldier. "Thin like starting a fucking fire? Or thin more like showing up at the compound of one of the five biggest drug traffickers in the world armed with nothing but a goddamn drone? Thin like those?"

"Fair enough."
"Let's go. We got maybe five minutes," says Ricky.
And then we're on the move again.

CHAPTER TWENTY-SIX

MADDIE

I can tell Tyler's in pain. I should have a million other concerns, but that's the one that's gnawing at me right now. I can see he's hurting, hauling Carlos along, and I hate it. I want to be able to heal him. Make him well and whole and transport us out of here. But I can't. So we keep on.

Just as we get to a door that exits out into... wherever, Ricky stops.

"As soon as we get out of here, we may encounter some resistance." He looks at Tyler. "Stay behind me with Carlos, and Maddie, you stay on Tyler's six. I'm hoping if they see we've got their boss, we'll be able to get past the main gate and out of here without any shots being fired."

"Can't you call in the cavalry? Like, I dunno, air support or something? However shit works?" I ask.

He shakes his head. "Again, almost nobody knows about this op or that I'm here, and we can't trust the local cops. Besides, it's Christmas."

"So?"

"DEA agents take holidays off and shit too," he says, like it's the most obvious thing in the world.

"Jesus Christ."

"What they're celebrating," he says. Tyler laughs at that. I look at him under arched eyebrows.

"What? Shit was funny. Good for you, Ricky Super-Soldier. I didn't think you had a sense of humor."

Why do I suddenly feel like I'm at a goddamned keg party?

"I've already called the one person I can call. She's arranging with the Mexican embassy to get a plane to pick us up at El Ciprés. It's only about three klicks out. We just have to get there. Where's your car?" Ricky asks Tyler.

Tyler doesn't say anything. Just stands there, shifting the still-unconscious Carlos around on his shoulders and trying to act like he isn't hurt in some way.

"Ty?" I follow up.

"What's that, now?" he asks.

"Your car, Ty? Where's your car?"

He gnaws at his lower lip for a moment before saying, "Uh. Know how you just started a fire to create a distraction?"

"Yeah?"

"I mean, you aren't the only person who had that idea." He winces as he adjusts Carlos again.

"Dude," says Ricky. "Was that your car they found burning across the road?"

"Had to find a way to get the gate guards' attention." Tyler stares at the ground. Damn. Even with the muscles, and the beard, and bad attitude, sometimes Tyler Morgan can look like a five-year-old who just got caught drawing on the living room wall.

"Fuck. Me," Ricky says on sighed breaths. "What is wrong with you two?"

"OK, whatever," I snap. "No car. Way it is. So what do we do now?"

268

Ricky rubs the barrel of the gun he's still holding against his temple, which makes me nervous as hell, but I guess he's just thinking. "When we walk out of here, we'll be at the fueling station. I've only been down here once before, but it was to pick up one of the trucks. It had the keys just sitting in the ignition. If we're lucky, that's protocol, and we'll grab one of those."

"Then what?" I ask.

"Then we'll drive a big fucking fuel truck through the front gate and hope that we can get the hell out of here and to the airstrip before we're all caught and murdered."

He doesn't say it with resounding confidence. He says it like it's the absolute worst of a very limited number of already bad options, but it's the only one we have left, so we have no choice. Or, I guess, we have the choice to just wait here to die.

"What about him?" Tyler asks, bouncing Carlos and grimacing.

"We bring him with us," answers Ricky.

"What about the cops?" I ask.

"El Ciprés is a military airport. We should be OK."

"Should?" I ask, with still more mounting incredulity.

"Hey, fire-starters!" he shouts unexpectedly. "This is what we got to work with!"

Tyler and I both mumble, "ok/yeah/sure/fine," in no particular order, Ricky nods, Tyler adjusts Carlos and scrunches up his face, and I wish all of a sudden I was wearing panties as we push open the door and head outside.

CHAPTER TWENTY-SEVEN

TYLER

I hope to fuck one of these trucks has keys in it, because I don't know how much longer I can keep carrying this fucking guy. I mean, I do. As long as I have to, is the answer. But I'd love to let him go sooner than later.

Nobody is immediately visible outside, so we gallop (they gallop, I lumber) by the fueling islands toward one of the trucks. This place is kind of amazing. If you didn't know it was owned by just one guy to operate his shitty criminal empire, you might think it was a small town all of its own. The fuel pumps are decorated with tinsel and lights and shit just like it's any old gas station anywhere.

They're probably about fifty feet away from me when they get to the nearest truck. Ricky jumps up into the cab and looks inside. "Fuck!" he shouts. "Nope!" He hops down and runs to another truck to keep looking. Maddie trails alongside him, her hair and dress blowing in the night breeze. She looks like something out of an old movie. Like Rita Hayworth in *Gilda*, only instead of in black and white, she's in full, living Technicolor. And I have this thought…

I'm going to marry this woman.

Which is fucking nuts.

We still have so much shit to work out, both between us and, I have a feeling, within ourselves (I dunno if she does, but I sure as hell do). We knew each other once, but there's so much filling in and catching up that still has to be done, and we've barely started. I never thought in a million years I'd ever want to see somebody's dumb face every morning for the rest of my life, much less marry it, but I want to see her dumb face every second of every day forever, because it's not dumb. It's perfect. And, oh, yeah, we're trying to escape the clutches of a murderous drug lord and his army of men right now, so marrying somebody is the last thing that should be entering my stupid, broken, crazy, rambling, tortured thoughts.

But it is. And just like when I thought of her when I set my apartment on fire (still haven't told her that. Again, lots to fill each other in on), thinking of her and about her and marrying her... gives me peace. Standing back, watching her run around in the night, looking for a way to find, literally, the key to our salvation... I can see nothing else.

Which I also mean literally. Because if I had been paying attention, I might have seen the bat swinging toward me a beat sooner, and I might have been able to avoid it before it came crashing into my already bruised and breaking ribcage.

CHAPTER TWENTY-EIGHT

MADDIE

"We have to hurry!" I hate that I say it the second it leaves my lips. Because it's the kind of thing dumb bitches say in movies and TV shows when some guy who's writing it thinks that it's what women say when they're panicked or whatever.

But we do have to hurry. So fuck it.

Finally, from inside the cab of the third truck Ricky checks, he turns back, holding a set of keys, and shouts, "Got it! Let's go!"

I breathe out the breath I didn't even realize I was holding, and turn to Tyler to shout, "Come on!" But I don't actually get the words out, because before I can, I see Logan, an insane look on his beaten face and what appear to be handcuffs with the chains hanging off them attached to his wrists, swing a baseball bat hard at Tyler's ribs. It makes contact and Tyler fights to stay standing, trying to keep Carlos on his shoulders, but he can't. He drops to his knees, letting him slide off and land on the ground beside him. It's almost like he's working to deliver Carlos daintily to the earth like a child being put into bed rather than just dropping him and letting his carcass crash down to the concrete.

273

And I probably can't, but I *think* I can hear the sound of the bat making contact with Tyler's side all the way over by where I'm standing. I know I can't actually feel it, since it isn't happening to me.

Except I can.

And it is.

"Ty!" I scream and start for him, but Ricky pulls me back. Just in time too, because I neglected to take into account the half-dozen armed men with Logan. All of whom are now pointing assault rifles in our direction. Ricky drags me around behind the passenger side of the truck we have the keys for and presses my back against the tire.

"Do not. Fucking. Move," he says. And before I can say anything, he's pinned himself to the front fender, rifle at the ready, and is shouting at Logan. "Hermano! No lo hagas!"

"Fuck you!" Logan shouts back, in English. "You fucking DEA dog, cockroach, rat motherfucker!"

So much for negotiating, I guess.

And that's when the shooting starts.

The sound of bullets hitting metal and echoing around makes it hard to even know where the shots are being fired from. I have no idea if Ricky has another gun, or more ammo, or what, but it doesn't matter. It feels like the whole goddamned world is shooting at us right now.

I cover my head—which is dumb, but I do it anyway—and peer around the truck tire to see if I can make out what's happening with Tyler. It's not good.

He's curled up in a ball, but Logan is fucking whaling on him. And each strike he lands feels like a shot to my gut. My spirit. My heart. I want to help him. I want to race to him. I have to fight every instinct in my body that tells me to run and help.

Fuck, bitch. I dunno what to tell you. The devil. On Christmas. Awesome.

Scarletton... Angel? Scarletton? What the hell? *It's a hybrid of Scarlett and Madison. Not the point right now. Listen. You can't. You can't go. You'll do nothing but sacrifice yourself and he'll still die.*

Shit, Devil says. *Feather-pussy and I might actually agree on something. But, y'know, self-preservation is my shit, so...*

I look at Tyler being beaten like Logan is a cruel child and Tyler is a turtle he found, and I start crying. Not sobbing. Just crying. Because the worst. Fucking. Thing. In the world. Is watching somebody you love suffer, and knowing that there isn't a single, goddamned thing you can do about it.

I know exactly what that feels like.

Maddie? the angel says.

What? I think.

You could pray.

What? That's me and the devil at the same time.

Pray.

To what? I silently scream. *To who?*

It doesn't matter. Whoever. There are thirty-five hundred different gods that people believe in around the world. Pick one. Or just pray to the universe. All prayer is in the transference of your life energy out into the world. The world is nothing but energy. And you're part of it. And Tyler's part of it. And you two are powerful together. I know you can feel that. So just send your power and your energy in his direction and see what happens.

This is the dumbest fucking shit I've ever heard. (I'm not sure if that's me or the devil.)

275

Maybe, says the angel. *But from where I'm sitting, chick? It looks like you're about out of moves.*

For fuck's...

I can't be sure, but it's possible a bullet may have just grazed the ground where I'm sitting. So. Fuck it.

I close my eyes. I try to tune out everything. Which is impossible, but I give it my best shot. I don't even know how to start. Or what to say. Or who to say it to.

So I just think of Tyler. I think of us as kids. I think of the scar that he gave me. And the selling-smiles-goldfish thing. And of summer vacations, and birthday parties, and Christmases all together. And I think of us now. And I imagine us in the future. Old and wrinkled and holding each other's hands as we walk through the park. And old, wrinkly Tyler trying to slip his old, wrinkly hand down to touch my old, wrinkly ass. I really see it. I imagine it with all my might. I try to wish it into being with every bit of force and strength and mountain climber's will I have inside me.

And that's when the explosion happens.

"Jesus Christ!" Ricky shouts, falling backwards, pulling me with him, and landing on top of me.

"What's happening?" I scream. "What the fuck happened?"

"I don't know!"

Shit is raining down from the sky all around us. There's a massive eruption where one of the fuel pump islands was a second ago. And I can't see anyone shooting at us anymore, because I can't see anything. Nothing but a raging wall of flames.

"Tyler!" I scream. I think. I can't hear anything anymore. Not because of the explosion, but because the whole world just ended and, as I know from science class, there's no sound when you're lost, floating endlessly in space.

The angel was full of shit. She's been full of shit this whole time. Maybe everyone is and always has been, so why should she be any different? There is no god. No universal power that holds things together and makes shit make sense. There's no nothing. There is pain, and suffering, and the tearing away of everything you come to love, and then it all just starts all over again.

Not for me. Not anymore. I'm fucking done.

I push Ricky off me, grab the rifle from his unsuspecting grip, and stand and round the front of the truck, ready to walk through fire and kill everyone still standing on the other side.

But I don't get the chance... Because of what happens next.

And suddenly I can hear again. But the only sound that makes its way into my eardrums is that of my own terrified voice still screaming...

"TYLER!!"

CHAPTER TWENTY-NINE

I don't know why I don't just throw fuckin' Carlos to the ground. Some sort of impulse, I guess. Maybe I'm remembering Nadir again? I wouldn't let him just crash down, so I don't let Carlos either.

Fuckin' feelings.

It ain't easy. Logan's really going all in on this bat thing. Maybe he's working out unfulfilled dreams of being a major leaguer. Who knows? All I know is that the shit hurts, and I'm not sure how much more I can take.

I get Carlos on the blacktop, and I do the only thing I can do... I try to wait it out. One of two things will happen. Either Logan'll get tired and quit, or he'll break my back and kill me. There is a third thing, I guess. He could just get bored and shoot me in the head. But my gut tells me at this point, homeboy's way more interested in making me suffer for a while than he is in just killing me.

"Fuck!" I find myself yelling. And not in a nice way.

And that's when I glance over and catch a glimpse of Maddie. I see her poking her head from by the tire where Ricky has stashed her and for which I am grateful. I think I may have been wrong to mistrust the guy so much. Maybe he's not a bad dude after all.

279

"Fuck!" And there's that bat again.

Shit. I don't think I'm gonna make it. I kind of laugh at that, in between getting hit and listening to the hellfire of bullets and whatever shit Logan's screaming at me in Spanglish. Of all the shit I've ever been through, I never thought this would be the way I would die.

In love, I mean.

Because I never thought I would ever be in love. Just didn't seem like it was in the cards for me. But. Here I am. In love and in big fucking trouble.

It's OK. I don't mind. I'm not scared or anything. I'm just... sad. Because I think I might actually have liked being happy. It didn't seem so bad. Some people change when they fall in love. I've seen it. Sometimes for better and sometimes for worse. But when it's right, when it works, when it's good, it doesn't *change* you. It makes you more... you. It's like that with Evan now that he's with Robert. He's always been the best guy, but there's a... light that shines off him now.

I wonder if it was like that with me these last few weeks. Was I lighter? Was I a better version of myself? I think I was.

I think I was.

Yep. I can feel it coming. My old, battered, beaten, scarred, mangled body has served me well, but I don't think it's got a whole lot left to give here. I've always thought that the body was just a tool, and that if the mind was willing, the body would find a way to push through whatever pain it was feeling and move on. But that's simply not true.

If that was true, Scotty would be alive today. He had more will and strength of character than anybody I've ever known. His body just couldn't respond. And he had to let go. There's no shame in it. It's OK. I don't want to leave Maddie, especially since I just found her, but it's starting to look like I may not have a choice.

All this whips through my mind in less than a fraction of a second, and as Maddie disappears behind the tire for safety, I decide that the only thing for me to do now is to try and transport my mind out of here so that my body can let it all happen and not feel guilty about it. And while I'm letting myself drift off, I will think of Maddie. I will think of her safety. And her protection. And her happiness. And her joy. I remember us as kids. Birthday parties, and holidays, and Christmases. Way better ones than this one.

And I think again about seeing her at Pete's for the first time. An angel, fallen from wherever. Because she is. She is to me.

And I try to imagine her old, and happy, and over me. Maybe moved on with a new guy who can give her what she deserves. Someone who'll love her the way I wanted to. And I'll just become a footnote. A long-forgotten someone that she knew for a little while and thought was kind of OK. Someone she saved. Someone she healed. Someone to whom she brought peace.

And I can see that life for her. I see it in my mind as clearly as I see the blood I'm starting to cough up. And I know it's real. I know she's going to be all right. She'll be safe. She'll be saved. And if my life is the cost for that, so be it. I'm so, so, so very honored to be able to pay it.

Thank you, angel. Thank you for everything. I'm sorry it all worked out this way. But it's OK. I love you.

I'll see you again.

And that's when the explosion happens.

It's like a fireball exploding from somewhere deep inside the suddenly molten earth. It puts a hard stop to everything else happening right now. It blows both me and Logan back about ten feet. The shooters too. It roils up and swoops over us like the devil himself is spitting at us in anger and frustration. Like he's pissed that we're disturbing his rest.

Maybe he's just trying to wait for Santa too.

The flames are all around us in both great, sweeping waves, and in tiny, standalone puddles.

What. The. Fuck. Just. Happened?

Doesn't really matter, as two of the shooters have turned and started to run back into the house/mansion/hotel/whatever-the-hell but are confronted by billowing smoke. Huh. I guess Maddie's little decoy fire must have gotten out of control in there. Shooter one and shooter two break left and take off around the side of the property and go running for the beach.

The other shooters are burning alive.

The flames catch them, either by the rapid way it's creasing a path along the gas-soaked concrete or in tiny fireballs that continue to spark and shower down all around us. I can't see through the fire in front of me. I can't tell if Maddie is OK. I can't tell if Ricky is either, but I care a fuckton less about that.

I can see that Carlos is still unconscious, lying right in the pathway of the spreading inferno. Logan is lying next to me where we were blown back and it looks like he's trying to stand up. I am too. The difference is that his bat is resting next to me now, and I can take it up and use it as a staff to help me get to my feet. So I do.

And, look, it's not cool, and it's not classy, and I'm not super proud of it, but I bring it down hard one time on Logan's stomach and he whines like the little twat-blossom he is. And again, not proud or dignified, but it feels fucking good.

What does not feel fucking good is everything inside my own body right now. But. Carlos is still there. And… goddamn it. I gotta fucking get him up before he's caught by this still-baffling eruption that keeps growing in our direction.

I race over to get hands on him, but as I do, another eruption of fire sends me back. *Where the fuck is this coming from?* I go in again and manage to get my hands on his wrists. The screaming of the other guys who are being burned up is super distracting. I know it'll stop in a second, but for now it's making it hard to focus.

I turn my head for the briefest of seconds and see Logan, now unconscious, and realize that I'm probably not going to be able to get them both. It's wild. The fire has spread in almost like a semi-circle around us. A literal ring of fire. Like the Johnny Cash song. *I fell in to a burning ring of fire. I went down, down, down, and the flames went higher.* Only less fun and without Johnny's sonorous baritone to bring it along.

Nobody could get to us if they tried, and I don't see any way out of this except back towards the ocean, where I know for a fact guys with guns have just skedaddled, or through the burnin' fuckin' ring of fire.

And then I realize…

This is like my DREAM. THE DREAM.

In that dream, I had to run through fire and burning flesh to reach my angel. But also, of course, in that dream, she blamed me for everything bad that had happened. Are

Maddie and I through that yet? If I run through this, are we through with that? The suffering and the pain? Could this be the last trial for us?

Shit, man. Let's fuckin' find out.

I eeny-meeny-miny-moe it to decide if I'm gonna try and drag Carlos or Logan out with me. Ultimately Carlos wins. Which is fair. Carlos is who Ricky wants to take down. Logan is just a dipshit I want to punch in the dick over and over. So I go in one last time and reach for Carlos. I get him, drag him up, and—with an unreal amount of physical discomfort—I sling him over my shoulders and see if I can find even a sliver of something that looks like a way of egress through the flames.

And I really wish I hadn't taken that extra second to try and figure it out, because in that moment of hesitation... Another explosion. I have no idea where this one emanates from, but it's a fucking doozy. It sends me back on my ass and causes me to drop the shit out of Carlos.

I look up at the clear, starlit sky and begin howling with laughter. Yeah. It's weird. I know. But it's what I do. And then I look over and see that Carlos is now engulfed in fire. He's still out cold, so he doesn't know it, and I'm glad of that. Getting burned alive is... Well, there's no one on the planet who doesn't have an idea of how horrifying that is. Until you've seen it, there's no way to even begin to *really* understand, but it's... it's bad.

Am I sad that Carlos is leaving this mortal coil right now? Nah. Not really. Just being real with myself. He was a bad dude and the world will be a better place without him. Plus, he repeatedly terrified and hurt the woman I love. So yeah. Fuck him.

But am I glad he's being spared a painful death? Yeah. I suppose I am. Because... Shit. I guess because there's enough suffering in the world. I dunno. I ain't no philosopher. I'm just me. But these are the thoughts I'm thinking as I watch him turn to ash.

Logan on the other hand... Yeah, I wouldn't mind sticking around and watching that cocksucker get barbecued. But I have to see if Maddie is still whole on the other side of this... flame tsunami. Or whatever the fuck it is. I'm not thinking right and out of words.

Oh. And also I just realized that my shirt is on fire. So I need to get the fuck out of here.

There is no way around it I can see except to just go straight through. I don't know how deep the wall is because I can't see past it, and I don't know if by running straight ahead, I'm just guaranteeing myself a grisly fucking end. But if Maddie is there, on the other side, then it'll be worth it. Because I don't know what waits for us down the line either, but I know the only way to find out about that is also by just running headlong into it. Shit. That worldview got me this far.

Whatever, motherfucker! You're on fire! Make moves!

OK. On three. One. Two. Oh, fuck it. Go!

And forward into an unknown fate, I flamingly charge.

"... Here." That's Ricky. He's holding a bottle of water and a Vicodin. I take the water. I wave off the Vicodin. "You're gonna want something for the pain."

"You work for the DEA and you're giving me a Vicodin?"

"It's not illegal."

JA HUSS & JOHNATHAN McCLAIN

"Yeah, well, maybe you guys should take a look at that. And anyway, I'm gonna try and lay off the scripts for a while and see how I do."

"OK," he says. "But you should probably get x-rays when you get home."

"X-rays, sex-rays," I say. Which doesn't make sense but makes Maddie smile.

"We'll be at McCarran pretty soon. If you guys wanna try and sleep…"

I wave that off too. "I'll sleep when I'm dead." There are so many different ways everybody could respond to that that nobody says anything. "How much trouble are you in?" I ask him.

Ricky shakes his head, takes a sip of his own water. "Dunno. Brought in an untrained civilian to a deep-cover op, burned down the estate of our target while simultaneously allowing him to suffer a fatal injury, thereby totally sandbagging years of work and millions and millions of taxpayer dollars? If I was a Congressman, I'd say I'd get off scot-free, but I'm just the guy putting his life on the line every day, so… probably pretty fucked. We'll find out." He smiles. He should smile more. It's nice.

"Well. Sorry," I say.

"It's all good," he says back. He's wrong. It's nowhere near all good. But I get it.

Emily, Ricky's little sorority cohort, comes walking down the aisle of the Cessna. "Agent Martinez, the assistant director is on the phone for you."

Ricky raises his eyebrows at me. "Yep. Guess we'll find out," he sort of sings, and then heads to the front of the plane to take his call. As he passes by Emily, their fingers touch. I think. Pretty sure. Not a hundred percent, but. Whatever. That's them.

"You doing OK?" That's Emily asking Maddie.

Maddie nods. Emily gives her a small grin, gives me one, and heads toward the cockpit herself. Maddie and I are facing each other. I've taken a few chartered flights. The facing each other thing is like my favorite part. I dunno why. Feels old-timey. Like you're on the Orient Express or something. Except you're in the sky. And usually there isn't some mysterious murder to solve. Usually.

Maddie's sitting back, looking out the window. It's still dark out. It won't be light for a couple more hours, so she's basically only seeing her reflection. I can't blame her. If I saw that in the mirror, looking back at me, I'd look at it all the time.

"Whatcha thinking about?" I ask.

She turns her head to me. Leans in. Takes my hand in hers. Looks at our intertwined fingers. Smiles. "Nothin'." she says.

She's still wearing my watch. Nadir's watch. "What time is it?" I ask.

She glances at it. "I dunno," she says. "It stopped."

"Really?" I look at it. She's right. It did. It seems like it stopped almost exactly three hours ago. Would have been right around the time I was trying to save Carlos. I think.

Honestly, I'm not sure. I decide not to think about it too much.

Instead, I just hold her hand in mine and decide that the only thing I'm going to think about is this moment. This one.

Right here.

Right now.

In the present.

CHAPTER THIRTY

MADDIE

What I saw when he came charging through that curtain of flame was impossible. It was terrifying. It was in competition to become the worst moment of my life.

Because there was simply no way he could survive. The fire was too out of control. The burning wall too thick to break through. The wrath of the inferno too savage to overcome.

But he did. He did break through. He did overcome.

He just ripped off the burning shirt he was wearing, smacked it on his legs to put it out, ran over to me, and said, "Hi."

Tyler fuckin' Morgan...

And so, I don't know how to tell him that what I'm thinking about now is that... I prayed for him. Not *to* any god or spirit or whatever, but *for* him. For him and me. For us. And that it may just have worked.

I don't tell him because I don't know if I believe it myself. It's too out there to be believed. If I tell him that I was imagining us old and together and still in love, and... Nope. Not gonna say it. It's weird. It's crazy. And we've had enough weird and crazy, so I'm just gonna let this shit sit for now. I do have a question, though...

"Ty?"

"Yeah, babe?"

"That explosion. The fire."

"Yeah?"

"What was that?"

He takes a sip of his water and nods his head back and forth. He winces a bit. I don't give a shit whether he wants it or not, he's getting fucking x-rays. "Yeah. Yeah. Yeah…"

"Tyler?"

"Yeah, I dunno. I've been trying to figure it out. I dunno."

"Well, we were standing on top of that whole fueling thing. Maybe one of the bullets started a—"

He shakes his head. "Nope. C'mon, babe. You've never seen *Mythbusters*?"

"No. What's that?"

"Show on TV. Fuckin' awesome. But no. That's bullshit. Movies and shit when something gets blown up by getting shot? No way. There's oxygen, and surface area, and heat diffusion and… No. Not possible."

"K. So what caused that?"

"I have no earthly idea. I've been studying this shit my whole life and I was thinking maybe the fire you started inside might have somehow done something to a fuel line that, in turn, was connected to the fuel reserves under the filling station, but… I dunno. None of it makes sense. Sure did blow the fuck up, though."

"Yeah. Sure did." I look back out the window to reflect on this. But I find that I can't. "And you saw Carlos die?" He nods. "Was it—?"

"Don't, babe," he interrupts. "It's… Don't. He's gone. And, no, honestly, it wasn't that bad. I can say with absolute confidence that he didn't feel it. K?"

I nod absently. Then, "Logan?"

Tyler sighs. "Uh, I didn't see him… go. But he was unconscious, and then it was all spreading his way, and… I dunno what to tell you, Mads. I was on fire and shit. I wasn't at my clearest level of thinking. But the point is, even if he somehow survived—which there's no way he did—it's done. This chapter of your life is over. K? I promise."

I nod, a bit less than certain. He leans forward and takes my hands again, wincing the whole time.

"You're getting a goddamned x-ray."

"OK, whatever, fine. Just listen." He looks into my eyes and holds my gaze. "We are going to leave the past in the past. OK? And I mean all of it. New Year's is less than a week away, yeah? OK, so I'm giving us exactly six days to take care of any unresolved bullshit that we need to take care of so that we can start the new year fresh and ready for whatever's next."

"Oh. *You're* giving us six days. Like, that's what *you're* doing. Is that, like, an order, or…?"

"Don't be a dick." He slaps at my knee. "You know what I mean. There's some shit I gotta handle and I wanna get it out of the way and be done, and if you can too, then… super. But hey, look, if you wanna keep being kinda miserable, be my guest. It's a good look on you."

I grin. Fucker. Then I reach up and tug at his beard. "This? Is this one of the things we're putting behind us, because I would be more than happy to see this shit gone."

"What? Are you crazy? I can't shave that! I'm like Samson. My strength is in my beard."

"Yeah, well then I may just have to Delilah the shit out of you while you sleep."

"Damn. You is a cold woman."

I laugh, lean forward, pressing onto his knees to support myself, and give him a long, well-earned kiss on his silly mouth. Then I sit back and look out the window again. I start giggling a little. I can't help it.

"What? What is it?" he asks.

And now my giggle turns into a chuckle, and my chuckle into a laugh, and before I know it, I'm full-on belly-laughing and snorting. Which makes him laugh too.

"Ow, ow," he says, laughing and holding his ribs. "Stop. It hurts. What are you laughing at?"

I let the laughter slow to a snicker again, breathe in, let it out, take a long look at him and say, "I dunno. I was just thinking... if this was Christmas... I can't *wait* to see what fresh hell New Year's Eve is gonna bring."

As it leaves my lips, we both crack up all over again. And as Tyler grabs at his side and begs me to stop making him laugh, I smile a big smile, glance out the window one more time, and quietly whisper to whatever mysterious force controls the universe...

"You know I'm only joking... Right...?"

END OF BOOK SHIT

JOHNATHAN

Let's talk about hope for a second.

I once had someone tell me that it seemed cruel to encourage patients with severe spinal injuries (paraplegics, notably) to believe that they could walk again. This turned into a broader conversation about chronic illness, terminal illness, and the like. The position being offered to me was that to encourage someone with virtually zero odds of recovery from injury or malady to believe that they could return to full form was just giving them false hope.

(For the purposes of what I'm talking about here, I'll choose to overlook the notion that "recovery" is, in and of itself, a fallacy – moments, once past, cannot be recovered; nor can one retrieve one's health, youth, or previous state of mind. Whatever form one currently occupies *is* one's full form, and to resist the given circumstances of a state of being is to exist in conflict with that state, which further reinforces individual suffering. But I digress...)

293

Here was my argument in return: All hope is false hope. So why not just choose to believe?

By which I mean that until something is proven true or "happens," it isn't real. So, relative to the *now*, there is no likely future. It simply doesn't exist. I mean, I hope I get to the end of this sentence, but there are no guarantees. (Oh, good. I did get to the end of it. Nice. I'll keep going then...) And so, given that lack of even the vaguest possibility that we can know what's going to happen as time continues passing, why not just *choose* to believe that the future can be the thing you *want* it to be? Because if you can grasp hold of that belief, you stand a chance of making the *now* a little more tolerable.

Here's where it gets tricky: You also have to let go of the *now*.

You have to see this moment as just an ephemeral blink of the universe's eye that has absolutely nothing to do with you, not take whatever is happening personally, and move on to whatever the next moment is that also has nothing to do with you. And this goes both ways. If you are sad now, but have been happy before, there is a reasonable chance that you will find cause to become happy once again. Obviously, the inverse is also true. Joy and suffering are by-products of the thoughts we think. And the thoughts we think are just tools we use. If the tools you are using are not accomplishing the job you want them to accomplish, you may want to investigate getting new tools.

Note: I grew up in a home with a mentally ill parent. My mother is a diagnosed paranoid schizophrenic who also suffers from bipolar disorder and potentially a whole other raft of issues. Hard to know for sure, as mental illness creates a paradigm in which it's tough to determine what is an accompanying illness and what is just a fabrication of the prevailing illness. But, my point is that my mother is simply not equipped with enough working tools to make the repairs on herself we would all like for her. And she's also not really in a position to acquire new tools. So, my whole premise is based on a certain foundational assumption of mental ability and capacity.

But. Even in bringing up the idea of my mom, I can tie it to the concept of hope. Because for years, I hoped that there was some way she would "get better." Or return to some version of the mother I vaguely remember from when I was very young, before she became recognizably ill.

And the hope that she would drove me fucking crazy.

Because it wasn't actually hope. It was desire. I *desired* that she would become different, or function differently, or behave differently. And I desired that because it would make *me* feel more comfortable. Which is fine, of course. I was a kid and shit. I hadn't yet worked out all the ways I think about things. But as I became an adult, I still held onto some of the feelings I had about what I wanted until I began to accept that … it just wasn't going to work out the way I wanted it to.

And that was when I changed my perception of what I hoped for. I began to hope instead for little things. Like, I hoped that if I got her on the phone on <u>this</u> day, that she would be having a good day, without torment and at peace. Or, hell, forget a good *day*, even that she would have a good couple of moments. And I hoped this for *her*, obviously. But I also still hoped it for *me*. There is a certain level of self-interest that is actually required in being a compassionate person. As they say, "put on your own oxygen mask first before helping others."

The characters in these books are driven by hope. They don't realize it of course, but they are. As are we all. If we weren't, we would just give up. In whatever way you take that to mean: Stop getting out of bed, quit our jobs, commit suicide, whatever. I realize there is an argument to be made that sometimes we just keep moving forward by habit and momentum and there's no "hope" to be found, but I would argue in return that just because you don't *feel* hopeful, doesn't mean it isn't baked in.

In the climax of this book, when things look bleak for Tyler and Maddie, ultimately it is their hope that gets them through. That they are saved from death is not the point, it's that both of them, in that moment, give over to a certain kind of acceptance while at the same time hoping for the outcome they desire. Their acceptance looks different to each of them, but their hope is the unifying force that keeps them going.

In the first book, *Sin With Me*, there is the sentence, "Fear implies hope." Tyler thinks that in the first chapter. Meaning, of course, that if you feel afraid it's due in part to the fact that you are still hopeful that whatever is threatening you won't harm you, or kill you, or harm or kill someone or something you love. His presumption is that once you've given up hope, you no longer have to feel afraid.

But what he hadn't learned yet is that acceptance and hope are not mutually exclusive. You can accept the reality of a negative circumstance and still remain hopeful that the circumstance can change.

Same goes for Maddie. She struggles in the first couple of books because of how much she's hoping for a better life. But the struggle isn't born of the hope, is born of her lack of acceptance of where she is *then*.

She struggles, he fights, but they are both just hoping for peace. In this book, WE hope we have brought these two that much closer to it.

As for my own hopes, they are many. But as relates to you and me, dear reader (my dear reader), when I took this project on with Julie, I hoped very much that we would wind up making something that might accomplish a couple of things.

1) I wanted to write stories that people would want to read.

2) I wanted to try and say something about the world and our place in it.

It seems to me that romance is kind of the perfect platform to try and achieve both of those goals. Romance readers are, by and large, excited and enthusiastic to get their hands on new stories (if you've read this far, presumably you are one of those enthusiastic readers), and stories of love, happiness, and hope are the ones that I'm interested in telling. I realize that what Julie and I are doing with this series is both in keeping with norms of the genre and at the same time somewhat apart from those norms. And I also realize that as a result, we may put off some readers.

But I hope... That anyone who discovers these books will find in them something that is special or identifiable or meaningful.

I hope... That anyone who reads these books will either love them or hate them, because indifference to art is, in my opinion, the greatest of all creative tragedies.

I hope... That, therefore, we have created a reaction in you that is strong and affecting and that stays with you after the last word has been tucked away in that magnificent toolbox you keep inside your head.

I hope... You'll return with us for the fourth book to see what becomes of Tyler and Maddie as they continue on their journey.

And.

For you...

I hope good deeds, a life as free from suffering as is possible, and kindness and compassion accompany you on your own journey as long and as far as that journey may take you.

Hopefully,
-JM

12 March 2018

JULIE

We're three joint EOBS's in and Johnathan hit this one out of the park, yes? I loved it when he sent it to me. We'd kinda come up with vague idea of doing these on hope and salvation and since his is filled with thoughts about hope, I'll fill mine with thoughts of salvation. Because that's really what this book was about.

Maddie was after revenge, and I get it. I think everyone gets it. We've all wanted revenge at one time or another in our lives. But I think back on the one time I really did get revenge and how it all happened and... it was really nothing more than karma, ya know?

You reap what you sow. Plain and simple.

I felt vindicated when all was said and done, but I didn't put anything in motion to get that result. It all just kinda played out.

The desire for revenge usually happens like this:

You decide to trust someone, you let down your guard, you give them the benefit of the doubt and figure since you play by the rules everyone else does too. And then they go and do something really mean, which—and this is the worst part—you weren't expecting because you trusted them.

So they did something really nasty. Something that just hurt you in your core. And they won. Whatever that prize was they were after (that you HAD, because let's face it, some people like to take instead of earn), they got it in the end.

Which is what really hurts. That this person you loved, or trusted, or cared for decided you were worth *less* to them that the object of their desire.

It's sobering. It's also debilitating and so this is how revenge pulls you in, right? You think... maybe I can get back what I lost?

But if you lost that thing because they took it from you, then fuck it, right? You earned it once, you can earn it again.

It's far easier to just let go.

I'd love tell you of my amazing revenge story, but I'm not gonna because the people involved don't deserve a place in my EOBS.

I will tell you this: It was quite diabolical. But I swear to God, I really had nothing to do with it. It was all karma.

So when I finally realized that it actually *was* revenge, it felt pretty good. But more importantly, it was freeing. Because I didn't do it on purpose. It kinda made me feel like good triumphs over evil and as long as I stay on my true path, be honest, and do my best—I'd be OK. (Even though in real life, it's the liars and the cheats who seem to win the most.)

I will tell you this as well—I think if I let myself go down a path of revenge I'd turn into a really terrible person because I think I'm capable of a lot more than people give me credit for. And not in a good way. I think if I wanted to fuck someone's life up, I could. Petty fuckin' bad too. And I'd get away with it. It would all be legal. I'm just kinda twisted like that. So I keep that part of me restrained to book plots.

So Maddie lost something she cared about. Carlos and Logan not only took Pete's from her, but Pete as well. But on a deeper level what they really took was the tenuous peace she'd found at the strip club and with Pete.

They rocked her world in the worst possible way and she wanted Payback with a capital P.

But I don't think she got payback at all. I think she got salvation. I think back on my revenge and think I got salvation as well. Because that outcome was the first step in letting go of people who were holding me down and allowed me to move forward.

I think a win every now and then is important. And that's what Maddie is looking for in this story. She just needed a win. And even though this is cliché, I'm gonna say it anyway. Winning isn't everything. Winning means you achieved something. Maybe the highest something. But unless your life is over after that win, there's still more to achieve. Maddie made some dubious choices, for sure.

But not because of the devil on her shoulder. Just because she was lost. And that's what the next, and final book, is about. Maddie and Tyler finding their peace.

Also, and this is the true point of this EOBS, salvation comes from forgiveness.

Maddie didn't need to forgive Carlos or Logan, so that wasn't her problem. Yeah, they were assholes and they did bad things but they weren't dragging her down, she was dragging herself down. So she needed to forgive herself, not them.

And once you can forgive yourself for not being perfect it's like a whole new world opens up. Because once you let go of the idea that you *have* to be perfect you allow yourself to make mistakes. And when you allow yourself to make mistakes you learn things.

I wrote a blog post about "imposter syndrome" last December. It was part of my Top Five Tips for Authors that I was doing on my website. And I said in that post that I've never felt like an imposter as a fiction writer even though I have no training. I never took a writing class and even though I have two college degrees, they are in science, not writing, or English, or literature.

But before I wrote fiction I wrote non-fiction. And that was all science stuff, which is my *thing*, right?

It was workbooks for kids on things like anatomy, and physics, and the lifecycle of a butterfly. And when I wrote that stuff—interestingly enough—I did feel like an imposter. Even though I had two science degrees and one of them was a masters. So when I'd publish these (I was self-published, even back then) I'd be so stressed about making typos because I would be *judged*.

I didn't have an editor—there was no way I could afford an editor back then—so everything that went out was all on me. It felt like a reflection on me as a person, and my brain too, because it was non-fiction, so I was being judged on my actual knowledge. On what I knew of the natural world.

And every once in a while I'd find a typo after I published and it would stress me out pretty bad. I'd feel stupid and small and quickly fix it before anyone noticed and sent me an email telling me I needed an editor.

But after a while I realized—ya know what? I'm not fuckin' Scholastic. OK? I'm not some big textbook company. I'm a fuckin' single mom working from home just trying to pay by bills. And once I cut myself some slack and allowed myself to be imperfect, I felt a whole lot better about things. I did better work. Letting go of the imposter feeling and allowing myself to make typos in a finished product actually led to me making better courses and spend that time learning new things.

So by the time I got to writing fiction most of that imposter bullshit was in the past. I know I have some typos in my books. Maybe not this series (Johnathan is much better at finding typos than I am) but in my solo books they're there. I have an editor and I have proofers… but again, I'm not Random House. I'm not Simon and Schuster. I'm not HarperCollins. I'm JA Huss. Just one person, sitting out here in the middle of nowhere Colorado, doing my thing.

I do my best to catch all the typos, but I choose to spend my time writing stories instead of pretending I'm perfect. And I think that's part of my success to be honest. What good are perfectly spelled words if the story sucks?

I have never felt like an imposter as a storyteller because I don't think storytelling and editing have much to do with each other. Yes, everyone wants a clean manuscript, but there's an acceptable level of imperfection allowed in my work and that's all there is to it.

So back to Maddie and her issues. :)

The other half of her problem was that she attributed all her failures to herself. She blamed herself for everything, when in truth, sometimes things just happen. Both bad and good. Sometimes shit just happens and there's nothing you can do about it except roll with the punches.

Sure she has to take some responsibility, but when you blame yourself for all the bad things in life you miss out on the bigger picture.

Which is... you are here to *learn* something. Something about yourself, something about people, or about the world around you. And you can do that a million different ways. You can help people, you can go to school, you can be a teacher, you can become a doctor, you can become a scientist, you can write books, you can raise kids, you can care for your elderly parents, you can cook new things, you can go new places, you can take pictures, or draw, or play music, or make jokes, or analyze movies, or be a motivational speaker, or hell, drive a different fuckin' way to work every week. There's an endless number of ways to learn.

But the best way to learn is to make mistakes. I think back on my success and you know what I remember most? All the times I fucked it up. And you know why I remember those the times the best? Because in fucking up I learned something new. How to do better next time, hopefully. But also that there *is* a next time. I think back on my biggest successes in books and I have no clue WHY those books sold so well. Like... none.

But you know what I remember about the books that didn't sell well?

All the mistakes I made. So I could try and fix them the next time.

And in making mistakes and fixing things you realize who you are as a person. You cultivate a story about what it means to be YOU, what you want, and how to get there.

Which was how Maddie saved herself. This book was all about accepting herself for who she is and allowing herself to move forward. It wasn't about kicking Logan's ass and taking Carlos down. It wasn't about allowing Tyler back into her life. It wasn't her quest for the perfect business.

It was her quest for SELF that saved her. What it actually meant to be Maddie Clayton. That's why she agreed to put herself in danger.

She didn't do it for revenge. She did it because she couldn't live with herself if she looked the other way and left the mess for someone else to clean up later.

Taking responsibility for something you don't have to, but NEED to, and forgiving yourself for the mistakes you've made is what leads to salvation.

She learned she had limits, she had courage, and she had convictions.

And she came to understand the most important lesson of all...

It not the typos that define you.

It's the story.

JA Huss
3-19-2018

Johnathan and I would like to thank all of you for reading our second book together. We hope you enjoy it just as much as all the books I wrote alone. Actually, we hope you like this better. :)

And if you've got a minute, and you liked the world we created, and the story we told, and the characters we gave life to... then please consider leaving us a review online where you purchased the book.

We are not traditionally published – WE ARE INDIE.

And we rely on reviews and word-of-mouth buzz to get our books out there. So tell a friend about it if you have a chance. We'd really appreciate that.

Much love,

Julie & Johnathan
www.HussMcClain.com

About the Authors

Johnathan McClain's career as a writer and actor spans 25 years and covers the worlds of theatre, film, and television. At the age of 21, Johnathan moved to Chicago where he wrote and began performing his critically acclaimed one-man show, Like It Is. The Chicago Reader proclaimed, "If we're ever to return to a day when theatre matters, we'll need a few hundred more artists with McClain's vision and courage." On the heels of its critical and commercial success, the show subsequently moved to New York where Johnathan was compared favorably to solo performance visionaries such as Eric Bogosian, John Leguizamo, and Anna Deavere Smith.

Johnathan lived for many years in New York, and his work there includes appearing Off-Broadway in the original cast of Jonathan Tolins' The Last Sunday In June at The Century Center, as well as at Lincoln Center Theatre and with the Lincoln Center Director's Lab. Around the country, he has been seen on stage at South Coast Repertory, The American Conservatory Theatre, Florida Stage, Paper Mill Playhouse, and the National Jewish Theatre. Los Angeles stage credits are numerous and include the LA Weekly Award nominated world premiere of Cold/Tender at The Theatre @ Boston Court and the LA Times' Critic's Choice production of The

Glass Menagerie at The Colony Theatre for which Johnathan received a Garland Award for his portrayal of Jim O'Connor.

On television, he appeared in a notable turn as Megan Draper's LA agent, Alan Silver, on the final season of AMC's critically acclaimed drama Mad Men, and as the lead of the TV Land comedy series, Retired at 35, starring alongside Hollywood icons George Segal and Jessica Walter. He has also had Series Regular roles on The Bad Girl's Guide starring Jenny McCarthy and Jessica Simpson's sitcom pilot for ABC. His additional television work includes recurring roles on the CBS drama SEAL TEAM and Fox's long-running 24, as well as appearances on Grey's Anatomy, NCIS: Los Angeles, Trial and Error, The Exorcist, Major Crimes, The Glades, Scoundrels, Medium, CSI, Law & Order: SVU, Without a Trace, CSI: Miami, and Happy Family with John Larroquette and Christine Baranski, amongst others. On film, he appeared in the Academy Award nominated Far from Heaven and several independent features.

As an audiobook narrator, he has recorded almost 100 titles. Favorites include the Audie Award winning Illuminae by Amie Kaufman and Jay Kristoff and The Last Days of Night, by Academy Winning Screenwriter Graham Moore (who is also Johnathan's close friend and occasional collaborator). As well as multiple titles by his dear friend and writing partner, JA Huss, with whom he is hard at work making the world a little more romantic.

He lives in Los Angeles with his wife Laura.

JA Huss never wanted to be a writer and she still dreams of that elusive career as an astronaut. She originally went to school to become an equine veterinarian but soon figured out they keep horrible hours and decided to go to grad school instead. That Ph.D wasn't all it was cracked up to be (and she really sucked at the whole scientist thing), so she dropped out and got a M.S. in forensic toxicology just to get the whole thing over with as soon as possible.

After graduation she got a job with the state of Colorado as their one and only hog farm inspector and spent her days wandering the Eastern Plains shooting the shit with farmers.

After a few years of that, she got bored. And since she was a homeschool mom and actually does love science, she decided to write science textbooks and make online classes for other homeschool moms.

She wrote more than two hundred of those workbooks and was the number one publisher at the online homeschool store many times, but eventually she covered every science topic she could think of and ran out of shit to say.

So in 2012 she decided to write fiction instead. That year she released her first three books and started a career that would make her a New York Times bestseller and land her on the USA Today Bestseller's List eighteen times in the next three years.

Her books have sold millions of copies all over the world, the audio version of her semi-autobiographical book, Eighteen, was nominated for an Audie award in 2016, and her audiobook Mr. Perfect was nominated for a Voice Arts Award in 2017.

Johnathan McClain is her first (and only) writing

partner and even though they are worlds apart in just about every way imaginable, it works.

She lives on a ranch in Central Colorado with her family.

Made in the USA
Middletown, DE
27 April 2018